SOLOMON
SPRING

ALSO BY MICHELLE BLACK
FROM TOM DOHERTY ASSOCIATES

An Uncommon Enemy

SOLOMON

SPRING

MICHELLE BLACK

FORGE®

A TOM DOHERTY ASSOCIATES BOOK
NEW YORK

SOLOMON SPRING

Copyright © 2002 by Michelle Black

This book is printed on acid-free paper.

A Forge Book
Published by Tom Doherty Associates, LLC
175 Fifth Avenue
New York, NY 10010

www.tor.com

Forge® is a registered trademark of Tom Doherty Associates, LLC.

ISBN 0-765-30465-1

First Edition: September 2002

Printed in the United States of America

0 9 8 7 6 5 4 3 2 1

For Ross, Brendan, and Krystle

ACKNOWLEDGMENTS

A special thanks to Marla Evert-Nye of the Mitchell County Historical Society for her help in researching the history of the Great Spirit Spring. Thanks also to Dale Walker and Nat Sobel, for your untiring help and support.

One

JANUARY 1879

HAYS CITY, KANSAS

The pale winter sun cast milk shadows on the brick floor of Brad Randall's jail cell. He had opened the wooden shutter to gain some fresh air. The draft was bracing cold, but at least offered a respite from the stale atmosphere of the coffinlike room that confined him. The remnants of dried urine and vomit from previous tenants seemed to live in the mortar between the bricks and endured despite weekly moppings.

Unfortunately, opening the shutter let in the unwelcome sounds from outside as well—the sawing and the hammering, the occasional shout of one workman to another. He did not need a reminder of what they were building—a gallows.

He ran his finger inside his collar to feel the tender flesh of his throat. What would it feel like? Would the drop through the trap door break his neck and kill him instantly? Or would he linger and jerk and slowly strangle while the hungry eyes of the onlookers watched with a mixture of horror and perverse pleasure?

How long would it take? How long before he slid into the peaceful void of oblivion, free from the burdens of thought and memory?

He had witnessed only a single public execution in his life. He had been working for the War Department in Washington City in the summer of 1865 when the conspirators to the Lincoln assassination were hanged. Some of his office cohorts had received coveted passes to the event from General Winfield Hancock and invited him to come with them to see the hanging after lunch. He would regret eating so much that noon.

He had been twenty-one years old and curious. The July sun broiled the crowd of two hundred as they watched the prisoners, three men and one woman, bound at the wrists, knees, and ankles before hoods and then nooses were pulled over their heads. One of the condemned men complained about the adjustment of his noose. Randall and his young friends had made rude jokes at this ironic turn.

Their high spirits melted in the noonday heat when the platform finally dropped. They watched one prisoner jerk and fight for five full minutes before his body went still. His bound knees drew up nearly to his chest again and again, then his whole body quaked and shuddered. Five long minutes. It seemed like an hour. Had the man been conscious all that time or did his body alone instinctively fight against its fate?

Another of the hanged men pissed himself. Randall grimaced at this embarrassing reminder of the frailties and limitations of the human vessel.

The date of Brad Randall's execution was set for noon the following Saturday. They chose a Saturday so that parents could bring their children to watch. No doubt the children would think they were attending a carnival or county fair. Entertainment of any fashion brought a welcome respite from the monotony and ceaseless labor of a prairie homestead. Vendors would probably stroll through such crowds plying the eager onlookers with refreshments and trinkets. Randall wondered if those children would be meaningfully improved by the lurid spectacle of his death.

He needed to write a letter to his own child. Four times he picked up the pen and four times he set it down again in frustration. He had to tell his son something. He could not let his only legacy to the boy be newspaper clippings. Frontier journalism was so tawdry—reporters seldom drew a line between fact, speculation, and editorial opinion.

But how could he explain to an eight-year-old boy with mere words on paper that he stood at this fearful precipice because of his love for a woman, a woman who was not his son's mother? How could he possibly make the boy, whom he loved so dearly, understand the impossible complexities that added up to a single human life, his life?

His thoughts traveled back to the first day of September last, barely five months ago. It now seemed like another lifetime. The events of that day had set in motion much of what had brought him to this sorry pass.

SEPTEMBER 1, 1878
WASHINGTON, D.C.

He had never once worried about the dangers of returning home from a business trip a day early, unannounced. He had heard the familiar jokes about such incidents, but had never stopped to consider that the jests might have been born of true-life experiences. As it turned out, he arrived only half a day early, but that was enough.

He had taken the evening train out of New York and fully intended to be in his own bed by midnight, but for the unplanned delay caused by the derailment of another train. The hours it took to clear the tracks caused him to arrive in Washington City at five in the morning.

He emerged from the dirty gloom of the railway station to savor the deliciously cool predawn air that heralded the coming of autumn. At this hour, even bustling New Jersey Avenue was comparatively tranquil. The inviting freshness of the breezes, as well as the fact that he carried only a small valise, convinced him to walk the sixteen blocks to his home; a comfortable townhouse located just north of Lafayette Square that his wife had inherited from her late father. How surprised Amanda and little B.J. would be to have him arrive in time for breakfast when they did not expect him until supper.

He would not venture to his office at the Department of the Interior until noon to allow himself time to bathe and shave and rest up from the hot and exhausting night in the uncomfortable coach.

When he rounded the corner of his street he noticed a hansom cab sitting directly at the base of his front steps. His pace quickened. He feared the doctor had been summoned to his residence. Only six months had elapsed since the tragic death of his little daughter and the thought that some illness or accident might befall B.J., his eight-year-old son and namesake, constantly tormented him.

Randall paused when he saw his front door open and the figure of a man emerge holding his hat in his hand and his top coat folded over his arm.

"Good-bye, my darling," said the man in a cheerful voice that Randall instantly recognized to be that of Clarkson, his young assistant at the bureau.

Clarkson leaned back in the door and kissed Amanda Randall on the lips, then turned and dashed, practically skipped, down the stone steps and disappeared into the waiting cab. The horse's hooves made a loud clopping noise against the paving stones that echoed in the morning silence. With a pulse pounding louder in his ears than the clatter of the retreating horses, he glanced up to his doorstep to see his wife, attired in her dressing gown, gaily wave as the hack withdrew from sight, then turn and shut the door.

Randall dropped his valise onto the sidewalk and drew several deep breaths. Though only thirty-four years of age, he thought he might actually suffer a heart seizure and fall over dead, just as his father-in-law had done three years earlier in their parlor after consuming a large Thanksgiving dinner.

He leaned against a lamppost for support and realized he was perspiring despite the morning chill.

A passing dairy wagon startled Brad when it pulled up.

"Are you all right, Mr. Randall?" called the milkman as he jumped down from the driver's seat and rounded his wagon to collect his milk tray.

He did not know the man's name and so was mildly surprised to be addressed by his. He had to remind himself that, as a public figure often quoted in the newspapers, he was frequently recognized in the streets of the nation's capital.

He drew himself up with a facade of recovered dignity. "Just fine, thank you."

"Coming or going?" asked the milkman cheerily. He apparently planned to accompany Randall up the steps as he made his morning delivery.

Randall glanced uncertainly at his door. It seemed to retain a shadow of the image of his wife kissing his young assistant, Clarkson.

"Going." He forced a polite smile and reversed his steps, heading now to his office. He would arrive there by at least seven and avoid seeing any of his staff, most particularly Clarkson. He would shut himself in his office and try to sort out his thoughts.

By the time he reached the large and imposing Doric edifice of the Patent Office on G Street which housed the Department of the Interior, clouds had gathered to spoil the fine morning. Thunder rumbled overhead and Randall took refuge under the eave of the entranceway just before the rain commenced. He hurried down the corridor and passed only a cleaning man sweeping the marble floor. The man courteously nodded in acknowledgment and was surprised that the young commissioner rushed by without his usual greeting.

Brad found the atmosphere in his office stale and stifling from his three-day absence. He struggled to open one of the two operable windows that bracketed the large view window behind his desk. The dampness in the air had swelled the window frame, but with enough yanking, tapping, and cursing, the sash finally yielded.

The rush of cool air bathed his flushed face. The fresh smell of the morning rain mixed with the dust on the windowsill and created an unpleasantly musty odor. He sat down in his upholstered chair and surveyed his surroundings dispassionately. His was a large and well-furnished office, befitting a man of his importance: commissioner of the Bureau of Indian Affairs. The very title itself resonated consequence with its cadence of prepositions. The work had consumed him in recent months, offering him much-needed solace after the death of little Sarah.

Had his long absences from home caused his wife to stray?

Damn it all! He would not blame himself for this. The fault was hers and no one else's. How would he proceed?

A divorce?

The word made him shudder. Being an important man in this grand office carried with it not only a certain privilege, but also an unpleasant loss of privacy. The esteemed commissioner of Indian Affairs suing his wife for divorce on grounds of adultery and naming as correspondent his own assistant—the press would dance with the story. His enemies in the War Department would feast on it.

He had barely been able to tolerate the news stories on his daughter's death. It galled him to read them, no matter how solemnly and compassionately written, in the news section of the papers rather than the usual obituary listings.

Now to face this . . . this hideous and unseemly scandal. How could he shield his little son from it?

What if he did nothing and pretended ignorance? Could he go on living with Amanda?

Before he could fully digest this line of thought the little clock on his desk chimed 7:45. The sound of his subordinates arriving at their posts distracted him.

With a cold stab of pain, he recognized Clarkson's voice calling hello to their shared secretary, Mrs. Post. The icy sting melted instantly into fury. He rose from his desk, strode across the large office, and peered out his door. Clarkson was nowhere to be seen, but plump Mrs. Post glanced up inquiringly from her pile of mail.

"Please send Mr. Clarkson in to see me at once," he barked.

"Yes, sir. Uhm . . . is everything all right, Mr. Randall?"

"Yes, fine." He closed the door before anyone else could see him. He realized from the look on Mrs. Post's concerned face that he must appear a fright. He had not combed his hair, had not shaved, his clothes were rumpled from a night spent sitting on a miserably hot, stalled train. He must seem very far from the dapper and well-groomed young gentleman who usually occupied this grand office.

The moment he sat down, Clarkson rushed in, smiling, then looked slightly confused as he glanced at his superior's disheveled appearance.

"Close the door behind you," Randall said.

The young man did as he was told, then took a seat in one of the two chairs that faced the desk. "We didn't expect you back so soon, sir."

"No, I'm certain you didn't." He studied Clarkson's slender, blandly handsome face. His slight build and medium height made him no physical match for his superior, who at six-foot-four-inches, towered over nearly all his associates. A decade earlier, Brad would have gladly looked forward to smashing in the impudent usurper's face. At this stage in his life, however, he felt a violent outburst beneath his dignity, especially when he forced himself to imagine the newspaper headlines such an incident would spawn.

15

Clarkson smiled nervously under his supervisor's scrutiny. Randall had previously liked the intelligent and witty young man. He was a Harvard graduate and had a fine career in public service to look forward to. Until now.

"Where was it you were born and raised, Clarkson? I don't recall it."

"A small town in western Ohio, sir. So small I doubt you've heard of it."

"Well, urgent family business requires you return there immediately. At least, that is what you will tell everyone as you empty your desk and pack up your belongings."

Clarkson frowned. Did guilt color the apprehension in his face? "I don't understand—"

"I saw you leaving my house this morning. I saw you kissing my wife."

Clarkson paled. "Oh, dear God. It's . . . it's not what you think."

"It's *exactly* what I think and we both know it."

The young man's Adam's apple bobbed several times. Randall wondered what Amanda saw in him. He always thought Clarkson's manner a trifle effeminate, though he had to admit that he was a popular figure with the ladies at social gatherings. He recalled seeing Clarkson surrounded by women on more than one occasion, and now that he thought about it, all those women clamoring for his attention had two things in common—all were married and all were a number of years Clarkson's senior.

"I'm sorry. I'm so very sorry. We never meant to hurt you."

"Don't say 'we'!" Randall shouted, breaking his promise to himself that he would not lose his composure. "Don't ever speak of my wife and yourself as a couple!"

"No, sir. I'm sorry, sir."

"In my own house! In front of my son!"

"Oh, no. B.J. was staying with your sister."

Hearing Clarkson speak so casually about his family caused

Randall to grasp the edges of his desk as he fought the urge to attack his young associate.

Clarkson wet his lips and asked in a contrite whisper, "What are you going to do to me?"

"You deserve to be horsewhipped." He was tempted to say, You deserve to spend the rest of your life with *her*. The wretched pair of you deserve each other. Instead, he said, "I'm firing you. Wasn't that clear?"

"Yes."

"Now, get out."

Clarkson rose unsteadily.

"Wait." A troubling new thought occurred to him. "Who else knows about this . . . this outrage?"

"No one, sir." Clarkson's tone turned groveling. "We—I mean, *I*—have been most discreet. I would never . . . I'm a gentleman, sir."

"I don't think a gentleman would seduce his employer's wife."

"No, sir. You're right. There is no excuse—"

"No, there is no excuse. Now get out."

Clarkson scurried for the door, but paused with his hand on the brass knob. He turned back, though he could not bring himself to make eye contact with the man he had so grievously wronged. "I cannot leave unless I have some assurance that Mrs. Randall will come to no harm on my account."

This minute act of chivalry served to further enrage Brad with its implication. Only by forcing himself to imagine those awful newspaper headlines, did he resist the urge to grab the young betrayer's skinny throat.

"It is none of your business, Clarkson, but I think you know that I am not a violent man." His voice issued as cold as iron, his words seemed to clank.

"You must not think your wife cruel or wanton, sir. She was just lonely and I was a friend to her. I suppose we simply let our friendship go too far—"

"Get out of my sight!"

Clarkson was gone before the words stopped echoing in the large office. Randall hurried to the door and tersely advised Mrs. Post he was not to be disturbed by anyone, except, of course, the secretary of the Interior. He then closed the door, turned the key in the lock, and returned to his desk. He watched the rain slap his windows and blur the view. He dropped back down into his chair as though his body weighed a thousand pounds and buried his face in his arms upon his large, cluttered desk.

He had not cried often in his life. He did not like the sensations it produced. His eyes stung as he wiped his face with his handkerchief and blew his nose.

He stared at the stack of correspondence that had accumulated during his absence. With little interest, he began to sort it into piles of various importance. He did not bother to read any of it until he came to the letter he had been expecting from the Secretary of the Interior.

The fact that their offices were situated only two floors apart in the same building and yet they felt the need to communicate only by written post spoke loudly to the professional difficulties between them. If their relations grew any more strained, Randall knew he would be looking for employment along with Clarkson.

After reading the contents of Secretary Carl Schurz's letter, he grew furious, though he had not expected a different reply. Schurz had outlined the reasons for his disagreement with the Honorable Commissioner of Indian Affairs, Mr. Randall, on the subject of the relocation of the Northern Cheyenne tribe.

When the Northern Cheyennes surrendered at Fort Robinson in 1877, they were persuaded to relocate to the Indian Territory and live with their southern brethren. They had reluctantly agreed when promised the right to return to their homelands in the north if the relocation failed. The secretary did not now feel inclined to acknowledge this promise in light of his insistence that the Bureau stay on budget for the next fiscal year.

The fact that the Cheyennes were starving, were not allowed to leave the reservation to hunt, were not given the promised rations, and were dying from malaria for which no quinine was made available apparently meant nothing to the esteemed secretary. But, by God, they were on budget.

"Damn him and every bureaucrat in Washington City," Randall said through gritted teeth as he shoved all his papers off his desk. Nothing in the Bureau had gone well since the convoluted election of '76. Though he had been one of the few political appointments to survive the shameful scandals of the Grant administration, his future now looked as cloudy as the Washington sky.

He grabbed his file on the Northern Cheyenne situation and marched directly for the secretary's office.

"Is Mr. Schurz expecting you, Mr. Randall?" asked the small, mouselike clerk whose desk sat in the receiving area of the secretary's large complex of offices.

"No, he is not."

"I'm afraid that—"

Randall stormed past the clerk and entered his superior's office unannounced.

"What's this?" Schurz looked up from his desk, startled and irritated.

"What gives you the authority to condemn people to death?"

"Sit down, Randall, if you please."

"I don't feel like sitting."

"Should I summon the security guards, sir?" asked the little clerk, peeking in.

"Leave us," Schurz ordered and, more unflappable than his assistant, sat back in his chair. "I suppose this involves some damned Indian problem."

"Given that I am the commissioner of *Indian* Affairs, I suppose you are right."

"No need for sarcasm, Randall. What's the trouble?"

"Precisely why do you seek to undermine my decisions and policies in the matter of the relocation of the Northern Cheyennes—"

Schurz raised a hand to silence him. "I am your superior and *I* will have the final say in all matters involving this department."

"Allow me to read from a letter I received from a Lt. Lawton at Fort Reno," Randall pressed on. "*They*—that is, the Northern Cheyennes—*are not getting the supplies to prevent starvation. Many of their women and children are sick for want of food. The beef I saw given them was of very poor quality and would not have been considered merchantable for any use.* On the subject of medical care, Lawton reports: *The post surgeon frequently locks up his office because he has no quinine to administer to the Indians and does not wish them to continue to call upon him*—"

Schurz interrupted, "Randall, you know that our appropriations are not sufficient to cover the stipulations of the various treaties—"

"Treaties whose terms *we* dictated and forced them to accept."

"For God's sake, man, lower your voice. Had your Bureau exercised the necessary economies—"

"These people are starving! I cannot manufacture food from stone."

"Commissioner Randall, *your* job is to carry out *my* will. We have not seen eye-to-eye on practically any policy since I took office. I am struggling to find a reason not to ask for your resignation." He paused for a brief moment and sighed. "Bradley, sit down."

Randall grudgingly did so. He studied the small, fifty-year-old man, an immigrant from Germany who had served in the U.S. Senate prior to his appointment. His passion was forestry, one of the many diverse spheres of the Interior Department's wide purview. That the interests of the many subagencies frequently conflicted with the Bureau of Indian Affairs did not make Randall's job any easier.

"Bradley, I have endeavored to make allowances for your— how shall I describe it?—acts of insubordination in these recent months." Though Schurz had lived in the United States since his youth, his speech still bore the halting cadence of his native land. "I know that you and your dear wife suffered a lamentable tragedy, but at some point, my patience with you must expire. I would never tolerate such behavior from any of my other department heads. You, however, are the hardest working, most dedicated man on my staff. I would not easily lose you, despite our many differences of opinion."

Randall shifted uncomfortably in his seat. He did not enjoy references made to his daughter's death. He could not govern his present emotions well enough to formulate a reply to his superior. He knew well enough that Schurz, for all his immediate praise, did not personally like him owing to an altercation on the secretary's very first day in office.

When Schurz was appointed to the cabinet by the newly elected President Hayes, he devised a test that all potential men in his employ had to take.

Randall had thought it impossibly demeaning to take a test like some schoolboy to retain his job when his own record of accomplishments as the youngest-ever superintendent of Indian Affairs, and later commissioner in the Bureau, should have spoken instead. He unfortunately voiced this opinion in the presence of not only the secretary, but members of the press as well.

The newly appointed secretary had publicly opined that Randall was afraid to take the test. With gritted teeth, Randall sat for the detested exam and, as though for spite, scored higher than every other appointee by a large margin, forcing Schurz to keep him on his staff to save face.

Schurz pulled off the little pince-nez spectacles that clipped to the bridge of his nose.

21

"Bradley, you are a very bright young man with an excellent career ahead of you. I hate to see you throw it all away over some misplaced sentimentality for a few Indians. I want you to carefully consider your position here. If you choose to come to this office tomorrow morning with an apology and renewed resolve to carry out the policies of this department, that is to say, *my* policies, then I will reconsider your future on my staff."

Randall stood up and for several seconds thought over what had just transpired as the secretary pretended attention to his paperwork. Without a word, he returned to his own office, moving slowly, as in a dream.

Once safely ensconced, Randall resumed his vigil at his desk with his large chair turned to face the view window. The rain had stopped and the sun had returned; the afternoon air was stifling.

He idly watched the workers who labored to construct a new wing for the office building across the street that housed the Department of Education. The site hummed with activity as the laborers swarmed about, laying brick, carrying hod, over and over in endless repetition. Most were Irish immigrants, potato famine refugees.

How simple their lives must be, he mused. Go to work, do your job—a strenuous job, to be sure, but one without much ponderous thought—then return to your home each night to eat and sleep, perhaps make love to your wife, then rise tomorrow and begin it all again.

And what would *he* do tomorrow? Apologize . . . and betray his principles? Or resign?

Mrs. Post tapped on his door and poked her head in. "Mr. Randall? The afternoon mail has arrived. I've opened it for you."

He did not turn to receive her, but continued to gaze out the window, transfixed by the workers building the new wing.

"Mrs. Post, have you ever felt shipwrecked?"

She placed the mail on his desk. "Excuse me?"

"Did you ever feel as though your life were shipwrecked and you were left alone in the ocean, clinging to a piece of wreckage, with no rescue in sight? Just floating out there, no ships on the horizon, no tropical paradise beckoning. The question would arise, How long would you hang on? At what point would you simply let go?"

"Are you feeling all right, Mr. Randall? You've looked tired all day."

When he failed to answer, she quietly withdrew. He thought about the teaching posts he had been offered by several universities after his treatise on the Cheyenne language and culture had been published two years earlier. He wondered where he had filed those letters and began to look for them when he heard a commotion outside his door.

"I need to speak with Captain Randall," came a man's voice.

Randall winced at the title "Captain." He knew that many used it as a sign of respect, but he preferred not to be reminded of his days in the military.

"I'm sorry, sir," replied the redoubtable Mrs. Post. "He is very busy. Perhaps if you would make an appointment and come back tomorrow."

Randall smiled at Mrs. Post's placid ability to handle every situation. A fifty-year-old widow, she had been employed in the bureau longer than anyone. She had been hired during the War years when the government was forced to hire women to fill the clerical posts vacated by the men who returned to their homes in nearby Virginia to join the ranks of the Confederacy.

"I need to catch a four o'clock train," said the visitor. "I was so hoping to meet the captain and speak with him in person."

"Perhaps one of the commissioner's assistants could help you, sir."

"No, the matter concerns a woman of Captain Randall's acquaintance of some years ago. When he served on the frontier under General Custer. He is really the only one. . . ."

Randall listened more intently now. He was curious about the man's reference, though still not anxious to receive him.

"If you could but inform Captain Randall that I come seeking information about a woman named Eden Murdoch, I'm sure that he would make time to see me."

Eden Murdoch! He had not heard that name spoken in nearly a decade and yet not a day had gone by in all those years that he had not thought of her.

Randall rushed to the door and opened it to see a young army officer, a major in the infantry by his uniform, standing before Mrs. Post.

"Come in at once, Major."

Two

"A man arrived at Fort Hays just over a fortnight ago. He was wildly agitated and we thought him a bit off, if you know what I mean."

Randall nodded thoughtfully as Major John Simon continued his curious story.

"He had a young boy with him. Early teens. The boy, by contrast, was a model of composure. He succeeded in getting his father to calm down enough to tell us the reason for his visit. It seems he longed to confess something that he had kept secret for fourteen years—as long as the boy had been alive."

"He committed a crime of some sort?"

"Most wouldn't really call it a crime. Many would consider it an act of compassion. Of course he should have told someone the whole truth of it, but he didn't want to hurt his wife."

"Forgive me, but you seem to speak in riddles."

"I'm sorry, sir. This bizarre story . . . well, it's not easy to tell. Let me begin again. I am so pressed for time." The mention of the need for haste caused the major to glance at his pocket watch. "I'm afraid I am running awfully close here. I must catch a train. And I did so need to talk to you about this."

"I am as eager to hear this story as you are to tell it, Major.

What would you say to my accompanying you to the station and we can talk on the way."

"An excellent idea, sir."

Randall informed Mrs. Post that he would not be returning to the office and guided John Simon down the long corridors of the building, pausing only to point out the fine collection of George Washington memorabilia on display along with an original, signed copy of the Declaration of Independence.

They emerged on G Street and Randall hailed a passing hack.

"No need for a taxi, Captain. It's such a short walk to the station."

Randall smiled. "My treat. We're on official business, are we not?" He wanted absolute privacy to hear this man's story and recalled his own army days well enough to remember how such simple luxuries as a seventy-five-cent cab ride could strain the wallet.

The muddy streets were noisy and filled with carriages at this hour. The progress of the horses stalled to a halt frequently, though the driver had been told of the need to hurry.

"The old man confessed that his son was not really his flesh and blood, but rather adopted," Simon continued. "He found the boy when he was just a babe, abandoned on the prairie. His mother had apparently been traveling on a stagecoach when it was attacked by Indians."

"Oh, my God . . . I know this story."

John Simon grinned. "My superiors thought you might. That's why they told me to call upon you. I would have come sooner but I was delayed—"

"Please continue. I didn't mean to interrupt."

"Well, the man found this baby and he had to assume that its parents were among the dead in the coach, which had been set on fire after the savages had done their worst. So he carried the little tyke home and presented it to his wife—the couple was childless, you see—like it was a Christmas present from heaven itself."

"They kept the child and told no one?"

"No one. They lived on a remote acreage and decided to pass the child off as their own. It was wrong and they knew it, but they thought, who's being hurt by it? Send the babe off to some distant relative who probably doesn't want it? Well, years go by with no one the wiser until the farmer reads a story in General Custer's memoirs and learns the truth of how that baby came to be on the prairie and how his parents are as alive as you and me. And I'm told you participated in the mother's rescue."

"The Battle of the Washita, back in '68. I was General Custer's aide-de-camp on that campaign." Randall smiled inwardly at the major's use of the word "rescue" in reference to his discovery of Eden Murdoch living in the Cheyenne camp they attacked. True, she had been abducted years before, but she had later come to live willingly among them and married a medicine man named Hanging Road. Randall had been instrumental in reuniting the couple and they had disappeared together, not to be seen or heard from again.

"This man, this farmer, Avel Vandegaarde, should have acted as soon as he read the story and knew the truth, but he didn't. His wife couldn't bear to give up the boy."

"What made him finally come forward?"

"The wife died. And the guilt was eating away at him. To be truthful, I don't think he's in good health himself. I think maybe he knows his time is nearly up and he wants to provide for the boy. It's obvious he loves the lad and raised him right all these years, however wrong his claim was."

"I suppose that's a small comfort."

"But can the parents be found?"

"I knew his mother once." Randall tried not to smile at his own profound understatement. He could have said, I loved his mother once. I asked his mother to marry me. I would have gone to the ends of the earth for the sake of his mother. But she left me anyway.

"Do you know how to reach her?"

"I haven't seen her in nearly ten years."

The major added awkwardly, "I feel compelled to mention that Colonel Ryan told me there was . . . well, once some gossip about you and this Mrs. Murdoch."

Randall pressed away a smile and looked out the window of the cab. "Yes, I imagine there was."

The officer waited, apparently hoping for some elaboration, but none was forthcoming. "And what about the father? Can he be found?"

Randall clenched his fists at the prospect of Lawrence Murdoch, Eden's husband, coming back into the picture. Eden loathed the man for reasons she never shared, but she was in the process of escaping from Murdoch that winter day fourteen years ago when her coach was attacked by Cheyenne dog soldiers.

His only recollection of Murdoch was a bad one. After the man was briefly reunited with his wife in the spring of 1869, his first action was to try and have Eden committed to an asylum so that he might secure a divorce on the grounds of insanity.

"I can't help you there, I'm afraid, Major Simon. I have no idea of the father's whereabouts." He felt guilty about this lie. The man, however despicable, deserved to know that his son was alive.

The horses halted in front of the busy railway depot, a station from which Randall had emerged only ten hours before, yet it already seemed part of another lifetime. The dense line of omnibuses and hacks, plus the scores of porters and drivers calling to the travelers on the lines of the Baltimore and Ohio, created a deafening cacophony.

He thanked the officer for his trouble and assured him that he would follow up on the matter directly. They exchanged addresses and John Simon disappeared into the crowd of passengers. The hack driver directed his horses toward Randall's home. His wretched day was far from over.

"How long will you be gone?" Amanda asked, still staring at the pattern in the Oriental carpet that separated her from her husband in their front parlor. She had not dared to raise her eyes to him since the moment he had coldly announced he knew about her affair with Clarkson. She had been shocked at first but then had adjusted to the news with surprising stoicism. She offered neither apology nor explanation.

"Quite a while. I don't know at this point. I haven't made a Western tour of the agencies in a long time. It's overdue. You'll still be able to draw upon your regular housekeeping money. Until another arrangement can be worked out, at least."

"You're divorcing me?"

"I don't know. My head is too muddled to think clearly at the moment. I know only that urgent business draws me to the Western territories and I may be gone quite a long time." He had decided, in a single blaze of inspiration during the trip to his house, that he would ask for a leave of absence from the bureau. He would plead the necessity of this tour of the agencies. The day-to-day affairs of his office could be handled by the undersecretary as they had been when he took two weeks off after Sarah's death.

The leave would afford him the opportunity to resolve, informally at least, the Cheyenne situation and thereby circumvent Secretary Schurz's decree on the subject. If he were successful, Schurz could ignore his small insubordination. Probably he would even take full credit for the triumph. If he were unsuccessful . . . well, what did he have left to lose? He would keep his soul if not his job.

He did not care to tell her that his other motive in going West was to locate Eden Murdoch and reunite her with her son. Before their marriage, when Randall had been sent out to the Western frontier with the army and had first encountered Eden, Amanda had grown suspicious of his feelings for this mystery woman . . . and with good reason.

B.J. burst into the room. "I'm hungry. When is supper, Mama?"

"Tell Dora to feed you in the kitchen, darling." Amanda did not even look up to talk to her beloved son, the centerpiece of her life since the day of his birth.

"But when will *you* eat?" he demanded in his usual forthright manner. Brad and Amanda Randall took a radical approach to parenting. They not only allowed their children to dine with them each evening, but carried on elaborate conversations with them as well, treating them with a dignity almost equal to that which they bestowed upon fellow adults.

"B.J., your mother and I need to be alone together just now. Please leave and go find Dora. She's certainly in the kitchen at this hour."

The boy frowned at the abrupt dismissal. He studied the strained mood between his parents. The temper of the house had been decidedly somber ever since his little sister, Sarah, had died, yet he had not seen his parents look quite this grim lately and it worried him.

"Is someone else going to die?"

Both parents turned toward their son.

"No, darling, not at all," said his mother.

"In fact, we're going to visit Aunt Jennetta tonight, son. You'll get to play with your cousins."

Amanda's eyes widened at this announcement.

"Am I going to sleep there *again*?" The child made an exasperated face.

Randall recoiled inwardly at this reminder of how B.J. had been shuttled off to his sister's house last night to accommodate Amanda's tawdry misbehavior. "Yes, that's correct."

The boy groaned. "I'll have to sleep with Lindal and he . . . *he wets the bed*."

"You can share a bed with me instead."

B.J.'s freckled face broke into a delighted grin. "You're coming, too, Dad? And Mama?"

Randall glanced at Amanda's questioning face. "No, just me. Now go tell Dora to feed you. Hurry off."

The boy frowned in confusion with his father's announcement as he watched the strain return between his parents like a dark cloud blocking the sunlight. Nevertheless, he dashed off to the kitchen.

"So that's how it's to be, then?" said Amanda.

"I can't take this house from you. It's yours, you own it. But I no longer wish to share it."

She raised her chin. "You can't take my son from me."

"Oh, can't I?"

"You wouldn't. You couldn't. He needs me. I'm his mother. You're not that cruel, for heaven's sake. You wouldn't dare separate us."

"I think the courts will see it quite differently. Adulteresses are seldom viewed as wholesome mother-figures."

Amanda's belated tears finally arrived. She sobbed loudly, covering her face with a handkerchief.

Randall left the parlor and went to his bedroom to pack. He glanced around the large and comfortable chamber, wondering if this would be the last time he ever saw it. The room had witnessed all the years of his marriage, all the love, the passion, the sorrow, and now the regrets. For half an instant, his anger subsided and he felt like crying again.

He remembered the day his son had been born in this room. He had not guessed that such joy existed in the world until the moment he had been invited in after the interminable wait and the doctor had placed the tiny, swaddled bundle in his arms. He had looked down at that bawling, red little face in utter amazement. *I have a son,* he had thought. *Amanda and I have created a whole new person.* This simple, ancient revelation had dazzled him.

He was forced to smile when he recalled Amanda's first words to him on that momentous day. "Don't look at me, I'm a mess!"

He had laughed at her vanity and kissed her sweaty forehead, assuring her she was still the most beautiful of women and that she had just given him the most spectacular gift on earth.

Six years later, Sarah had been born here. Dear little Sarah. A painful knot in his throat still formed at the mere thought of her. And the awful memory of the day she died. He and Amanda had never been able to speak of it. What happened that day was a well of darkness between them, a festering sore that would never heal.

"Are you saying that there is no hope?"

The doctor sighed. "There are those who would say, where there is life there is always hope, but that is a rather hollow comfort."

A hideous new possibility arose as he sat down on the bed. Had Amanda and Clarkson shared this room? What a profoundly sickening thought. She would not have had the audacity to defile their marriage bed, would she?

He instantly stood up as though he feared he would somehow be contaminated by mere contact with the guilty mattress.

He grabbed clothes and personal items from the wardrobe and the bureau drawers. Most of the items in the room belonged to him as Amanda had not slept here since the day Sarah had fallen ill.

The fact that she had begun to sleep on a cot in the nursery seemed natural enough at the time. But she had not returned to their bedroom after Sarah's death. And neither he nor Amanda had ever even remarked on the matter.

After placing all he could fit in his large portmanteau, then picking up the small valise he had not yet had a chance to unpack from his recent trip, he extinguished the bedside table lamp and left.

He determined not to think about Amanda or Clarkson or the secretary of the Interior or any of the other irritating complexities that were currently eroding his soul. From that moment forward, he resolved to think only about finding Eden Murdoch.

Three

The world starts over with each new day, Eden Murdoch reflected as she sat waiting for her daughter to get ready for school. How many times would her life start over? At least this current new start was of her own choosing. And it was going to be a good thing, she could sense it.

Still, she could never feel safe anywhere. Security was an illusion. Only fools believed they were safe. A person could be standing under a clear blue sky and still be struck by lightning. She knew that for a fact.

"*Hadley Rose Murdoch*, hurry up!" Then she muttered to herself, "It would hardly do to be late on the first day."

The tall nine-year-old ran from the one-room sod house to join her mother in the wagon.

"What have you forgotten?"

The girl slapped her hand against the top of her honey blond head with a groan and ran back into the house to retrieve her hat. She returned and pulled herself up into the seat next to her mother.

"Good-bye, Pink," Hadley called to her big, old mongrel dog as he loped along beside the wagon until he got tired. She watched him recede into the distance and said, "He's going to be so lonely without me, you know."

"He'll survive," said Eden with a nervous smile. She felt anxious for her daughter on the first day of school. Hadley had never attended a real school and Eden desperately wanted everything to go well for her. She had spent the summer schooling her as best she could. She had no books but picked up a discarded newspaper in town whenever one came her way and tried to teach her to read.

Would the other children be kind or cruel? Her daughter outwardly resembled the others, but she was a far cry from them in so many other ways. Born in a Cheyenne camp along the Tongue River, raised by her Cheyenne stepfather to be Indian in every sense, could the child successfully make the transition, given such odds?

Eden had never planned to return to the white world, but the world had other plans for her and now she and her daughter must adapt. The death of her husband Hanging Road and the surrender of almost all the remaining Cheyenne bands to reservation life dictated her departure.

"*Henova'e he'tohe*, Mama?"

"In English, Hadley."

"What's that?" the girl repeated. She pointed to an object on the southern horizon.

Eden squinted to make out the mirage-like image. "If I didn't know better, I would say—"

"It's a tribe, Mama! Is it *our* tribe?"

"No, dear, of course not. You know better." The sight did look for all the world like the dust cloud raised by a mass movement of people and horses traveling at high speed across the parched plains. The strange vision could have been mistaken for a buffalo herd, but the buffalo were long gone from this territory now.

A longing for happier days had drawn her back to the fork of the Solomon River after a decade's absence. She had followed the Solomon once again to find the Sacred Spring. The last time she had made a pilgrimage to the spring she had been carrying Hadley in her womb and had prayed there to be delivered of a healthy child. Her prayers had been answered and so she had given her the Cheyenne name of *Maheo Maape*, Medicine Water.

The natural—or supernatural—wonder that was the spring never failed to amaze her. The silvery blue circle rose out of the prairie like an ancient remnant of the primordial sea that had once covered the vast plain. Why the sea vanished and left in its place only this round well of salty water perplexed and confounded innocents and experts alike. The spring never froze in winter, nor flooded with the torrents of spring rain, nor did its surface recede in times of drought.

Its mineral-laden waters seeped over the edges of its circular bank in steady and even proportions year after year, decade after decade, slowly increasing its own basin. Higher and higher it grew above the prairie floor surrounding it as the minerals laid down their deposits for centuries to create an imposing and enormous limestone dome.

The day Eden and her daughter had returned to the area they chanced to meet an elderly woman named Mrs. Redding in the nearby ghost town of Waconda. She stopped to chat and ask for a ride back into Bluestem, two miles away. On the short journey, she had told Eden of an abandoned homestead claim with a house and a corral. Eden would learn much later that the homestead had once, long ago, belonged to Mrs. Redding. She had given it up and moved into town when her husband passed on.

Eden had hesitated on whether to even look at the claim that day. She had not been certain she was ready to take on the work and responsibility a farm would demand, but to be polite she had gone out.

The little sod house needed a great deal of work. She had decided she and Hadley might as well stay the night, given that the sky looked like rain.

She liked the location. The humble soddie sat near a good stream, but high enough above it that there should be no fear of a flash flood. And trees—that most rare and precious commodity on the open prairie—a fine stand of cottonwood trees lined the creek which flowed into the Solomon, two miles up.

There had been some rough furniture strewn about the dirt floor, a table, two chairs (though was one broken), a partially collapsed rope bed, and a serviceable-looking iron cookstove whose flue needed only a small repair.

"Look, Mama, a cradle," Hadley had said. She pulled it over and brushed out the dust and the cobwebs. "If you have a baby, he can sleep here."

Eden had looked up from her own inventory to chuckle at this idea. "I'm afraid there's no chance of that. You have to have a husband in order to have a baby."

The girl had defiantly placed her hands on her hips. "Hanging Road was your husband, but he wasn't my father."

"Who said that?"

"Everyone."

Eden sighed. "Babies are a gift from heaven."

"It takes more than heaven to make a baby."

"I've lost interest in this conversation, Hadley. Now help me lift this dirty, old mattress. We'll carry it outside to give it a good shake."

"We're going to have to talk about this sometime," the girl had warned.

———

At three in the afternoon, Eden picked up her daughter from school and headed home in the wagon her nearest neighbors, the Laytons, had loaned to her. She owned three horses inherited from her late husband, but her neighbors insisted she needed a proper wagon. Eden thought the neighbors were uncomfortable with her use of an Indian travois to transport her belongings. She had never made a secret of the years she had lived among the Cheyennes—indeed she had to frequently explain why her daughter spoke English with a slight accent—but she did not wish to offend her new friends, so she had gracefully accepted the loan of the wagon.

She had made a promise to herself when she moved here that she would do everything possible to fit in and be accepted, for Hadley's sake. She knew this was a foolish wish. They would never accept her. She had returned from the dark side of the moon, in their view. She could feel their penetrating stares and disapproving glances whenever she walked down Wisconsin Street in Bluestem. She heard the whispers from groups of matrons when she passed— young married women who in another life might have been friends with her. In a matter of weeks, she knew she would never be asked to join their sewing circles nor to help at their church socials. To have willingly married a man of another race—especially a race they considered barbaric—was to have cast herself beyond the realm of social acceptance forever.

She and Hadley were halfway home and busily chatting about the events of her first school day when they saw the mysterious cloud again, only now it was at least ten miles closer. It was a tribe of Indians all right and they were now between Eden and her homestead. In a quick reflexive action, she slid her hand down under the seat of the wagon to check for the loaded shotgun she stowed there whenever she and her daughter crossed the open prairie. She carried it not so much for protection as for an opportunity to hunt.

"Hadley, take the reins."

The girl heard the urgency in her mother's voice and instantly did as she was told.

Eden removed the shotgun from its hooks and sat it across her lap.

"They might be friendly," Hadley offered, squinting into the distance.

"I hope so, honey, but this is very odd. All the friendly tribes have surrendered by now and their reservations are far from here."

A fully armed party of a dozen men came riding toward them at full speed.

"Hadley, climb in the back of the wagon and hide. Quickly!"

The child jumped over the back of the wagon seat and huddled behind it without a word. She pulled a filthy horse blanket over her as her mother sat stiffly waiting for the Indian party to ride up.

Eden did not think she recognized any of them as they came closer. They were poorly dressed, not a handsome and fierce war party at all, though they certainly bore arms. Two had rifles, four had lances, and the rest, bows and arrows. Eden's simple shotgun was no match for them, though she was determined not to show fear. She held her reins in one hand and braced her shotgun against her side, with her hand on the trigger and her elbow pressing the butt into her waist.

She clearly heard one man announce to the rest in the Cheyenne tongue, "Just a woman, alone." The men quickly assembled in a half-circle in front of her wagon.

She felt bathed in an instant relief. "You are *Tsitsistas*?" she asked in pitch-perfect Cheyenne.

A shocked murmur rolled through the group. To be addressed in their own language by a white woman was an event they had clearly not expected. A middle-aged man rode forward to question her. He did not smile, but he showed no hostile intent.

"How is it that you know how to speak to us? Are you a missionary?"

Eden chuckled, but ducked her head to avoid eye contact as tribal courtesy demanded. "I lived among the *Tsitsistas* for many years. Hanging Road was my husband. Have you heard of him?"

They spoke among themselves, then one man came forward. "I know of him. A holy man, a healer. I heard of the remarkable manner of his death."

"Yes. You must be northerners? I thought you were living with your southern brothers in the Indian Territory."

"That was a bad place," said the older man nearest Eden. "We are returning to our homelands in the north."

"Then please camp on my land tonight. There is a fine creek with good water. We don't have much food, but what we have we will share."

"*Ha-hoo*," said the older man, using the universal Plains Indian word for "thanks." Eden judged from his manner that he must be a chief.

She tapped Hadley on the shoulder and the girl resumed her seat next to her mother as they rode toward home trailed by the rest of the band.

"They promised us that we could return to the north if we were not happy in the south," said Morningstar, their leader. "But once we got there, they starved us and treated us like prisoners."

Eden and Hadley sat with a large group around a bonfire made from an old wooden fence that had long since collapsed. They had all shared a simple meal of stew made from an elk recently shot by one of the men of the tribe. Eden contributed several loaves of bread to the meal, plus her entire harvest of tomatoes and corn. She and Hadley needed these provisions for winter but when she saw the starving condition of the children in the group, she decided they needed the food far more. Still, it did not begin to meet the needs of the nearly three hundred who now camped at her homestead.

Another elderly chief called Little Wolf spoke up. "The land there was so poor that when they finally gave us back some guns and horses to go hunting, all we could find were a few miserable coyotes."

"We cannot tolerate that hot and humid climate. It is a place of constant sickness," Morningstar continued. "The fevers killed two-thirds of our tribe the first year alone."

"*Two-thirds?*" Eden repeated with shock.

"The white government in Washington are all liars. They won't be happy until we are dead. Every one of us. And no one will speak our names when we are gone because we will not have died a noble death."

"This fills me with sadness," Eden said. "I know the man in charge. At least, I once did. I thought he was a good man. An honest man who cares about the welfare of Indian people."

"I have seen no evidence of this," said Morningstar with regret. "That is why we must go north at all hazards."

A noisy disturbance interrupted their conversation. Several young men a short distance away had begun to speak in loud voices, arguing about something, but Eden could not catch their words. The two elderly chiefs glanced up apprehensively and both rose to join the arguing group. More angry words were exchanged.

Eden turned to the young woman who sat on her right, Morningstar's daughter-in-law, and asked what the problem was.

"My father-in-law wants us to avoid the *ve'ho* settlements and not seek trouble. The younger men do not agree. They want to raid. We are all starving and now, since the last battle with the soldiers, we have lost most of our horses."

The young woman then related the recent debacle at a place called Punished Woman Creek. A contingent of soldiers had been following them for several days. Whenever they got too close, the young warriors drove them off rather easily with a volley of shots. Though the soldiers always retreated, they continued to follow.

Three days before, the Cheyennes had reached the sheltering canyon at Punished Woman Creek. They saw a perfect opportunity to lay a trap for the soldiers and be done with them. Possibly they would capture some horses in the bargain.

The women and children hid in a several small caves and crevices deep in the narrow canyon while the men took offensive positions around its rim and waited for the soldiers to approach. The plan would have been flawless had not one young man fired his weapon an instant too soon.

The soldiers, alerted by the blast, avoided the trap and fought all day. By nightfall, the soldier chief lay dead and the troops retreated but not before coming upon the untended Cheyenne pony herd. They shot or scattered what they could and now all the tribe had left was thirty horses, one-third the number they had upon leaving the Darlington Agency. The next morning, the Cheyennes had vanished from Punished Woman Creek and were on the move again.

"There's talk of vengeance, too," continued the daughter-in-law. "Many of our tribe were killed near the Sappa River Valley three summers ago. Attacked without mercy. Many of the men want to avenge that wrong."

Eden shook her head and placed her arm around the young woman's shoulder to comfort her. She now noticed that the younger men had stopped their quarrel and instead their two chiefs, Morningstar and Little Wolf, argued between themselves.

When Eden and her daughter retreated to their tiny sod house, Eden brought Hadley's dog in with them. She did not want to tell her daughter, but she sadly feared someone might eat him.

As they climbed into the small bed they shared, Hadley asked, "Who do you know in the government, Mama?"

"I once knew the man who is now running the Bureau of Indian Affairs in Washington. His name is Bradley Randall. I haven't seen him in many years—since before you were born—but the man I knew was caring and compassionate. Not callous. Not the sort of man who would do the things these Cheyennes describe. I can't understand it."

They were awakened before dawn by the sound of gunshots and a thundering of horses' hooves against the hard prairie earth. Eden made Hadley hide under the bed while she peeked out the window. The entire Cheyenne encampment had packed up and left. Only a few stragglers were still visible in the northern horizon and a contingent of hard riding soldiers appeared to be chasing them.

Several of the soldiers who rode in support of a pack train of wagons approached Eden's homestead. She wrapped a blanket around herself to cover her nightgown and stepped out in her bare feet to investigate. Pink barked and ran in circles around her.

"Are you all right, ma'am?" called one of the troopers as he rode into her yard.

"I'm just fine. What is going on?"

"We're chasing that bunch of Indians. Didn't you see them? They were camping right on your land."

"With my permission. Why are you firing on them?"

"We're under orders. We're out of Fort Dodge. They left the reservation without permission and we gotta haul 'em back any way we can."

"By whose authority?"

"I don't think this is any of your concern, ma'am, but it's orders from Washington. Good day, now."

The pack train and its escort disappeared in chase of the Cheyennes and Eden returned to her house and sat at the little table.

"Mama, what is it? Your hands are shaking."

"I'm upset. Confused and upset. I'm going to have to do something I swore I would never do."

"What's that?"

"I'm going to have to write a letter to a man that I once knew."

"The man you talked about last night?"

"Yes, I have got to find out why this is happening. There must be some explanation. I need to write this quickly so that we can post it on the way to school. Wash your face and fix your own breakfast this morning, all right?"

She located some paper and a pen and ink, but soon found the ink had dried up into crumbling curls inside the little bottle. She mixed in some water and sat down to begin her letter.

The pen froze in her hand. She did not even know how to begin the salutation. Dear Commissioner? Dear Captain Randall? Dear Mr. Randall? Dear Brad?

Four

Brad Randall's request for a leave of absence was met with un-disguised relief by his superior. He knew Secretary Schurz longed to replace him with a more compliant bureau chief. This leave allowed him to do so without the unseemly formality of a dismissal or a forced resignation.

Randall did not really mind. He was determined to head off the likely bloodshed that was destined for the Northern Cheyennes. He had received word before leaving his office that they had carried out their threat to leave the Darlington Agency and return to their homelands in the north, most likely the Montana Territory. They were already being pursued by the army though they had displayed no hostile intent in their flight thus far.

Randall's pleading telegrams to his callous replacement had gone unheeded. His only hope to help the Cheyennes was to go out there and talk with the military personnel and hope to convince them to let the tribe return in peace.

Then there was his second mission, of a more personal nature: To find Eden Murdoch and reunite her with her long-lost son. He loved to repeat the phrase "long-lost son" in his mind. It sounded like something out of a fairy tale.

The one motive he did not acknowledge to anyone was a desire to see her again—not that he had anything to hope for in that regard. She was still married to the Cheyenne medicine man, Hanging Road, a man he had risked his life and his military career to set free. His ill-fated affair with Eden had begun during one climactic winter that changed both their lives. She had been told her husband was dead and she and Brad had grown closer and closer.

Back in '69, when he had discovered Hanging Road was still alive, he could have easily hidden the fact from her. He could have broken his engagement to Amanda and persuaded Eden to run away with him, but he did not. If he had won her through deception, how could he ever have enjoyed such a victory?

She returned to her husband. There was never any doubt of that outcome. Still he dreamed about her like a lovesick schoolboy. Her skittering image represented the only glimmer of light in the ruined landscape of his life.

"Do you really think our horses will be all right, Uncle Brad?"

Randall's reverie ended abruptly with attention demanded by Christopher Randall—"Kit" from birth—his twenty-year-old nephew and traveling companion. They had just settled into their compartment on the train leaving Washington for points west.

"They'll be fine. And you don't have to call me 'uncle' if you don't want to. We're just two men traveling together, you and me. Equals, partners . . . friends."

Young Kit grinned. "Right, right. That's right."

Randall sighed. Kit seemed intelligent, but he had an annoying habit of constantly repeating himself that was already grating on his nerves and they had only just commenced a journey of more than a thousand miles.

Of course, he knew Kit probably viewed him as just as tiresome. At thirty-four, he must seem ancient to a college boy. Kit was the son of Randall's older brother, Grant, who had been killed in the War of the Rebellion. Kit was only three when his father died and Grant's young widow continued to live with the family on the Vermont dairy farm Randall's mother owned.

Kit had grown up almost a sibling to him and his sister, Jen-

netta, though Randall had left home when Kit was still a youngster in grammar school.

"I just never thought of putting a horse on a train."

"They'll be fine," Randall said. "We used to do it all the time
in the cavalry. You could never depend on the quality of the
horses the army might provide. We've wrapped their legs and
hobbled them. There's nothing more we can do. I gave that
freight-car boy six bits to take extra notice of our mounts. He
didn't seem to speak much English, but I think he understood."

"That's good. I'm sure that's good, Uncle—I mean, Brad." Kit
relaxed back into the comfortably upholstered couch that would
fold out into a bed come nightfall. "I've never traveled first class
before. This is grand. Just grand."

"Money may not buy happiness, but it certainly buys comfort."
Randall glanced up to admire the clerestory windows overhead
beaming down refreshing sunlight into their large compartment,
trimmed in exquisitely detailed carved walnut. The large window
at their side was hung with deep green brocade curtains bearing
heavy gold fringe. He mused on how spoiled he had become
during ten years of marriage to Amanda. How easy it was for
luxuries to become necessities. He had enjoyed his wife's money,
he could not deny it. That plus his comfortable salary at the Bureau afforded them an enviable life by anyone's standards.

Two years before, when he had received those offers from
universities and had mentioned them to Amanda, she had scoffed,
"I'd love to see *you* live on a teacher's salary."

However much he hated to admit it, she was right. Luxury
could be as addictive as morphine. He wondered if the seductive
tyranny of the former would be as confounding to break free of
as the latter.

A knock on their compartment door brought a young girl selling sandwiches and fruit.

He watched with a bemused smile as his young nephew flirted
with the girl. Deep dimples appeared in Kit's cheeks whenever

he smiled and he employed them shamelessly in the presence of the opposite sex. Brad was the only member of the family lacking the notorious Randall dimples, a fact for which he was grateful. He thought they pleasingly enhanced his sister's face, but caused both his late brother and Kit to look juvenile.

Kit set the young miss to giggling with his elaborate compliments and teasing remarks. She blushed, but stood up to his banter and ended by selling them four ham sandwiches and half a dozen apples.

"At this rate, we won't need to visit the dining car tonight," said Randall as he unwrapped his sandwich.

"Oh, yes, we will." Kit seemed to inhale his first sandwich and had begun his second when he decided finally to ask what had been on his mind since they had first planned the trip. "So I guess you and Aunt Amanda are going to get a divorce?"

Randall stopped chewing and said with a mouth full of bread, ham, and pickles, "Who told you that?"

"Jen and Bob. Well, not in so many words, but isn't that why you moved in with them and had them keep B.J.? I mean, you've got that perfectly big townhouse, twice as big as Jen's little place."

Randall tried to swallow. Twenty-year-olds were not necessarily known for their tact. Everything that entered the boy's head apparently came out his mouth unedited. Randall had no interest in revealing the intimate and humiliating details of his marital crisis with this impudent puppy.

"Kit . . . I don't feel comfortable . . ."

"I think you're doing just the right thing, although . . . I suppose this happens all the time. And given how Aunt Amanda looks and all."

"*What?*"

"The perils of being married to a beautiful woman. If you two weren't married, I'd make a pitch for her myself. To hell with the age difference. She's a good-looker."

"You are speaking of my *wife*."

"Don't get mad. I meant it as a compliment. Jen thinks Aunt Amanda has just come a little unraveled since Sarah, well, you know. And, if you ask me, I think that fellow in your office took advantage of the situation."

That his sister had breached his confidence outraged Randall. And he did not fancy getting marital advice from a twenty-year-old bachelor. Yet, surprisingly, Kit had independently come up with a remarkably similar explanation to what Clarkson, himself, had offered to excuse his transgression.

"Jennetta told you *everything?*"

"No, Bob did. We had a little man-to-man chat, I guess you'd say." Kit winked. "He thought I had a right to know what I was dealing with here. I mean it's not every day you get asked to keep an eye on a relative who's so much older and all."

"Excuse me? You've been asked to do what?" He could not imagine what Kit was talking about. Jennetta had virtually ordered him to take their young nephew along on the trip. Kit had been Jen's nonpaying boarder throughout his Georgetown University career and was apparently quite comfortable there, in that he had shown no sign of looking for employment since his graduation. Jen and Bob had begun to wonder if he would ever leave their house.

"You'll be such a good influence on him, brother," she had said when Randall balked at the idea. "He needs maturing, seasoning."

"You make him sound like inedible meat," he had groaned at the time. Now he felt like groaning again.

"Bob said you had gone through hell with all that had happened and that you might be . . . well—" Kit made his hand into a mime of a gun, aimed it at his own temple, and pulled the "trigger."

"Oh, good God!" Randall did not know whether to take this as a joke or an insult.

"Sorry, Brad. She and Bob gave me this big speech on how I just have to go with you because there's no one else to go. She's worried about you. I thought it was the least I could do since she and Bob have put me up all these years. I don't mind coming. Really, I don't. It could be interesting."

Randall continued to chuckle and shake his head. His sister was a clever woman, solving multiple problems in a single action. "I promise you, it will be interesting, one way or another."

Kit made good on his threat to visit the dining car. Brad was amazed at just how much food the boy could consume, given his small, wiry build. As his young nephew sliced into his third piece of apple pie, Randall outlined their itinerary.

"All our mail will be forwarded to Fort Hays. I know the postmaster there and he'll take care of us."

"Fort Hays is where you got stabbed."

Randall looked up with a grin. "You remember that?"

Ten years before, he had gotten stabbed in the chest while attempting to free Eden Murdoch's Cheyenne husband from captivity. Hanging Road had been held along with the other Cheyenne prisoners the Seventh Cavalry had taken at the Washita Battle. An elderly Indian woman in the stockade had mistaken the rescue and, thinking she was saving the medicine man, attacked Randall with a hunting knife that she had hidden in her clothing. He had nearly died of the massive wound.

"Sure I can. I must've been ten or eleven when it happened. That was pretty big news. We thought Grandma was gonna have a stroke over it. Then you got married right afterward and that about gave her another stroke."

Randall chuckled wickedly and said half to himself, "Proving I was sound of body, if not mind."

Amanda, still just his fiancée at the time, had defied her father—and social convention, for once in her life—to rush all the way out to Fort Hays to nurse him back to health. They had gotten married as soon as he was released from the hospital.

Kit frowned in confusion over his cryptic remark, so Brad thought it best to alter the subject. "Elopements are a family tradition among Randall men."

"Did my father—?"

Randall nodded. "Him, too. Do you remember your dad at all?"

"Not really. I think I remember what he looked like, but I guess I've just seen that photograph so often, the one that Grandma keeps in her bedroom."

The daguerreotype he referred to had been taken of Grant Randall the week before he was killed. There remained a long-running battle between Grant's mother and his wife over whom he had actually intended to receive the photograph. It had simply arrived one day with no letter and addressed only to "Mrs. Grant Randall." Brad's brother, being the namesake of their father, left two Mrs. Randalls to fight over the picture. His mother had ultimately prevailed in that she represented the young widow's sole hope for future support.

"I'm almost the same age he was when he died," Kit said pensively. "I've been thinking about that a lot lately."

"He died too young. That's for certain."

"At least he died covered with glory. I'll have no chance of that."

Randall did not think dying facedown in the mud of Shiloh, Tennessee, had very much glory in it, but he said instead, "Better to live gloriously, don't you think? We can all be heroes, if we try."

Kit shrugged.

Randall returned to more immediate concerns. "At Hays we'll leave the train and start riding."

"Riding where?"

His uncle unrolled his map with a frustrated sigh. "That's a good question. We may head toward the Indian Territory. There's trouble down there that I hope I can help resolve. If I'm not already too late, that is. I want to get in touch with all the agencies dealing with the Cheyennes. I'm looking for a woman."

"Aren't we all?"

Randall chuckled at Kit's randy tone. He could remember well enough what it was like to be twenty. "I'm looking for a *particular* woman."

"I can't afford to be that choosy."

Randall longed, for half a second, to say, Be careful what you wish for. Or perhaps just, Be careful. My brother had to marry at eighteen because of you, years before he was financially or emotionally ready. And in the spring of 1861, when Mr. Lincoln called for volunteers, Grant Randall had been only too happy to enlist. The War allowed him to escape his domestic prison with at least the veneer of honor, but after a year of war all he gained was a flag-draped coffin.

He said instead, "Please pay attention. I'm counting on your help on this trip. It's not going to be a pleasure outing. We have work to do."

"So who is this woman you're looking for?"

"A ghost woman."

Kit's dark, merry eyes danced at this strange reference.

"Ghost Woman was the name the Cheyennes gave her. She has proven to be every bit as elusive as that name would imply."

———

Randall prepared for bed as the light outside the train grew dim. He found his toothbrush with no problem, but had a devil of a time locating his tooth powder. He was not good at packing. Amanda always packed for him. She had a genius for organization when it came to filling a portmanteau.

In his digging through his clothes he came upon his .44 caliber Colt revolver, a trusty old friend from his army days. He ran his finger over the "BJR" carved in the handle. He remembered the rainy afternoon of exquisite boredom in his tent in the panhandle of Texas a decade earlier when he had been so lost for entertainment he crudely scratched his initials into the handle with a nail.

He pulled on his nightshirt, but found he was not as sleepy as he thought. He savored finally having a moment to himself. Kit had decided to roam the various cars, looking for a card game in progress. Jennetta had warned him the boy had much too much a fondness for gambling.

He sat back down in his seat and leaned his cheek against the cold glass of the window to watch the farmlands of western Pennsylvania roll past in the twilight.

He tried to remember the word Kit had quoted Jen as using in regard to Amanda. *Unraveled.* That was it. He felt like that word described him as well. His whole life was unraveling. It started the day Sarah died and it just would not stop.

Maybe if he found Eden again she would loan him some of her strength. She was a woman who could survive anything. She had been blessed or cursed with the ability to withstand the worst life had to throw at her. She could help him make sense of it all. If only he could find her.

He tried to imagine the measure of Eden Murdoch's joy when he delivered his marvelous news—that her son was still alive. He had known in the abstract how much she had suffered over the assumed death of her son, but only now did he fully comprehend the exquisite pain the loss of a child can bring.

His grief was like a silent companion, ever-present, a dependable companion, in that regard. If it left him, he would feel like some part of him was missing, like when one unconsciously senses he has left a glove behind in a public place and knows instantly that something is gone before he even realizes what it might be.

And then there was the one terrible memory of Sarah's death that could not be spoken of aloud. The incident from which neither he nor Amanda could ever free themselves, the shared secret that drove them apart.

Is that why he thought more often of this woman, Eden Murdoch, whom he had not heard from in a decade, when so many more pressing issues should occupy his mind? He wondered why it was that he did not suffer the anger and jealousy and sense of betrayal he ought feel after Amanda's stunning falseness.

Instead he felt only a pervasive sense of . . . dare he admit it? Relief. An excuse to end it. Was he to be like his brother before him, longing for his freedom and now jumping at the chance fate had bestowed?

He cursed himself for thinking such thoughts. He settled into his sofa-turned-bed and tried to shut out the day.

"Are you saying that there is no hope?"

The doctor sighed. "There are those who would say, Where there is life there is always hope, but that is a rather hollow comfort. Her illness has not yielded so much as an inch to the remedies I have employed thus far. An inflammation of the brain such as this typically has three stages: violent excitation, then stupor, then, lastly, profound unconsciousness, which we call coma. This last stage progresses steadily to a fatal termination. I can tell you that, in my thirty years of medical practice, I have not personally witnessed a patient recover after reaching the third stage."

"How long does she have?"

"I cannot say."

A loud banging on his compartment door jerked Randall awake.

"Mr. Randall? Are you there, sir?" came the Pullman porter's voice.

"Uh, yes, what is it?"

"It's the young man, sir. I think you'd better come right away."

He quickly pulled on his trousers and tucked in his nightshirt as much as he could. He opened the little door of the compartment as he shoved his bare feet into his boots. "What's happened?"

"A problem in the parlor car, sir. There's been a fight."

Oh, god. He glanced around for his jacket, could not find it, and decided to leave the compartment without it. If anyone were offended by the sight of his suspenders, they would just have to get over it.

He followed the quick pace of the porter, all the while trying to work one of his heels into his boot. They arrived in the crowded, smoky parlor car to find Kit on the floor and a much larger man being restrained by two others.

Kit's nose bled and his upper lip had already swollen to grotesque proportions. He sucked in air through his mouth while blood soaked his shirt front. A man who must be the bartender stood over him to ensure he would not try to get up and fight again.

Randall made his way through the elaborately decorated car with disappointment that this might be his only visit. He had looked forward to spending some time here himself, lounging about, enjoying a drink, perhaps conversing with an interesting fellow passenger. Now he supposed he might not be welcome owing to Kit's misadventure.

He hauled his nephew to his feet. Kit tried to stand, but his legs wobbled precariously, so Randall pulled the boy's arm over his own shoulder and propped him up enough to walk. With some difficulty, the pair negotiated the course of overturned chairs and tables. A brass spittoon had spilled its nasty contents in their path.

Kit yelled, "You son of a bitch," to his adversary.

The restrained man tried to take another swing at Kit as Randall dragged him past, but he was a few inches too far from striking distance. The men restraining him tightened their grip and he succeeded only in kicking one of them in the shin.

"You're a dead man!" Kit shook a threatening finger at his attacker over Randall's shoulder.

The bartender shouted at Randall, "Get him out of here and don't come back!"

As the two made their way to their compartment, Kit hung his arms around his uncle's neck since he could only sporadically support his own weight.

"I think he broke my nose," Kit said. "My face hurts so bad."

"It'll hurt even worse when you sober up."

They had to squeeze by another Pullman porter on the way. "Can I be of help, sir?" asked the elderly black man.

"A pitcher of cold water, please?" Randall gave the porter the number of their compartment.

The man nodded and scurried off while Randall continued to half-drag Kit through the narrow aisles and corridors until they at last reached their destination.

He sat his nephew down and gave him a towel to hold against his nose.

"He said I was cheating at cards and I called him a damned liar and he smashed me with his briefcase before I knew what happened." Kit's comments were barely audible through the wad of toweling.

"You're lucky he didn't pull a gun on you."

Randall gently removed the towel for a moment and examined his nephew's damaged nose. It now lay against his left cheek, pointing in a southeasterly direction. "Hold still."

"What are you—"

Before Kit could stop him, Randall had taken hold of the errant nose, gave it a hard jerk and—with a scream of pain from its owner notwithstanding—returned it to its original alignment.

He examined his handiwork. "There, that's better. It's nearly straight again."

Kit fought back tears of pain, but said nothing more. He just rocked back and forth in his seat, holding the towel to his face.

This is going to be a long trip, Randall thought as he pulled off his bloodstained nightshirt.

Five

Eden trudged out of the Bluestem post office and climbed up into the wagon seat.

"Still no letter, Mama?"

She shook her head with a dejected sigh.

"Let me drive," said Hadley.

She handed the reins over to her daughter, but was too downcast to start a conversation.

"He'll write back. I'm sure he will. You were his friend. It would be impolite not to answer your letter. Maybe he's just really busy."

"It's more complicated than that, honey." Each day that passed without a letter from Brad Randall, Eden sunk a little deeper into despair and occasional anger. She had analyzed a hundred times in her mind what his reasons might be for ignoring her. Had he forgotten her? Her pride chafed at this unlikely occurrence.

Was he angry with her? She had indeed deserted him in what some would think a heartless manner, though she trusted him to know that she had done what the situation demanded. She had done what was in *his* best interest, not necessarily hers.

Did he simply not care? Not care about the situation, not care about her opinion? This possibility made her the angriest. He was the commissioner of Indian Affairs. It was his duty to care.

They made their way down the main street of Bluestem, a growing city of six hundred souls, representing the largest dose of civilization Eden had exposed herself to in nearly a decade. The town had everything—several grocery stores, dry goods establishments, and livery stables, plus tin shops, harness shops, wagon shops, hotels, restaurants, a brewery, a dairy, a fine school, which impressed Eden most, and they were building a circulating library. Eden could hardly wait for the library. She and Hadley would fill their tiny house with borrowed books.

All had been moving along so smoothly for them until this problem with the Cheyennes had arisen, and brought the complication of Brad Randall back into her life.

"Hadley, I think I might have to go on a very long trip."

"Oh, wonderful, a trip!"

"No, just me, honey. It will be awfully expensive and I can't afford for us both to go. Besides, I don't want you to miss school."

The girl halted the horses. "But I hate school! It's awful."

"We're not going to start that discussion again, so forget it."

With a pouting face, Hadley set the team in motion again. "Will I have to stay by myself?"

"Don't be silly. I'll ask Mrs. Redding to keep you. But you'll need to check on the farm every day and feed the animals. I'm leaving you in charge."

"Mrs. Redding smells funny."

"She dips snuff. A terrible habit and let that be a lesson. But she is a nice woman and kind and trustworthy. And you know how much you love her lemon cakes. I just hope she feels up to keeping you."

"But I want to come with you. Wherever it is."

Eden sighed. She would be wretched the entire time she was away from her beloved girl, but even if she could afford it, she would not bring Hadley. Brad Randall and her daughter must never meet. That would be disastrous.

She hated to admit it, but she wanted to see him again. She

longed to see him. Even just a glimpse from across a street or hallway would be enough. She would do whatever was necessary to see him. At all hazards . . . as the fleeing Cheyennes had said. *At all hazards.*

She tried to clear her mind of such romantic drivel. He was undoubtedly married and had half a dozen children by now. He had no interest in seeing her or he would have answered her letter.

She rehearsed the meeting in her mind. She would govern her emotions with precision and remain totally businesslike in attitude. She had important matters to discuss and she must keep that foremost in her thoughts.

All the way home from Bluestem to the abandoned town of Waconda she meditated on which of her three horses to sell to finance this trip. Rail fare all the way to Washington and back would cost a lot. Plus meals, plus at least one night's stay in a hotel while in Washington City.

And then there was the matter of her clothes. Her plain attire would look shabby on the streets of Washington among all the fashionable ladies. She had never been too concerned with fashion when she lived there years ago, during the War of the Rebellion. She had worked as a nurse at one of the army hospitals and all sorts of social rules were relaxed or ignored during the War. Today's world would be another matter entirely. Her vanity would not permit her to appear in plain serge farming clothes before the grand Commissioner Bradley J. Randall, Esquire, who considered himself so exalted that he could ignore her letter.

Her horses were good ones, well-trained and of fine age and health. The sale of one should fetch a reasonable sum.

As they drove through the ghost town of Waconda, Eden turned to her daughter, "Head over towards the Solomon Spring. I want to stop there a moment."

"Oh, Mama," Hadley said, "you know that going there always makes you sad."

"It's not sadness, honey. I go there to think about things. To *contemplate* things. You'll understand about contemplating when you get older."

"That's what you say about everything."

"Drop me off there, then, and I'll walk home."

Hadley guided their team of horses up to the bizarre limestone dome that created the base of the Sacred Spring and Eden jumped down. Mother and daughter exchanged conciliatory smiles before miming a kiss in the air to each other.

She watched Hadley drive off and reflected on her daughter's comment. It was true that she appeared downcast whenever she visited the spring, though her feelings were more complex than a single word could describe.

She made her home in Mitchell County at the fork of the Solomon solely to be near the spring. Though she disliked the commercial use the current owner made of the property, she still found solace there.

She hugged her woolen shawl tightly around her shoulders to ward off the gathering chill of the late afternoon. Autumn was in the air, no doubt of that.

The minute she reached the top of the limestone dome, she observed several men, including the one who bottled and sold the mineral waters of the spring as a cure-all under the label, *Solomon Spring Miracle Elixir*, engaged in an operation which for all the world looked like dredging. She rushed around to the opposite edge of the spherical pool of sparkling water.

"What are you doing?" she cried.

Mr. Phineas Claypool, the owner of "The Solomon Spring Company," looked up from his team of mules who pulled a long series of ropes out of the waters. "Oh, it's you. We're minding our own business. Might I suggest you do the same?"

"Good day, ma'am," said a short, plump gentleman with more solicitude than his cohort. He drew off his narrow-brimmed hat politely. "I'm Clyde Summerfield. I don't believe we've met."

Eden nodded to return his courtesy, though she did not bother to introduce herself. Rather she renewed her demand.

"We're dredging this here pond, ma'am," said the portly Mr. Summerfield. "Full of all kinds of treasures. Look here and see." He motioned for Eden to look inside a large wooden barrel. Amongst the muck and mud she could make out beads, jewelry, arrowheads, some moccasins, a large object that looked to be a blanket, and miscellaneous bones and other ritual items offered for sacrifice.

" 'This here pond,' as you call it," said Eden, "is a sacred place, a shrine."

"Only to a bunch of Indians," said Claypool with disdain.

She narrowed her eyes at the odious man. The tight, rigid features of his thin face illustrated a hardness of soul to Eden's eye. Sharp cheekbones, dark, narrow eyes, a jaw that could cut glass, he was every inch a man who worshiped greed before all other idols. His only passion outside of making money was the amateur theater company he founded in Bluestem. Eden thought his looks suited him to play the villain in his productions but he was always billed as the hero in the posters she had read advertising his self-written dramas.

"If you found the stable in Bethlehem where Jesus was born, would you loot that, too?"

"I would if there was a buck to be made, lady," said the portly man with a grin.

"That's hardly a fit comparison, Mrs. Murdoch," snapped Claypool.

"Who is this woman, Phin?" asked the third man in their midst. He was a tall, well-dressed gent, a businessman by his haberdashery.

"A widow and a busybody, among other things. She farms some acreage south of town. She comes over here and feels free to give me hell whenever the notion seizes her."

She wanted to shake her fist at the men and call them all Philistines, but the allusion would no doubt be lost on them. Instead, she indulged her curiosity. "How deep is it?"

Once again, the stout man responded cordially. "At least thirty feet, maybe thirty-five."

Is that all? Eden wondered to herself. She had always imagined the spring to be bottomless.

"Mrs. Murdoch, this is my land you're on and I'd appreciate you standing aside, *if* you don't mind."

"With pleasure, Mr. Claypool. But you should all be ashamed."

"You're too pretty to be so serious," called the plump man after her.

"Forget it, Clyde," said Claypool.

Eden retreated to the opposite side of the mineral pool, seething with annoyance. The world was changing and she would have to get used to it, at least some of it. She tried to do what she had come here to do—think, meditate, feel close to her late husband, but found it impossible to concentrate in the presence of such mindless blasphemy.

The Sacred Spring, still an important religious site to all the tribes of the Plains, had passed into white ownership only a few years before when the government had decided to unilaterally rewrite several treaties.

The whites called the strange body of water the Waconda Spring or the Solomon Spring. Eden assumed the name "Waconda" was some white man's corruption of an Indian word related to the spring. The word sounded Lakota to her ear. In any case, she had never heard it applied to the springs by Hanging Road, a medicine man intimately acquainted with all types of legend and lore.

Ameo, she whispered in her mind, using her pet name for him, *for once I'm glad you're not alive to see this.* Everywhere around her she saw outrage and obscenity.

She looked over at the men and their dredging and felt sick with contempt. Claypool represented everything she disliked about living back in the white world. Had Brad Randall turned into yet another Phineas Claypool? If he had, she had better not visit him after all. She did not think she could bear it.

She walked back to Bluestem and stopped in at one of the livery stables and told the man in charge that she needed to sell a gelding. She described the horse, his age, his temperament, and level of training. She wanted two hundred dollars for the horse.

The stable manager opined that she could not expect more than one hundred and fifty, but that he should have no trouble finding a buyer over the next week or so.

She left with a hidden sense of indignation that she was being cheated because she was a woman, and worse—a woman alone in the world, but there was little she could do considering her need for haste.

She next marched directly for the boarding house where Mrs. Redding lived.

"Just in time for some tea, dear," said the elderly woman with a warm smile. Eden followed her into the shared parlor and waited for her to return with a pot of hot water.

The sight of old Mrs. Redding always made her smile. She was no bigger than a tall child. Her back and shoulders were rounded with age, but her dark eyes remained bright and inquisitive.

"You've been a busy girl," said Mrs. Redding as she returned with coffee instead of tea. Mrs. Redding often said one when she meant the other. "Gossip travels fast in so small a town."

"I think, at thirty-seven, I'm too old to qualify as a girl."

"When you've seen the worst side of seventy, thirty-seven sounds downright juvenile."

"I'll take it as a compliment." Eden then began to ask her special favor—to watch Hadley for nearly two weeks. As if this was not enough, she also requested the use of her friend's sewing machine, so that she could create a decent traveling garment for herself.

Mrs. Redding said yes to all of it, though she chided Eden for being so mysterious on whom she was visiting in Washington City and the exact nature of the visit.

As Eden left the boarding house, her hostess issued a stern warning, "Eden, dear girl, you don't need enemies the likes of Phineas Claypool. I heard about your quarrel today. I told you gossip travels fast. You're the talk of the town."

"Oh, that ridiculous man. I'm not afraid of him."

"You should be."

Six

Dearest Sister,

Our nephew and I arrived at Fort Hays this morning and found lodgings in a little hotel in Hays City. We could not get a private room and must share a bed with another man for the duration of our stay here, which, pray God, will be short.

As Western hotels go, it is not too bad though it is located too close to the Kansas Pacific depot to allow for a quiet night's sleep. The K.P. line has grown since the last time I had occasion to ride it. It now calls itself the Golden Belt Route and boasts a mere twenty-three hour trip from Kansas City to Denver.

Kit arrived much the worse for wear, I'm afraid. He got into a fight over a card game on our very first night on the train. He suffered a broken nose and two eyes so blackened he has much the appearance of a raccoon. Please don't let on that I said this if you write to him. He is terribly sensitive about the whole affair.

I'm just grateful the altercation kept him quiet the remainder of our rail journey. He was so self-conscious about his ruined appearance he refused to leave the compartment, but to visit the convenience, and even then he came sulking back once because his looks had frightened a little girl in the aisle and she ran screaming to her mother.

I rather tired of carrying all his meals to him like a personal servant, but I remember what it is like to be young and vain. His swelling has gone down considerably now, though his eye sockets will carry colorful reminders of his misadventure for some days to come.

Still, his presence is not without its compensations. He always manages to have something clever to say. Upon arriving here, he stood upon the rail platform long after our train had pulled away and surveyed his new surroundings by turning in a complete circle.

"It's so flat!" he proclaimed in amazement.

"Welcome to the Great Plains," said I, knowing full well how difficult it is for someone raised in the East to comprehend the overwhelming vastness of the prairie on first sight.

"More like the Great Pancake," he rejoined.

I hope he behaves himself while we reside in this dusty, notorious little town. My memories of its wildness in the late sixties are enough to fill a dozen dime novels. All manner of gaming, drinking, and debauchery were for sale on its streets back then (and do not ask me how I know this, Sister!) Now the town has grown and prospered into a much more formal place. Whether its wild side has grown as well has yet to be determined.

I wish I could say I was cheered by your letter, but you know I am not. I apologize for all the trouble with the school. It is unlike B.J. to do so poorly in his studies. And rudeness to his schoolmasters? He has never been like that before. I wish I were there to deal with this. In fact, I frequently wish I had brought him along on this trip. (He might have proved less trouble than my current traveling companion!) Had it not been for my fears for his safety and my desire for his school term to progress uninterrupted, I would surely have done it.

I apologize as well for the daily grief Amanda has caused you. I have written her again, as has my attorney, advising her to leave you in peace.

I simply cannot see my way clear to relent on this issue. I don't care how much she begs and pleads, the fact remains she has forfeited her right to be thought a decent and fit parent to my son.

Another letter waited for my arrival at Fort Hays which caused me concern. Mrs. Post, my trusted secretary at the Bureau, wrote to inform me she has resigned. She had a family illness that required her to return to her home in Maryland. Now I do not know what will become of my personal correspondence that I relied upon Mrs. Post to forward to me.

Nothing about this trip seems to portend a happy resolution to date. I shall write again as soon as I can.

Your loving brother,
Brad

He sealed his missive to post, then thumbed through the rest of his mail. There was a message from his lawyer with more advice on his contemplated divorce and a stack of letters from Amanda, none of which he read after the first one, which contained no protestations of love nor pleadings for forgiveness, not even so much as a simple, goddamned, "I'm sorry." Instead, she begged endlessly to be given access to their son.

He decided to find Kit and get something to eat. He almost hoped his nephew did not want to join him for dinner, in that he looked forward to rereading B.J.'s three letters to him. He felt awash in homesickness for his only child and just looking at the pages of B.J.'s awkward, boxy cursive gave him joy. Included with the letters was a colored chalk drawing of a caterpillar—they were studying insects in science class—and a funny rendition of his two little cousins.

Randall had solved the issue of his son's bedmates by asking Jennetta to allow the boy to sleep in Kit's old bed in the attic. B.J. wrote that though he found the attic a bit scary at first, it was still preferable to sharing sleeping quarters with Lindal, the bedwetter.

His son closed each letter with a new entreaty that his parents stop their quarrel and kiss and make up and why can't he go home and live with his mother since she misses him so much and he could be a lot of help to her since she was all alone and Auntie Jen's house is much too small and if this fight is because of him he is really, really sorry.

Those were the only parts of the letters Randall did not enjoy.

The Randalls, uncle and nephew, ordered dinner in a restaurant near their lodgings called the Prairie Sunrise Cafe. The fare was well-prepared, though not so elegantly presented as in the first-class dining car on the train. Both men enjoyed the attentions of their waitress, a pretty young girl with the fairest hair Randall had ever seen.

She could not have been more than sixteen, seventeen at the most, and looked as thin and pale as a long winter. Her hair was blonder than corn silk and hung in a single, thick braid to her waist. The lashes that rimmed her pale blue eyes were so fair they almost seemed invisible.

"What might your name be, miss?" Kit asked, with the Randall dimples on full display.

His uncle frowned at him for being so forward, but the young lady did not take offence.

"Solange," she answered with a demure smile.

"Is that a French name?"

"My grandmother was born in France. I'm named for her."

"Parlez-vous Francais, mademoiselle?"

She did not answer, but looked worried that perhaps Kit was

making sport of her. She picked up her tray and left the table.

Randall tried not to grin. "That'll teach you to show off your education, Nephew." He was surprised to find people of French descent in Hays City. Every immigrant he had met so far seemed to be Volga German in heritage.

They commenced their meal with a tasty beef and vegetable soup, accompanied by fried oysters that were not quite as fresh as Randall would have wished.

"So how did you spend your afternoon, Uncle?"

"Entirely in the company of my correspondence, I'm afraid. I didn't get a chance to meet with any of the people I've come to see here yet." Randall knew Kit had no real interest in how he had spent his day, but was instead angling to be asked about his own afternoon activities. Randall declined the opportunity. He had a strong suspicion that his young nephew had visited one of the numerous brothels that flourished in the shadow of Fort Hays. The lad had returned to their hotel fairly reeking of sex. That Randall had not himself smelled like that in a long time filled him with self-pity.

There was a time when his marriage to Amanda had been charged with passion, a passion that had continued despite her decision after B.J.'s birth that she did not want any more children. Though he had always envisioned them raising a large family, he would not ask her to undertake such hardship and danger un-willingly. On the other hand, he did not find the prospect of a celibate marriage appealing. That did not prove to be the case, however, thanks to Amanda's best friend Millie, who had just returned from Paris with a marvelous little invention she called the French Sponge.

The fact that all such contraceptive devices were illegal in every state of the union only served to add an illicit glamour to their bedroom activities. He took a wicked pride in the idea that he could make love to his wife *and* violate the Comstock Act at the same time.

The party came to an end five years later when the French Sponge experienced its first failure. Amanda had informed him there was another Randall in the offing with the same tone of voice usually reserved for announcing a terminal illness, the death of one's mother, or a crash of the stock market.

After an evening spent rambling from one saloon to another, Randall and Kit finally made their way up the creaky stairs to their hotel room. They both enjoyed the freedom of being off the train and able to walk in all directions at will. Randall insisted they drink only beer that night in hopes they would stay sober enough to find their way to their lodgings, which they did, but only just.

They discovered their roommate sitting up in bed, sound asleep, with a lit cigar in his mouth. An enormous ash had formed, making it impossible to remove it from its owner's lips without showering his shirtfront.

This did not deter Kit, who plucked the cheroot out of the man's mouth without a moment's hesitation. Both Randall and his nephew were surprised that this did not wake the man up. Instead, he merely made a grumbling, snorting noise, slid down under the patchwork blanket, and began to snore. They both laughed out loud, but this did not wake him either.

Kit drew a puff on the nearly played-out cigar before erupting into a coughing fit. Randall chuckled at this while the two, tipsy and off-balance, pulled off their clothes and prepared to retire. After a momentary disagreement over who had to take the middle spot in the crowded bed, Randall pulled rank—he being the financier of the trip. Kit reluctantly climbed in first.

Randall extinguished the oil lamp at his bedside and tried to ignore the reverberating snores coming from their bedmate. The man's beaklike nose produced sounds of inhuman proportion, rattling the very bedframe. He included in his repertoire not only the traditional grind of a snore, but little, high-pitched whinnying sounds as well.

After twenty minutes of trying to get to sleep with the din, Kit sat up in exasperation. Randall sat up, too.

Kit whispered, "Maybe we could smother him with a pillow. Put him out of his misery."

Randall immediately got out of bed and stood in the darkness, staring at nothing and breathing hard.

"What's wrong?" Kit said.

Brad did not answer, just ran his hands through his hair and over his face in a distracted fashion.

Kit strained to make out what he was doing in the faint light of the room. "I was just kidding, for christsakes. What's wrong with you?"

"Nothing's wrong. I just . . . never mind. I need fresh air. Want to get dressed again and go for a walk or something?"

"Anything's better than lying next to old Buzz-saw here."

As they prepared to leave the noisy room, Randall hastened back and grabbed his revolver from his traveling case.

"Is that a gun?" Kit whispered, trying to see what his uncle had just slipped into his large jacket pocket. It did not quite fit, but he no longer owned a holster for it.

"My old army Colt. Hays used to have a pretty wild reputation. I thought we shouldn't be rambling the streets at this hour unprotected."

"Can I see it?"

Randall handed over the gun to Kit once they reached the sidewalk. The young man examined it and held it up to the light coming through the hotel windows.

"Your initials?"

"Yes. You can see why I never took up a career as an engraver. Be careful where you point that thing! It's loaded."

Randall slipped the pistol back into his pocket before anyone saw him. He was not sure what the gun laws were in Hays, but he knew that all firearms had been banned in the city of Wichita for several years in response to the general lawlessness of the Kansas cowtowns.

———

The night air was refreshingly cool and served to clear both men's heads as they walked along the darkened streets. Soon they found themselves out on the far western edge of the city. Three miles to the south, they could see the glow of the huge fort. Strains of music drifted through the undulating switch grass.

A large thunderstorm was brewing in the distance, still at least thirty miles away. Silent lightning sparkled on the western horizon again and again. Kit finally yawned, stretched, and headed back for town, but Randall stood for nearly half an hour transfixed by the celestial display. He tried to count the lightning strikes, but kept losing track. The jagged bolts lit up one spot, then another and another, sometimes several at once. They performed a haunting dance across the wide flat prairie that was both sinister and dazzling.

That's her, that's Eden, he thought. *The ghost woman. Eden. She's alive. She's calling to me.*

Without realizing it, his hand had slipped into his coat pocket and now caressed the cold metal of the revolver. How tantalizing and terrible the thought that all his problems and cares could be so quickly and permanently foreclosed. He touched the revolver a long time, but did not take it out of his pocket.

Seven

"What do you mean he isn't here?" Eden was so stunned she nearly shouted the words back to the clerk at the Bureau of Indian Affairs.

"Mr. Randall left many weeks ago on an extended leave of absence. Did you have an appointment to see him?"

"Why did he take a leave of absence?"

"I'm not at liberty to say, ma'am. That is, I don't really know the whole story. I'm new at this office and it would be most indiscreet of me to speculate."

The young man sat before a large window. Too much morning sun shining through it reduced him to a mere silhouette and caused Eden to squint. "I can't believe this. I've just traveled a distance of fifteen hundred miles—at great personal expense—to see him."

"But you did not have an appointment?"

"No, I did not have an appointment!"

"No need to shout, ma'am."

"I'm sorry, I'm sorry. I know this is not your fault." She glanced around frantically, fighting tears of frustration as well as exhaustion.

"Please don't fret. I'm sure the acting commissioner can be of some assistance. Someone on his staff would be happy to receive you if you will but make an appointment."

"Just tell me why Mr. Randall left. Please. In confidence?"

The clerk sighed and leaned forward to speak in a lowered voice. "It is said that Mr. Randall's departure was not entirely voluntary. Rather that the Secretary of the Interior *asked* him to take some time off." The young man sat back. "That's just gossip. Don't quote me. No one quite seems to know except the secretary and Mr. Randall himself."

Eden whispered, "You mean to say he was in some sort of trouble?"

The clerk shook his head. "No, good heavens, no. I'm told Mr. Randall enjoys a peerless reputation among his associates, though he was known to be outspoken in his opinions and thought to be a bit radical in his views. He had some enemies, I'm afraid. Both in the Interior and in the War Department. They felt he had lost his perspective. Too sympathetic toward the Indians. After the Little Bighorn, he lost all support for his liberal views. The tide of public opinion, you know. His policies and programs were deemed too expensive and unworthy."

These words gave Eden some comfort that the Brad Randall she had once known had not vanished, nor lost his principles.

"Again, this is just gossip," he said, "but several of his former staff members told me that he weathered a personal tragedy of some sort—I don't know what exactly—but that he was much altered by the experience."

"How so?"

"His moods were . . . unpredictable. Though I've never heard of him abusing a member of this own staff, they say he was quite contentious in his dealings with his superiors."

"Where is Mr. Randall now?"

"I'm not at liberty to say."

She nodded, then looked up and gave him her best pleading look.

The clerk shuffled his papers and glanced around uncomfortably. He then pulled out a blank piece of paper and inserted it into an odd-looking mechanical device. Eden watched with fascination as he pushed small, black keys with his fingertips that in turn caused printed letters to form on the paper with a resounding clack.

He saw her studying his activity and announced with noticeable pride, "It's called a typewriter. It allows me to create printed documents all on my own." He pulled the paper back out of the machine and slid it to her side of the desk.

"I've been forwarding Mr. Randall's mail to his home. If I were to deliver it *in person*, I would walk to this address."

Eden read on the paper, *Number 302 K Street.*

"It's just a few blocks north of Lafayette Square."

She smiled broadly and whispered, "Thank you."

Eden walked up and down K Street six times, trying to work up the nerve to knock on the door marked Number 302. She was impressed with the grandeur of Brad's neighborhood. Elegant stone and brick townhouses, three stories each, lined the street. Maple trees, displaying their fine autumn colors of red and orange, bordered the broad avenue on both sides. Hardly a five-minute walk from the resplendent dwelling of the president himself.

Well-dressed children played on the brick sidewalks. Three young girls about Hadley's age skipped rope nearby. They chanted an old rhyme that brought Eden back memories of being at school. She would have to teach Hadley to skip rope. That would help her make new friends among the other little girls in town.

Several boys played baseball in the street, though they were often interrupted by the passage of smart carriages traversing the lane and tradesmen calling upon the houses on K Street. Eden watched a poultry merchant work his way up the avenue, knocking upon each door. She waited for him to arrive at the Randall residence, curious to see who might answer the bell. She stood across the street and held her breath as the poulterer carried his wares up the steps to Number 302.

To Eden's dismay, a plainly dressed, middle-aged black woman appeared at the door, obviously a maid or a housekeeper. What had she expected? That a lady of fashion like Amanda Randall would answer her own door? She had forgotten the manners of the city.

Eventually, her heart stopped racing and she had to make a decision. She could simply go home and achieve nothing, after selling a horse she should not have sold to buy a train ticket and fabric for a traveling dress she could not afford . . . or she could get it over with. She could march up to his door and satisfy her curiosity.

She had never in her life flinched before a challenge. Was she now so cowardly she would prefer never to see him again rather than face some awkward or humiliating scene? She, who had faced perils worse than death itself?

She drew a deep breath, walked across the street, and rang the bell.

The black woman again opened the door. "I told you we don't need—. Oh, sorry, ma'am, I thought you was somebody else."

"Is this the Randall residence?"

"Yes, it is, but Mrs. Randall is not at home to callers this aftern—"

"Is *Mister* Randall at home?" Eden interrupted.

"No, ma'am, but if you would like to leave your card—"

"Who is it, Dora?" called a woman's voice from inside the house.

Dora turned her head and Eden heard her tell someone, "A lady to see Mr. Randall. I told her—"

A tall, attractive woman with honey blond hair immediately replaced the middle-aged servant at the door. She was elegantly, though simply attired in what could only be mourning clothes, given their lack of ornament. Her carefully draped polonaise set off her trim, statuesque figure and she seemed to Eden's eye like a fashion illustration come to life. She looked down on Eden with a haughty disdain. "I am Mrs. Randall. What is your business with my husband?"

"I simply came to pay a social call on Mr. Randall."

Amanda Randall narrowed her large blue eyes. "I have never heard of any woman, unescorted, paying a social call on a married man. Am I allowed to be informed of your name?"

"My name is Mrs. Lawrence Murdoch." Eden had not used her former husband's name for so long the word "Lawrence" almost stuck in her throat.

The woman's eyes now widened. "So *you* are the famous Eden Murdoch."

Eden blanched at the woman knowing her first name and did not care at all for her hostile and sarcastic tone. The hair on the back of her neck began to prickle and she now regretted her boldness in coming to the Randall house.

"I don't think I'm famous."

"Well, you *are* in this house. Come in. We need not discuss such matters on the porch." Amanda Randall opened the door wide and gestured Eden to enter.

She hesitated, feeling like she was being invited into a lion's den. Or perhaps that of a lioness.

"Come, Mrs. Murdoch. Don't be shy, for heaven's sake."

Eden followed her hostess into the parlor and felt immediately underdressed. Her plain, dark traveling frock was no match for such elegant and stylish surroundings. Rich brocades adorned the furniture and grand velvet draperies curtained the large bay window. The tooled leather dado gave way to an embossed wallcovering in a bold robin's-egg blue which bore a stylized garnet and moss green floral pattern in the style of Eastlake. A rich Turkish carpet repeated the colors of the wallpaper.

A coal fire burned in the grate of an elaborately carved marble fireplace. Blue and white Oriental ginger jars decorated the mantle.

Brad Randall had done well indeed. A beautiful wife, a beautiful house. She wondered where all the beautiful children were. The house was so quiet it threatened to echo. And for whom did Amanda Randall wear mourning black? This must be the personal tragedy alluded to by the clerk at Brad's office.

Amanda motioned for Eden to sit in a chair opposite the settee, where she seated herself. "I'll ask Dora to prepare us some tea. Or do you prefer coffee?"

"I don't expect I'll be staying."

"Don't be silly. I'll be right back." Amanda rose and left the parlor, apparently to seek her servant.

Eden could not restrain her curiosity and began to explore her surroundings. Just off the parlor, she poked her head into a room that must be Brad's study. It was a small, dark, and masculine room with a heavy desk and a comfortable chair. The walls were lined floor-to-ceiling with shelves of books, hundreds of volumes. Eden wanted to weep with envy for the possession of so many books.

Next her attention was drawn to a small fireplace across from Brad's desk. On its carved walnut mantel sat numerous family photographs. She rushed over to examine them. The handsome Randall family obviously enjoyed posing for the camera. Most were portraits of Amanda and a little boy, at various ages from infancy to seven or eight. Some were of the boy by himself. One showed an elderly man sporting grand white side whiskers, posed with great formality in a military uniform. Eden did not recognize him, but knew he must be someone's father. Probably the wife's father in that Brad had never mentioned his own father and she assumed he had died when Brad was a child.

Another picture showed Amanda holding a baby in a long and elegant christening gown with the boy—at about five years of age, Eden guessed—standing next to them.

Finally her eyes fell upon the last picture in the group, a small portrait of Brad Randall himself. The sight of him staring out at her after an absence of so many years made her catch her breath. He sat for his portrait in a studio setting, his head and shoulders stiffly aligned before a simple drapery backdrop. His face no longer appeared so boyish, yet his features had taken on a pleasing maturity. The broad brow and hooded gray eyes had not changed. His long, draped mustache from the postwar years had given way to a closer-clipped, more current fashion, accompanied by long side whiskers bracketing his face. His golden brown hair appeared darker than she remembered, but perhaps that was the fault of the photographer's lighting.

The small likeness was displayed in a more restrained frame than the other pictures, all of which bore elaborate gilt filigree and ornament. Brad's picture was small enough to fit in the palm of her hand.

She impulsively grabbed the photograph and shoved it in her jacket pocket just as she heard the rapid click of Amanda Randall's heels returning to the parlor. She hurried back to the main room like the thief that she was and resumed her seat, trying to appear more composed than she felt.

Amanda carried in a lovely china tea set on a silver tray and sat it on the marble-topped table near Eden's chair. Eden watched her hostess serve their tea and was astonished to note that Amanda Randall's hand trembled as she poured. The delicate blue and white teacup rattled against its saucer as she held it out for Eden to take. Was she really making such a formidable and imposing woman nervous?

"Please don't go to such trouble on my account, Mrs. Randall. I came to see Mr. Randall and I've been told he's not at home."

"You mean you don't know where he is? When I realized who you were, I assumed you came here to gloat."

"I don't understand."

"My husband left last month for a tour of the Indian agencies in the West. Has he returned to the city or not?"

Eden was thoroughly perplexed by this odd statement. Why would Amanda Randall not know the whereabouts of her own husband? "I think there has been some kind of misunderstanding.

I have not seen or spoken to Mr. Randall in nearly ten years. I do not understand your remarks and, frankly, I find them offensive."

Eden glanced into her lap and realized the outline of the stolen photograph pressed itself clearly against her jacket pocket. She dropped one hand into her lap so that her arm shielded the guilty pocket from view.

"You find them offensive? How interesting. Well, perhaps you could instruct me on the proper manner in which a wife should receive her husband's former mistress? If 'former' is the correct adjective."

This remark stunned Eden to the core. Brad had actually told his wife about his brief affair with her all those years ago? How could he have been so incomparably indiscreet? They had never even discussed it between themselves. Though he had professed his love for her several months after the fact, he had never verbally acknowledged the one night they had spent together as lovers.

Perhaps frankness about premarital indiscretions was the new fashion among young married couples these days. Eden had been away from civilization a long time, she reminded herself. Still, such unbridled candor seemed altogether too . . . *French*.

"I take issue with your implication. I assure you that you are mistaken. If you'll pardon me, I'll take my leave." She stood and placed her teacup back on the tray beside her.

"My husband's feelings for you are no mistake. I can assure you of that. Before our marriage, he would fill whole letters to me with discussions of *you*. Extolling your virtues and your noble triumphs over adversity. Do you think I enjoyed those letters? And do you know he has created a scrapbook full of newspaper clippings about you?"

"I must be going." She hurried for the door.

Amanda was right behind her. "He doesn't know that I know about that scrapbook, but I do and I intend to make fair use of it. Oh, yes, rest assured I will. Two can play his game. I may not be blameless, but neither is he!"

Eden dashed down the front steps and walked as fast as her feet would carry her. She did not want to run. That would not be dignified. Neither did she dare look back until she had placed a good three blocks between herself and Number 302 K Street.

Eden headed straight to the nearest telegraph office and sent a message to Mrs. Redding:

COMING HOME EARLY STOP WILL ARRIVE 4 PM MONDAY NEXT STOP LOVE TO HADLEY—E. MURDOCH

She sat in the dingy railway station waiting to board the train. She had not spent even one full day in her former home of Washington City and yet she was so anxious to leave already she could hardly contain her impatience.

What folly this trip has been, she thought to herself as she sat on the hard wooden waiting bench. *Thank God, in one hour I will board the B&O and in four short days be home again. I will think myself back in heaven—to be away from this accursed thing called civilization and return to my simple life.*

She found it hard to sort out her thoughts amid all the noise and bustle of the station. She tried to eat an apple she had bought from a street vendor, a poor legless War veteran, but she still had no appetite after her unsettling encounter with Amanda Randall. What had all that been about anyway?

She pulled Brad's photograph out of her jacket pocket in a surreptitious fashion, still afraid his wife might send a policeman after her for her theft. She could only hope the woman did not venture into her husband's study often enough to notice the photo's absence. She gazed down at his picture and wondered what all had happened to him in the last ten years.

She recalled the first time she saw him. What a terrible day that had been. He was a captain in the Seventh Cavalry, aide-de-camp to the famous Boy General, George Armstrong Custer. The seven hundred men of the Seventh had swooped down upon the peaceful Cheyenne camp of Black Kettle on the day after Thanksgiving in 1868.

Eden had watched in horror as her Cheyenne sisters, Hanging Road's other wives, were killed before her eyes. She might have suffered the same fate, had her white skin not been discovered in time.

Brad Randall had been placed in charge of finding her family and helping her return to life in the States, a task she did not make easy for him. Yet gradually they grew to know each other better, trust each other, learn from each other. As their friendship blossomed, Brad's loyalties subtly shifted. Before that long winter ended he no longer believed in a military solution to the Indian Question. He decided to work for peace and she admired him for it.

To others, she would use words like "admire," but secretly she knew at some point she had begun to love him. She never once expected him to return those feelings and had been shocked when he bluntly announced them the day they parted forever.

How did he feel about her now? Why did he keep a scrapbook about her? She supposed she should feel flattered by such interest. His actions had obviously inspired jealousy in his wife. Instead, all she experienced was a chilly sense of unease. The only thing she knew for sure was that there was a great deal she did not know at all.

Her train arrived and she boarded, still lost in her puzzling thoughts. She had settled into a seat next to an elderly woman who did not seem to speak English. This pleased Eden in that she planned to buy books with the money she had saved by not staying overnight in a hotel. To pass the long traveling time engaged in reading a book made her look forward to the tedious hours ahead.

The newsboy came through the car with his tray of enticements—books, newspapers, candy, tobacco. Eden's eyes fastened on *The Writings of Mr. Henry David Thoreau.*

Eight

Randall spent the morning at Fort Hays, speaking with the post commander about the Cheyenne situation. The lieutenant colonel hated to admit that the Indians had managed to elude the army for so many weeks.

"General Pope at first refused to believe that the tribe had even made it as far as Kansas. He detailed a small contingent to pursue them. About two hundred and fifty men in all. Captain Lewis was in charge. An excellent soldier. He brought a much needed vigor to the situation, but sadly, he was killed at a place called Punished Woman Creek. Since the depredations on the Sappa River, the complexion of the situation has finally changed."

"What manner of depredations?"

"Quite bloody, I'm afraid. Settlements raided. Livestock stolen. Men killed. Women outraged by the devils. Even a child as young as *nine* did not escape their lust. One poor girl was kept by them through a night and they pulled out all her hair—in addition to whatever else they did."

Randall winced to hear these things.

"They're reported to have already crossed the Platte River in Nebraska. General Crook has dispatched parallel columns to the Sand Hills. More than thirteen thousand troops, in all."

"Thirteen thousand against three hundred? Two-thirds of whom are women and children?"

"General Pope believes the Cheyenne women and young boys can fight as well as men. If I were you, I would head for Camp Robinson. That's where you would find out the latest developments. The post commander there is Caleb Carlton. A good man. I'm sure you'll like him. He would share your sympathies on the matter, I feel certain."

"What will happen if they are caught?" Randall asked.

"*When* they are caught," corrected the commander, with a sly smile. "When they are caught, I assume they will be transported back to the Indian Territory. Sheridan is still in charge of this military district and you know how he feels on the matter."

Randall frowned to acknowledge this assertion. "But this is not a military matter, Colonel. The Bureau of Indian Affairs still governs this situation."

"That's not how General Sheridan views it, Commissioner. The Cheyennes have been declared renegades. The matter is settled. In any case, you know better than I how policies have shifted in the Bureau with the new administration."

Randall nodded and thanked the commander for his time. He and Kit would soon be leaving for the Nebraska Sand Hills, it seemed. He had only one more mission to accomplish before leaving Ellis County. He wanted to meet Eden Murdoch's son in the flesh.

He had been waiting nearly a week for Major John Simon to return from a patrol. He hoped the major would accompany him out to meet Eden's son, who lived on a farm northeast of the fort. For some reason he felt odd going out there by himself.

In his pursuit of Eden Murdoch, he had wired every Indian agent who had dealt with any Cheyennes, requesting information on a white woman who might be living among them, married to a medicine man. His search had yielded nothing. How could she have disappeared so completely? He could not consider the possibility that she might be dead.

He wandered over the fort grounds filled with nostalgia. The place had more than doubled in size since he had spent the spring and summer of 1869 there.

As he passed by the blockhouse and the mess hall, he heard a bugle call that he recognized as "First Sergeants' Call"—one o'clock. He saw the sergeants filing into the Adjutant's Office in the blockhouse and smiled at still being able to remember such things.

Nothing brought back the old days at Fort Hays quite like hearing that bugle call. As a young officer during the War, he was required to memorize nearly a hundred battlefield signals. At least the garrison calls were not so numerous, fewer than two dozen, but so frequent, one seldom needed to carry a watch to know the time of day. The ancient nature of some of the calls gave him a pleasing sense of continuity with the past.

He had been told that "Tattoo," the call that sent the men to retire to their quarters and notified sentries to begin making their challenges, dated back to the Thirty Years War. It signaled the men to "turn the tap to"—in other words, no more beer for the night. This call had been apt for his hard-drinking brother officers in the Seventh.

He looked for the log stockade that had been the setting of his near-fatal stabbing, but found it had been replaced by a more formal and secure building. He wandered over to its former location and found traces of the old stockade's foundation. The original structure had consisted of a circular row of logs driven straight into the ground with a sentry walk ringing its upper edge. Now only the "stumps" of those logs remained, barely visible among the overgrown prairie grasses. He walked the circle in a ritual fashion as though he could somehow summon up the past.

How clearly he remembered the last time he had been here. He thought that day would be his last on earth. He recalled sitting on the dirt floor of the place, gushing blood from a stab wound to his chest. He had slipped into unconsciousness feeling the pressure of Eden Murdoch's warm lips on his forehead, kissing him good-bye before she left with her Cheyenne husband.

The oddest thing he recalled from that day was his lack of fear, despite his certainty that he was about to die. He felt a sadness, a kind of floating wistfulness, but not dread. To lose one's fear of death at so young an age was a splendid gift indeed. Another of Eden's benefactions to him, though he doubted she knew it.

A very different flavor of memory lurked around another corner of the bustling fort. He could not resist walking down Officers' Row and pausing before the third dwelling. He gazed up to the second-story bedroom window on the right side of the house—the room in which he and Amanda had spent the first week of their marriage.

The Seventh Cavalry had been bivouacked in tents three miles south of the fort that summer, but one of the Fifth Infantry officers and his wife had graciously agreed to vacate their quarters for a week to allow the newlyweds to start their marriage in some semblance of comfort and privacy. Hays City, in those wild and raw days, had no decent rooms to let, at least none fit for a bride.

The quarters had been nearly new in 1869, with shutters on the windows and an attractive covered porch that spanned the entire house-front. For a frontier posting, the accommodations were not bad at all, a fact lost on Amanda who let him know the frame dwelling which housed two officers' families with a shared kitchen in the back was not up to her standards.

"You have not lived in a tent yet, dearest," he had reminded her.

He recalled waking up before dawn the morning after the wedding, quite early given he had slept less than three hours. The predawn light had lent shape to the room, but not much color yet. Amanda lay naked next to him in the little bed sleeping silently. He watched the even rise and fall of her breasts as she slumbered.

The humidity of another miserably hot June day had risen before the sun causing her porcelain skin to glow with a dew-like patina. He picked up her little ivory fan from the bedside table and gently waved it over her. The cooling breeze he created caused her soft pink nipples to tighten into perfect little buds. He longed to kiss them though he hated to wake her from such a peaceful and much-needed sleep. At the wedding ball, nearly every officer in both the Seventh and the Fifth had demanded a turn on the dance floor with his beautiful bride. And when they had finally been allowed to retire to their humble bridal suite, sleep had been the last thing on their agenda, at least on his agenda.

She looked like an angel, lying there. Exquisite. Flawless. His.

This is it . . . this is marriage, he told himself. *No turning back now, no second thoughts, this is forever.*

He knew he loved the woman he had wed, but with a small sigh, he acknowledged that he had not wed the woman he loved the most. This shameful admission, however secret, caused the first morning of his marriage to dawn with a poignant tinge of regret.

———

An officer's wife appeared in the door of the house he stood before. She peered out at him with an anxious scowl.

He smiled at the woman awkwardly. "I'm sorry to be staring. I used to live here, you see. A long time ago."

The woman continued to frown.

"I didn't mean to disturb you." He tipped his hat and hurried on down the little limestone walk of Officer's Row. He thought, with a chuckle, that he should have added, "I'm harmless," in that the look on the woman's face indicated she thought him a lunatic.

Enough of this foolishness, he lectured himself. Time to get something done. He mounted his horse to ride out to meet Eden Murdoch's son.

John Simon had given him general directions to the farm where the boy lived. He was to ride north out of Hays until he reached the Saline River, then follow its course east for several miles. The ride took nearly an hour, but a farm finally came into view. He squinted his eyes against the wind and sun.

The farmhouse and outbuildings looked well cared for and stoutly made. Four horses, big Belgian draft animals, grazed in a fenced pasture. Lowing from a large barn indicated some number of dairy cows. That sound was all too familiar to him from growing up on a dairy farm.

Neither he nor Jennetta had had any interest in running the Randall Dairy after his mother's death a few years back, so they leased it out. The rentals currently provided him with his only source of income and if he was careful, he could live on it for a while.

He wondered when he and his sister should finally break down and tell Kit that he shared in these profits. He was entitled to his father's one-third portion. The money was placed in a trust each month and had financed his Georgetown education. Brad and Jennetta originally kept Kit's money a secret to prevent his mother and her new husband from squandering it. Now they hesitated to tell him for fear he would become even more worthless than he was already.

As he neared the farmhouse of Avel Vandegaarde, a teenaged boy with thick dark hair could be seen chopping firewood. He noticed Randall's approach at about the same time.

He set down his ax and shielded his eyes from the autumn sun to see who his visitor might be. He was tall for his age and sturdily built. Randall rode near and dismounted.

"Is this the Vandegaarde farm?"

The boy did not smile, but merely stated, "This is the Vandegaarde *Ranch*. We mostly run cattle."

"And you must be Marcus Vandegaarde?" Randall strode forward with a forced smile and extended his hand.

The boy tightened his grip on the top of his ax handle and refused the friendly greeting. "Yes."

"I'm Bradley Randall. Is your father about?"

"My father died last night. If you want to see him, you'll find him at the undertaker's."

"I'm sorry. I had no idea."

The boy said nothing more. He was a good-looking young fellow, with nice regular features, startling green eyes, decent teeth, a well-cut jaw. A closer inspection revealed red, swollen eyes. Randall knew he had chosen a poor day for his visit and felt badly about it.

"Why are you gawking at me?"

"Was I?" Randall glanced away, sorry for this. He was searching the boy's features for traces of Eden. Instead he found only echoes of the boy's real father, Lawrence Murdoch. He recalled Murdoch being a handsome man. Eden had once described her husband as a nightmare wrapped in a pretty package.

Like so many couples during the War years, theirs had been whirlwind courtship followed by a hasty, ill-advised marriage that proved disasterous to them both.

"What was your business with my father?"

"Actually, I came here to meet you."

The boy frowned at this and jutted out his chin. "If you're selling something, you may as well know, I don't have any money. Not yet. My inheritance is going to be all tied up in the courts for a long time because I'm underage, so you've wasted your ride out here."

"I just wanted to meet you, Marcus. I'm a friend of your mother's."

"My mother died last spring," he said.

"I mean your real mother. The woman who gave birth to you."

This announcement caught the boy's attention. He scrutinized his visitor with new interest.

"Where is she?"

"I'm not quite sure. I've come out here to find her for you."

"Save your time. I don't need her . . . or anyone."

Randall sighed. "You may be forgetting the possibility that it might be *she* who needs *you*."

The boy frowned at this, then resumed his wood chopping, but not before Randall caught sight of a tear quickly blinked away. He decided to leave the sullen child alone for now, knowing he would wish to grieve without an audience.

Nine

Eden arrived back in Bluestem just as Hadley's school day ended. When she drove her wagon near the school yard she envisioned her daughter running to greet her. They would talk happily, sharing stories of the previous two weeks and Eden would bestow her traveling gifts—three books and a new pair of gloves, plus some peppermint candy.

Instead a much less welcome sight greeted her travel-weary eyes. Hadley stood in the center of a circle of children, both boys and girls. Considerable shouting was heard, though Eden was still too far away to make out their words. She hoped they were engaged in some sort of game, but when she saw her daughter's furious face, she knew something far more sinister was transpiring.

She snapped the reins against the horses' backs to urge them into a fast trot and headed them directly onto the bare dirt of the school yard, startling the gang of children and causing many to scatter. Jumping down from the seat, she rushed toward Hadley and found two larger boys holding her to the ground while a third smeared stripes of mud on her face.

"Get out of here now, before I call the marshal," Eden shouted as she grabbed the shoulder of one her daughter's tormentors.

All the children ran for their homes, while Eden helped Hadley to her feet. They walked to the pump in back of the deserted schoolhouse and Eden wet her handkerchief so that the girl could wash her face.

Hadley held her feelings in until they cleared the last street of Bluestem, then she started to weep. Eden placed her free arm around her and wanted to cry, too.

"Tell me what happened, honey."

"It started three days ago. I couldn't remember a certain word in English and I let a Cheyenne word slip out. Teacher made me stand in the corner until recess, then all the kids on the playground started calling me 'Squaw Girl' and saying things like, 'Where's your feathers' and 'why don't you wear warpaint?' I told them they were stupid and didn't know anything, but that just made it worse."

"The teacher punished you for saying a non-English word?" This act upset her much more than that of the school-yard bullies.

"She says we all have to speak good English or else."

"And does everyone in class speak perfect English?"

"Everyone but me and Anna. She's from Germany and she can't hardly talk English at all. Teacher punishes her almost every day."

Eden's temper cooled slightly. It seemed Hadley was not being singled out after all.

"It wasn't fair that Teacher punished me. I just made a tiny mistake. I try so hard."

"I know you do." Eden's eyes ached from fatigue. The journey had tired her more than she cared to admit and now this nasty school incident made her want to cry along with her daughter. "We'll talk about this more at supper tonight."

As they passed near the Sacred Spring on their drive home, they caught sight of a large gathering of people standing at the top of the limestone dome.

"Let's go see, Mama."

Eden was as curious as her daughter, despite her longing to get home. She pulled the wagon up, set the brake, and the two scrambled up the embankment. As they approached the group of well-dressed men and women, they heard a deep, raspy voice: Phineas Claypool was addressing the gathering.

"The Indians consider this place to be owned by the Great Spirit himself," Claypool announced with an authoritative air. "They say that Coronado visited here in 1540 on his quest to find the Seven Cities of Gold. We know for a fact that Zebulon Pike stood here in 1806. The trappers and traders who passed these ways called it the Devil's Washbowl."

Claypool's audience chuckled politely. Eden moved closer, wondering who these people were and why Phineas Claypool felt compelled to entertain them. He noticed her standing to the side of his little group and cast her an annoyed glance. He even momentarily lost his train of thought, something that pleased Eden in an ornery way.

"The Indians have an interesting and romantic legend about this place which I am sure you have all heard about."

"Oh, do tell us the story, Mr. Claypool," asked one of the ladies. "As the owner of the spring, you must know it best."

Eden smirked at this assertion, but kept her peace. She glanced about and saw Hadley playing near the base of the huge limestone dome that held the spring. She did not seem to be finding any mischief to get into so Eden relaxed and stayed to listen to the philistine Claypool defile the legend of the Solomon Spring.

"Ages ago," Claypool began with unctuous drama. He removed his top hat and slicked back his hair. "A beautiful Indian maiden named Waconda, the daughter of a chief, chanced by here one day and saw an injured young warrior who hailed from an enemy tribe. She nursed him back to health and fell in love with him. When he dared to ask her father for her hand in marriage, a great war broke out between the two tribes. Waconda saw her lover shot by an arrow on the very edge of this spring where we stand now. He fell into its bottomless waters and Waconda dove in after him, calling to the gods to give her back her beloved. The Indians say her spirit still resides in the magical depths of these waters and she has the power to cure all those who come here with a pure heart."

Eden shook her head at Claypool's shameless overstatement, calling the spring "bottomless" to please and enthrall his audience when he had dredged it out only last month to plunder its artifacts. His experience on the stage was being employed to an extravagant degree.

With dramatic flourish, Claypool added, "It's also said that if an evil man dares to step close to these sacred waters, a great geyser will swell up to swallow the man and drown him."

Claypool's audience dutifully clapped their gloved hands in appreciation of either his story or his drama in telling it. One of their number was the portly man Eden recalled from the day she came upon their dredging operation. He caught sight of her standing there and stepped over.

"Well, good day to you, Mrs. Murdoch, isn't it?" He tipped his green felt hat.

"And you are—?"

"Clyde Summerfield. We've met before. Do you recall it?"

"Only too well." Eden tried to force herself to be friendly. This man obviously liked to flirt. She thought she might as well put his attentions to practical use. She whispered so as not to interrupt the proceedings. "What is all this performance about?"

"Oh, big doings. These folks have money. Investment capital. Mr. Claypool is looking for investors for his health spa."

" 'Spa'? What is that? I do not know the word."

"It's a resort where people go to get healthy, you know, take the cure."

"Like a sanatorium?"

"More or less. Only the folks who'll come here are probably not that sick. It's more like a holiday for them."

They both quieted to listen to Claypool continue his presentation. "The spring is fifty-five feet across and rises thirty-five feet

from the floor of the valley below. The waters are highly medic-
inal in nature. A fact well-known to the Red Man long before the
arrival of civilized persons to the area."

"What does the water contain?" asked one of the men. "Have
you had it scientifically analyzed?"

"Indeed, I have, sir. An excellent question. Sent off a sample
to a chemist at the University in Chicago. Highly mineralized,
these waters are. Sodium chloride, sulphate, and bicarbonate,
magnesium sulphate, calcium and iron bicarbonate, and silica. All
known and recognized as Nature's healers."

Several of the audience now conferred among themselves and
nodded approvingly.

Eden noticed the approach of an Indian family. She thought
perhaps they were Kanzas, the tribe which formerly lived nearest
this place before the government relocated them to the Indian
Territory. A man, perhaps thirty years old, carried a child of four
or five in his arms while a woman followed, bearing a large,
folded blanket. Eden knew without being told why they were
here and what they planned to do.

The child was obviously sick and the parents had come here
to make a sacrifice and perhaps allow the child to drink or bathe
in the sacred waters.

"Oh, my," said a lady in Claypool's party when she noticed the
approach of the Indian family.

"It's all right, my dear," said one of the men, probably her
husband.

"But they're not coming near us, are they?" the woman fretted.
"Are they wild Indians? Like on the Sappa? We don't know what
they might do."

"I'll take care of this," said Claypool with a gallant flair. He
marched over to the family and began to shout and wave his arms
at them.

Eden followed him. "Mr. Claypool, I'm sure these people mean no harm. They're just coming here for the same reason you sell the water in bottles—for its healing powers."

"Stay out of this, Mrs. Murdoch. I don't need to deal with you today." He turned back to the Indian family. "Get outta here, I said. Leave here before I call the marshal!"

When the father holding the sick child refused to move and indeed took a step closer to the spring, Claypool shoved him in the shoulder hard enough to knock him off his balance, given his filled arms. Both the man and the child tumbled backward and fell onto the hard limestone surface of the dome.

"How dare you?" screamed Eden. "If I had my buggy whip, I'd lay it on you, you . . . you scoundrel!"

Both Eden and the Indian mother stepped to the side of the man and child. He had managed to protect the child from the fall, though the little boy whimpered in fear or pain.

The child's face was covered with crusting sores. Measles? Eden wondered. Or smallpox? The thought of exposure to the dreaded pox caused her to distance herself a bit. She had faced all manner of contagion while working as a nurse during the Civil War and had assisted her medicine man husband in treating the ill, but now concern for the safety and health of Hadley caused her to be more cautious.

Claypool's well-dressed group gathered about them to view the commotion, though the one woman whose fretful remarks had occasioned the whole incident hung back at a fair distance.

"No trouble," the Indian man managed to say in English. He pulled himself up as he handed the child to his wife. "Please, no trouble."

"Leave them be, Mr. Claypool," said Eden. "They've just come here to try and heal their child."

"Well, this is *my* land and I'll say who comes around or not."

"But you know they consider this sacred ground. The Indians have been coming here for centuries."

"Not anymore, they won't. I'm going to build the finest health spa west of the Mississippi and it won't be dirtied up by redskins. You can bank on that."

"Mr. Claypool, your incredible callousness astounds me every day more."

"What's all this, Claypool?" asked one of the group.

He tried to swallow his anger and make a good face of it. He turned a spectacularly false smile on his guests. "Nothing, nothing to worry about. Let's all go back to my office in town. I'll show you the blueprints and the financial projections. And tonight we will all dine together and forget this little misunderstanding."

Claypool ushered the group back down the limestone hill and into their waiting carriages.

Clyde Summerfield tipped his hat to Eden once again to bid her his leave. "Mrs. Murdoch, you mustn't rile Phin so. He's got a nasty temper. Trust me. You'll want to stay on his good side if you're planning on living around here for long. When a fly pesters him overmuch, he gets real creative in how he sees to getting rid of it."

"I'll keep that in mind. Good day, Mr. Summerfield."

Ten

Randall woke up with a monstrous hangover such as he had not experienced since the day after Sarah's birth, when he had celebrated by emptying two bottles of champagne. So much for his being a good influence on his nephew. In fact, quite the opposite situation prevailed during their sojourn in Hays City. Kit seemed devilishly determined to corrupt him and he spoke with such authority on the merits of the various brothels in town, he wondered if he had spent his time doing anything else. They ended up drinking the night away, but Randall ultimately resisted the temptation of "horizontal entertainment," as Kit called it.

He could not tolerate anything more than coffee for breakfast and even the clatter of the cup being set before him caused him to wince in pain. He knew Kit was much the worse for their carousing as well. He had gotten up many times in the night after they had finally made it back to their hotel.

Kit eventually joined him at the Prairie Sunrise Cafe with a mournful expression. With his dark, curly hair in wild disarray, his slovenly, unshaven appearance caused the little blond waitress with the exotic name, Solange, to avoid their table for once, letting her burly father take their order instead.

"You, too?" Randall asked his nephew.

"Huh?"

"Hangover?"

"Oh . . . yeah." Kit's manner seemed to imply something worse than a headache or a queasy stomach.

"What's wrong? Are you sick? More than the whiskey, I mean?"

The boy glanced up at Randall, then quickly down again. He whispered, "I've got something bad wrong with me."

Given how Kit had spent the last week, his uncle had an awful suspicion what his problem might be. "At the risk of sounding indelicate—does this involve a burning sensation in an unmentionable location?"

Kit immediately looked up, startled by his uncle's perceptive diagnosis. "God, yes. It nearly kills me to take a piss."

So much for delicacy. He leaned in to speak in a still lower voice. "It sounds like you've caught your first case of the clap. This is why sensible people don't frequent whorehouses." Though a mere fourteen years older than Kit, Randall felt a surge of paternal emotion for him. "Don't worry, it's not fatal. Just unpleasant."

"You've had this, too?"

"No, thank god, but some of my friends did when I was in the army. I'll take you over to the post hospital and call in a favor or two in order to get one of the surgeons to take a look at you. Army doctors see lots of this sort of thing, so don't be embarrassed. They'll set you right."

Randall decided not to tell him that he had heard the cure was almost worse than the complaint. One of his friends once told him he fainted in the doctor's office during the treatment.

Kit grimaced at the thought of visiting a doctor, then said, "You're not going to tell my mother, are you?"

"Good Lord, no. The family would skin me alive if they knew what I've been letting you get up to." Randall could not resist adding, "You know, when St. Augustine said that it was better to marry than to burn, well . . . it kind of takes on a whole new meaning in this context."

Kit groaned.

Randall wondered if they would have to delay their departure for the Sand Hills of western Nebraska due to Kit's malady. Though his nephew insisted he could sit a horse, he looked feverish on the short ride over to the post hospital.

He dropped Kit off in the head surgeon's anteroom with a hasty farewell and an encouraging pat on the back, but sneaked a glance back at him before leaving the building. The boy had dropped his lusty posturing and now resembled a scared rabbit. He looked more twelve than twenty sitting there with his hat in his lap and his dark, unruly curls hanging in his face.

Randall went to the mess hall to see if he could get a cup of coffee and sit at a quiet table where he could spread out his maps and railway timetables to plot out the next leg of his journey.

When he returned to the post hospital, he found Kit lying down in the infirmary, resting. While he waited for him to dress, the surgeon motioned for Randall to step into his office.

"I wish I could admit him as a patient, Captain, but I'm already bending the rules just seeing him since he's a civilian."

"I appreciate your help, Major. And I understand."

"I have some good news to report. His infection is merely an inflammation of the bladder. Not the dreaded 'clap,' as the boys call it. Though it's quite likely he caught it in the same manner." The surgeon dolefully shook his head. "Damned bawdy houses."

"No one exactly forced him to go there."

"He'll think twice after this, I can assure you. But he took his treatment like a man. Some of them whimper like little girls. If he follows my prescribed regimen, he should be right as dodgers by week's end. See to it he drinks a pint of water every hour. That will help flush out the contagion."

Randall thanked the doctor once again as he and his nephew departed.

"He says I need three more days of treatment." Kit looked ashen and a little shaky as they walked to the post livery where they had tethered their horses. "Uncle Brad, I don't think I've got three more days in me. You can't believe what's involved—"

"I'd rather not hear about it if it's all the same to you."

"But you just can't imagine what that doctor—"

"Kit! I don't want to hear about it. All right? Just *imagining* what that doctor did to you is giving me cold chills." He had survived two wars and had unflinchingly witnessed nearly every manner of carnage human beings were capable of inflicting upon one another, but when he spied on Kit's medical chart the words, "urethral irrigation," he thought he might swoon.

"The doctor thought your St. Augustine joke was a lot funnier than I did."

"I'm glad I was wrong about the diagnosis."

"Me, too. There's something else, though. I lied to the doctor. Was that wrong?"

"Lied about what?"

"He asked me how many women I'd, you know, been in bed with."

"I expect most men lie about that."

"I told him two. I didn't want him to think I was a degenerate or something."

"God forbid."

"The true number was eleven."

"Eleven?" Randall was astounded. "In one week?"

Kit nodded sheepishly.

"Eleven women. In one week." Randall repeated it just to try and comprehend it. He had been intimate with exactly three women in all his thirty-four years.

"I was trying for an even dozen, but I ran out of money."

"Do you have *any* funds left?"

"No. In fact, I told the surgeon that you'd pay for my treatment. Is that all right? I'll pay you back somehow. I swear. I'll . . . I don't know . . . find a job or something."

Randall groaned. This seemed a remote possibility in that Kit had never worked a day in his life. "It sounds like we'll need to delay our journey to the Sand Hills. That's in Nebraska."

"No, let's go. Let's leave tomorrow."

Randall felt powerfully conflicted. He hated to postpone his journey north to the Platte, but Kit's condition would slow him down. On the other hand, he felt duty-bound to look after him. He was his dead brother's son and surely Grant would have done the same for B.J. if necessary.

"I'll be fine, Uncle Brad. The surgeon gave me these pills for the pain." Kit produced a little brown bottle and Randall examined it.

"Morphine. Be careful how much you take. You don't want to end up like me."

Kit looked to his uncle for an explanation as they mounted their horses.

"They gave me morphine in the hospital here after I was stabbed. I used to inject the stuff into my veins with a needle. After five years, my arms looked like pincushions. I've still got scars."

"You're kidding."

"I wish I were. It used to give your Aunt Amanda fits to watch me jab myself. It's hard to stop though. Whenever you try, you get horribly sick. All I'm saying is, be careful. I hated the drug . . . but I loved it, too. It's like *wanting* a snake to bite you."

B.J. was the reason he eventually stopped. He would never forget the look of horror on B.J.'s little four-year-old face when he walked in on him one morning while he was preparing for work. Using the brass and glass syringe was as much a part of his morning routine as brushing his teeth or shaving his chin. He was pulling the needle out of his forearm when he heard his little boy gasp to see the droplet of bright red blood appear with the needle's exit. B.J. ran from the bedroom, terrified, before Randall could explain.

"There seems to be no end to what I don't know about you, Uncle." Kit rolled the little brown bottle between his thumb and forefinger and studied it for a long time.

———

He insisted Kit return to the post hospital the next day for more treatment. He accompanied the balky young man to make sure he got there and quietly resented his nursemaid role.

As he left the infirmary a clerk from the post commander's office ran out from the limestone headquarters building and hailed Randall with waving arms.

"Captain Randall, we have news." The young corporal dashed up, breathless.

He waited anxiously, assuming the corporal referred to news of Eden Murdoch.

"Some of the Cheyennes have surrendered at Camp Robinson."

"Well, I'll be damned."

Eleven

Eden could not sleep for thinking of the confrontation at the Solomon Spring. She had begun to call it Solomon, as did everyone else in town, though it would always remain the Sacred Spring, *Maheo Mahpe*, in her heart. That, in addition to Hadley's problems at school burdened her heart immensely.

She wondered if she should try to apologize to Phineas Claypool, not because she thought she had done wrong, but to gain his good side. She might be able to persuade him to see matters her way if she could somehow erase the bad blood between them.

Clyde Summerfield certainly seemed to like her. Maybe she could convince him to put in a nice word for her with his partner or boss, or whatever Claypool was to him.

On the other hand, why should she ingratiate herself with such a despicable man as Claypool? Her current idol, Mr. Thoreau, was not so meek and diplomatic. Since she could not sleep, she decided to make positive use of her time. She rose and lit a lamp so that she might re-read Mr. Thoreau's essay on civil disobedience. Although her quarrel was a private one, not involving the government, as Thoreau's was, she thought he might have some insight to lend her nonetheless.

In half an hour's reading she had her answer,

Action from principle—the perception and the performance of right—changes things and relations; it is essentially revolutionary.

After dropping Hadley off at school, Eden headed for Claypool's Bluestem office. He lived in town with his wife and her sister and maintained an office on the street level of his dwelling, out of which he conducted many of his business affairs.

The house stood out from the others with its sixteen lightning rods of every style and description gracing the many-eaved roof of the Italianate frame dwelling.

Claypool told everyone that his wife feared thunderstorms more than the devil himself, but town rumor said that it was actually Phineas who mortally feared them. According to gossip, Claypool was once getting his hair trimmed at the local barbershop when a fine spring storm swept down the prairie with little warning. As the storm became louder, Claypool grew more agitated, according to the other patrons of the shop. When a bolt of lightning struck close enough to make the windows rattle, he jumped out of the barber's chair and ran for his home, ignoring the fact that only half his head had been shorn. He drew many stares when he returned the following day to have the barber complete the cut.

Mrs. Claypool informed Eden that her husband could be found at his bottling works next to the spring. Eden thanked her, though the woman virtually slammed the door in her face. Apparently Mrs. Claypool did not hold her in any higher regard than did her husband.

When Eden arrived at the spring, the sight she beheld caused her to toss aside her determination to calmly reason with her nemesis.

Claypool was directing a team of three workmen engaged in the construction of a wrought-iron fence around the spring.

Though the filigreed ironwork fencing was attractive to look at, it had but one purpose: to control who came and went from the spot.

He stood with a group of onlookers, several of which Eden recognized from the day before. They were some of Claypool's prospective investors.

She ran toward him, breathless and agitated, "Mr. Claypool, you cannot do this!"

He drew an irritated breath through his long, thin nostrils. "I can and I will, Mrs. Murdoch, and if you do not leave immediately, I'll have you thrown off this place as a trespasser!"

"Now, Phin . . . settle down," said one of his investors, obviously embarrassed by the scene.

"This is a holy place. You cannot treat it like a curiosity or tourist attraction. It's a sacrilege."

"What do you mean, Madam?" asked the would-be investor.

"This is private property," said Claypool to Eden, but turning a nervous, placating smile on his group of investors. "You have no right to be here and I have every right to develop the property in any way I see fit!"

"You're sure you have title to this land, Mr. Claypool?" asked another of his potential money men.

"Of course, I have title, dammit."

"No need for profanity, Mr. Claypool," rejoined the man, who looked to be a banker or a lawyer.

"Sorry, sorry. You must forgive my ill temper. This annoying woman has me quite vexed, I'm afraid. Please allow me to deal with this situation and I will return at once to continue our discussion." Claypool made to grab Eden's elbow, but the first investor held up his hand to halt him.

"Madam, why do you care so passionately about this issue?"

"She's a damned Indian lover," Claypool spat out. "Used to live with the Indians, married to one of 'em, so I hear. Not that a heathen could enter into any sort of real and legal marriage."

This revelation caused a low rumble of conversation among the men in the little group. Claypool eyed them nervously.

"I don't know how you came to know so much about my personal history, Mr. Claypool. If you find me so interesting, I really must invite you to tea sometime."

Every man but Claypool saw fit to chuckle at this remark.

"I'd be available for tea on any given day, Mrs. Murdoch," spoke up plump Clyde Summerfield as he approached the group.

"Sirs," Eden began, "What is happening here is simply wrong. This is a sacred place. A shrine. To turn it into a commercial venture mocks the laws of God and all that is right and honorable."

Claypool broke in, "Before she goes any further, I think you good gents should know she isn't talking about the Christian God."

"Is that true, madam?" asked the banker-lawyer.

"This place existed before Jesus Christ walked upon the earth. Do you have the right to stop people from coming here to be cured by its healing properties just because they're not Christians?"

"All *paying* customers can come here," said Claypool. "As long as they meet my standards. I propose to build a first-rate resort. Catering only to the finest in society. I won't have the place sullied by any dirty Indians, I can assure you gentlemen of that much."

"You're asking for trouble," Eden said.

"What are you saying, madam? Would there be trouble with the wild Indians if Claypool here carries out his plan?"

Eden considered her answer carefully. She knew the honest response to this question was probably "no," yet it would serve a higher purpose to play upon the fears that were recently inflamed by the Cheyenne depredations along the Sappa River Valley.

"Possibly," she said.

"That's a damned lie," said Claypool, losing his composure once again.

His investor frowned with doubt. "But we all read those horrifying stories out of Decatur County in the papers last month. The savages killed men, outraged women, tortured little children—"

Claypool turned to Eden. "I'm going to have to ask you to leave. Now! And don't even think about coming back!"

"You can't stop me from coming here!" Eden had never once considered the possibility that she would be banned from this spiritual site, a place so full of memories, she did not want to imagine a world in which she could not visit it.

A thin smile stretched over Claypool's narrow face. "What do you think that fence is for?"

"I'll show you what I think of your fence!"

She headed straight for the workers putting up the iron barricade. They stepped back in surprise when they saw this wild woman sprinting over to them.

She grabbed a section of the fence and began to work it loose from its foundation.

"Hey, stop that, lady. The mortar ain't set yet," yelled one of the men.

Claypool and company reached her just as she succeeded in pulling the six-foot-long piece of fence free of its moorings.

She raised the section of wrought iron and held it before her like a shield, "Don't come near me!"

Claypool shook a long, skinny finger at her. "Put that down and get the hell out of here or I'm calling the law."

"Do whatever you need to do, Mr. Claypool, but I'm not moving until you agree not to build this fence." Her breath came in short bursts, both from the excitement of the moment and from the exertion of keeping the heavy fence aloft.

The iron was at least forty pounds in weight. Though she was as strong as any woman accustomed to performing hard labor, this reached her limit and marched a little beyond. The muscles in her shoulders and forearms trembled with the stress. Two of the workmen stepped closer and she jerked the fence at them as though she might throw it. She was not strong enough to actually accomplish such a feat, but she counted on them not knowing this.

Clyde Summerfield was ordered by his boss to fetch the town marshal. He rode off on horseback while the standoff continued. Eden lowered the railing and braced it in front of her. She looked as though she was staring out of a jail cell door already, though the bars ran the opposite direction.

Clyde Summerfield returned with the local law in a surprisingly short time. Much to Claypool's dismay, a number of curious citizens arrived with them.

Eden recognized among their number the man who wrote articles for the weekly *Bluestem Echo*. As the group approached, led by elderly, white-whiskered Braxton Bunch, the marshal of Bluestem, Eden repeated in her mind the words of her hero, Mr. Thoreau, "Action from principle, action from principle, action from principle. . . ."

"Now, ma'am, let's calm down," said Marshal Bunch. "Turn loose of the fence before you hurt yourself."

"No. Not until Mr. Claypool agrees not to build it."

Claypool shouted, "Get her off my property. She's trespassing!"

"Come on, now, Mrs.—what's her name again?"

"Murdoch," offered a fretful Clyde Summerfield.

"Mrs. Murdoch, I'm going to have to arrest you if you don't settle down."

Eden glanced at the reporter from the *Bluestem Echo*. He was busily jotting notes on a little pad of paper with a pencil. "Do whatever you need to do, Marshal. I'm willing to go to jail for my cause."

"All right then, Mrs. Murdoch. I'm going to arrest you for . . . trespassing and disorderly conduct. Will you come now?"

Eden nodded and set the railing down on the limestone at her feet. The marshal allowed her to mount her own horse but he insisted on taking her reins and leading her horse behind his own all the way back into Bluestem.

The entourage of gawking citizens followed and they had all the appearance of a parade. Mr. Summerfield seemed most upset by the matter.

"Mrs. Murdoch, what about your little girl?" he asked just before Bunch escorted her into the jail.

"Do you know Mrs. Lavergne Redding?"

"That little old widow lady? Lives in the Colton boarding house?"

"Please tell her what's happened. She'll know what to do."

Eden was placed in the jail's only cell and told she would appear before the city magistrate in the morning.

Mrs. Redding brought Hadley by the jail immediately after school was out. The girl was upset to see her mother behind bars, so the kindly marshal opened the cell door and allowed mother and daughter to share a reassuring hug and a brief talk.

"Hadley, remember the night the tribe of Tsitsistas came through and camped with us on our land?"

The girl nodded and wiped her tears, trying to make a brave face so as not to disappoint.

"Remember what their chief, Morningstar, said? That they would go north at all hazards because they knew it was the one right course and once you know the one right course, you must follow it no matter what the odds or what the cost."

"And that's why you're in jail?"

"I feel I'm doing something important. I want to stop that man from preventing the Indians from making pilgrimages to the Sacred Spring. My goal is clear to me and I know that achieving my goal will come with a price."

"How much?"

"It's not a price you can measure in dollars, honey. But I must do it, even though it may cost me in other ways, like being separated from you. Do you understand? Does any of this make sense?"

Hadley shrugged.

———

Court was held in a meeting room of the bank building. The entire affair lasted less than ten minutes.

"This is an outrage!" said Phineas Claypool when Eden pleaded guilty to the charges against her, but refused to pay the ten-dollar fine assessed. The magistrate instructed Marshal Bunch to confine Eden in jail for a period of thirty days.

Claypool paced back and forth in Bunch's little office while Eden stood a safe distance behind the marshal's thin, bent form.

"I'm going to sue you, that's what I'm going to do," Claypool said, seething in his starched white collar. He shook the latest edition of the *Bluestem Echo* at them. The front-page story of Eden Murdoch's little protest and subsequent arrest had the whole town talking.

"Calm down, Phin," said Bunch. "Just get over it."

"Calm down? Calm down? My investors backed out this morning! They didn't want to be part of a project that was so 'controversial.' " Claypool spat the last word out as though it were a june bug flown into his mouth. "That's why I was late to court. I've already got limestone ordered, stone masons under contract. What am I supposed to do?"

Eden's amber green eyes glittered with excitement. *I've won*, she thought. *I've actually made this happen.* The fact she had to spend the next month in jail seemed a small price to pay.

"I'll sue you for every penny you've got. You won't get away with this!"

"You can sue me if you wish," said Eden, trying not to gloat, "but I think you'd be wasting your time. I don't have any money."

"I'll get a writ against your land."

"Go right ahead. I don't own that either."

Phin Claypool looked so exasperated, he seemed on the brink of tearing out his greasy black hair. He opened his mouth to speak one last time, but thought better of it and stomped out.

Old Braxton Bunch turned to his prisoner, "You're quite a little pisser. Having you in jail is downright entertaining."

———

Claypool came back the next day to make peace.

"Mrs. Murdoch, I just want to know what you have against me. I'm an honest man trying to make a living. I have broken no laws—"

"Mr. Claypool, there are many laws not found in any law book that we still must follow."

"Why are you trying to ruin me? I have never done anything to you."

"I'm not trying to ruin you. I don't even know you, really. This isn't a personal matter. It's about doing what's right."

"And I say what's right is to build people a fine resort, a sanitarium where they can get cured of what ails them and enjoy one of nature's wonders in the bargain."

"You shouldn't *exclude* people. We all should have the right to enjoy the 'wonder,' as you call it. No one loves that place more than I do."

"I love the place, too. Don't say I don't."

"You love the *profit* it brings you."

"So what if I do? This is America."

Eden sighed. "Yes, I know." America, of railroads and Manifest Destiny and greed and the lust for more and more. To Eden's way of thinking, "America" had come to be synonymous with "insatiable."

"I never complained when you bottled and sold the water—"

"Yes, you did."

"Well, only a little. Can't you satisfy your need for profit using that venture alone? I didn't complain to anyone else about that, did I? Besides, I imagine few people in town agree with me."

"Did you read this article in the *Echo* today?" He slapped the folded paper against the palm of his hand.

Eden shook her head, bracing herself for the latest news.

"This reporter thinks you're some kind of modern Joan of Arc!"

Eden laughed in delight. "Joan of Arc? Really? How flattering. Ridiculous, but flattering."

With an irritated sigh, Claypool threw the newspaper on the floor of the jail and left.

Eden saw the headline that had enraged him: "Will Mitchell County Martyr Its Own Joan of Arc?"

Claypool returned for yet another visit the following day.

Eden rose and greeted him with mock enthusiasm. "Why Mr. Claypool, if we spend any more time together, we will become the subjects of gossip."

This time he brought his assistant, Clyde Summerfield, who courteously removed his hat, though his employer did not.

"I've come to talk business, Mrs. Murdoch," said Claypool. "I've got a lot of money riding on this deal and I am not about to have some Indian-loving bluestocking ruin it for me. Like I told you the other day, because of the mess you've stirred up my investors have backed out on me. I am already on the line for nearly *forty thousand dollars.*"

Eden's eyes widened to hear such an enormous sum. She had never known anyone capable of getting into so much debt. Her personal liquid assets of the moment amounted to thirty-seven dollars and change.

Claypool lowered his voice, "So I am putting it to you straight—how much do you want?"

"What?"

"Mr. Claypool is prepared to offer you a handsome sum to—"

"Shut up, Clyde. I'm prepared to offer you a handsome sum to make this problem go away."

"I don't think so," said Eden.

"All you'd have to do is have another of your famous little chats with the *Echo*. Say how you and I now see eye-to-eye and that it was all just a big misunderstanding and you're not going to cause any more trouble. You do that and I will write you a check for one hundred dollars. I'll go to the bank and give it to you in cash if you want."

"You really don't understand."

"All right, two hundred, that's it."

"I don't want your money. I want you to stop your plans."

"Three hundred, but that's my final offer."

"Three hundred dollars is a lot of money, Mrs. Murdoch," said Summerfield. "Think what-all three hundred dollars could buy."

Eden paused. Her head began to swim in the unholy seas of temptation. Three hundred dollars would buy her and her daughter a great deal of security. But then she thought of Claypool shoving that poor Indian father and his sick child to the ground. "You can make it three thousand and I still would not agree."

"You're a damned fool," growled Claypool. "You'll regret this day."

"If I were you, I would confine my theatrics to the stage. Oh, but I forgot—you always play the hero, don't you?"

Claypool narrowed his dark eyes to slits and said in an utterly quiet voice, "I'll make you sorrier than you can imagine."

The utter malice echoing in his words frightened her. She dropped her saucy pretense of bravado.

"Marshal?" Eden called. "Can you make these men leave? I don't have to have visitors if I don't want to, do I?"

Marshal Bunch made his appearance. "Sounds like it's time for you to go, boys."

Claypool nearly knocked the old man down with his exit, but plump Clyde Summerfield paused and whispered to Eden, "I told you before, Mrs. Murdoch, you mustn't vex Phin so. He takes pride in getting even. A drummer once cheated Phin in a business deal, so he invited him to share a drink of whiskey, like they was celebrating, and he put some kind of acid in the fellow's drink that burned his lips right off and took half his tongue as well. That caused a stir. I mean, everybody knew the drummer was a rogue and a cheat, but still it's not like he deserved—. Well, anyway, Phin laughed about it for weeks. He said, 'That son of a bitch'—excuse my language, but I'm quoting—'will never forget the day he cheated Phineas Claypool.' "

Eden felt a strange twitching in her stomach. "Are you threatening me, Mr. Summerfield?"

"Oh, Lord, no. You're such a nice lady. I don't want anything bad to happen to you, ever."

Twelve

Randall exalted at being on the road at last—to ride over open country, to sleep under the stars, to eat next to a comforting campfire, and even to piss on the ground as he pleased. Just breathing in the fresh, cool air gave him immeasurable pleasure—a joy that could only be fully appreciated by one such as he who had filtered in city air for a decade soiled by ten thousand coal flues.

He had not felt so happy in months. He had not felt so free since . . . he could not remember when. After a couple of hours, he paused to water his horse in a slow-moving stream. He smiled down at his own reflection and mentally crowned himself king of all the Western Territories.

When he finally left the train at Julesburg, Colorado, and got his poor horse retrieved from the livestock car, he had loaded up and headed north though he only had a few hours of daylight left on the unusually cold October day. His horse, Night Sun—a bay mare named after the Cheyenne expression for moon—seemed as eager as he was to hit the trail.

The only time he found in recent years to be out in the wilderness had been his once-a-year hunting trips with Kit and Jennetta's husband, Bob. Those trips had been filled with fun, the least of which being the actual hunting. Amanda and Jennetta always wondered aloud why their husbands never seemed to have much game to show for their efforts, not realizing the main purpose of the trip was to sit around the campfire at night, swapping tall tales and drinking beer. Sleeping late the next morning usually spoiled their chances for hunting success, a fact that seldom bothered them.

Randall still worried over his decision to leave Kit on his own in Hays, but he needed someone to stay there in case important mail or telegrams arrived for him.

He had managed to secure better lodgings for the boy prior to leaving. The little blond waitress, Solange, had offered him the use of her family's attic at the modest rate of two dollars a day. Since this included all Kit could eat, the arrangement paid for itself.

Randall could tell that the young girl was smitten with his nephew and he could only hope Kit would exercise some discretion for once. Her father looked like a formidable sort. Grant Randall had gotten married with a shotgun at his back, or at least the threat of one. His son seemed headed for a similar destiny.

Randall had never before thought about how he and Bob were the closest thing Kit had ever had to a father. The boy's stepfather had been less than a positive addition to his life several years ago. When his mother remarried, she did not even extend an invitation to her son to live with her and her new husband. Kit was never heard to refer to the gentleman without including the phrase "son of a bitch" in the sentence.

Of course, Randall, too, had largely grown up without a male parent. Come to think of it, he had not seen his own father since he was B.J.'s age. The elder Randall had emigrated from England as a young man and met and married Brad's mother, but then got so homesick for his native country, he moved his young family to Liverpool when Brad was five. They lived there for three years, but his mother was just as unhappy in England as his father had been in America.

One night, without a word, his mother woke and dressed eight-year-old Brad, twelve-year old Grant, and two-year-old Jennetta. She walked them to the docks in the dark and the fog. Though that seemed odd enough, the scene grew stranger still when he heard his mother give a false name to the captain as they boarded the ship. He never saw or heard from his father again.

He did not want the same fate to befall B.J. He would remain in his son's life, no matter what. The effect on B.J. of Amanda's forced absence was not a topic he had yet considered.

He thought about the contents of his brother-in-law's letter that he had received just before leaving Hays and to which he had not yet figured out a response.

Dear Brad,

I write you this letter because your sister cannot. She fears you will disapprove of our actions in regard to your son, and surely they are in contravention of the explicit instructions you left with us, but know that we are acting, we believe, in the best interests of all parties here.

B.J., as you know, has become increasingly difficult to manage. He misbehaves at every opportunity and has taken to the most cruel and outrageous treatment of Lindal and little Bert. We are reluctant to discipline him in that he is not our own child and given all he has been through—well, suffice to say it's quite worrisome and we are at a loss.

Now I must tell you our solution. We have begun to allow Amanda access to him. We really had little choice given the fact she had taken to waiting for him to return from school each day on the corner at the end of our lane.

Jennetta had no alternative but to invite her in to tea. We actually feared she might "kidnap" the boy. None of us want the authorities involved, for heaven's sakes. Though it is difficult for either Jen or myself to even be civil to her after the miserable way she behaved to you, we force ourselves to be polite for the sake of B.J., who is overjoyed by her daily visits.

His behavior seems much improved in recent days, though he frets most terribly each evening when his mother must return home without him.

I hope you will be understanding about all of this, Brad. Trust us to cope with the situation as best we can. We love little B.J. and want the best for him.

Your concerned brother-in-law,
Bob

A brisk wind blew down the prairie and Randall was forced to tie his woolen scarf around his head to keep his ears from freezing. He yanked his hat down and rode on, looking for a suitable place to camp.

He had to forcefully urge the balky Night Sun to cross a shallow river. He patted the mare's neck afterwards.

"You've become a spoiled city horse," he said. "Just like your master."

Night Sun was used to a pampered existence, well cared for in a full-service stable, groomed and exercised by stable boys, and ridden by Randall only once a week. He took her out on a bridle path every Sunday morning, in all weather except pouring rain, while Amanda attended church.

Being occupied by a desk job five and even six days a week left him little time for amusement. At least he had managed to keep up his boxing skills. Three times a week he visited the Men's Athletic Club and pummeled a canvas punching bag until he was sore and sweaty. He found the activity a marvelous release from the tensions of the day.

He had once been quite proud of his boxing talents—they had supported him through his first year of college. He had not fought a human being in nearly a decade and wondered if he still knew how. Time and again, in recent weeks, he had entertained himself with fantasies of beating young Clarkson's face bloody.

By early evening, he reached a fine, free-moving creek to make camp. The cottonwood trees that grew along the ravine provided plenty of dropped limbs for firewood. While watering his horse at its bank, he saw a wedge of geese honking overhead. They landed not fifty yards away on a broadening of the creek that amounted to a small pond.

Seized with the prospect of a camp-roasted goose for dinner, he tethered Night Sun and pulled his long-barreled old .44 out of his saddlebag. Though he had recently loaded the gun, he had not fired it in years and certainly had not practiced his aim in too long to matter. Still, he thought to give it a go, confident he could sneak up on the geese at close enough range to insure success.

Using the low brush for cover, he crouched and leveled his sights on an unlucky goose that blithely swam within ten feet of him. He pulled back the hammer and squeezed the trigger.

At the flash of black powder, Randall dropped the gun with a shout of pain and surprise. The revolver had managed to discharge two cylinders at once—one sent a lead ball through the barrel and the other exploded in his hand.

He dove to the edge of the pond and plunged his injured hand into the icy water. A few seconds later, the throbbing wound had numbed enough for him to relax a moment and wonder what the devil had happened.

The flock of geese, now high above him, honked so loudly he felt sure they were laughing at him. He withdrew his hand when he could no longer stand the cold and examined the burn. He had taken off a large piece of skin in the valley between his thumb and forefinger. When sensation returned, the throbbing of the burn began again, so he broke off a tiny crust of ice from the pond's edge and bound it to the raw flesh with his pocket handkerchief.

After unsaddling and grooming Night Sun, he built a small

campfire in the fading evening light. The dancing flames cheered as well as warmed him. He opened a tin of peaches and gobbled them down, then drank the sweet syrup they were packed in straight from the can. Next he heated up a tin of hash on his little fire and ate it straight out as well.

Though disappointed that he could not dine on roast goose, he laughed to think how good the slightly burnt hash tasted. Just eating it outdoors under the gathering stars, made all the difference. The yeasty rolls he had purchased from the Prairie Sunrise Cafe had grown stale and tough, but he loved them anyway. The circumstances transformed the humble meal into a feast. He, who had dined with presidents and senators and foreign dignitaries of every rank and description, could not remember enjoying a meal more than this.

He even forgot from time to time the pain in his hand, though he replaced the little ice chip occasionally. He knew he had not maintained his old Colt as well as he should have. Now he was paying the price. Soon he would be at Camp Robinson where he could have a professional gunsmith take a look at it.

The night sky opened up clear as glass. He decided not to set up the tent he had brought and to sleep out despite the cold. After he had settled into his sleeping roll, he spent a long time gazing up into the endless prairie night, watching the stars come out.

Soon the bright band of stars that Eden Murdoch called the Hanging Road emerged. She had once told him her Cheyenne husband's name derived from the star path which they believed the dead traversed across the sky to reach *Seyan*, their own version of Heaven. Had little Sarah trod the Hanging Road?

———

"This last stage progresses steadily to a fatal termination. I can tell you that, in my thirty years of medical practice, I have not

personally witnessed a patient recover after reaching the third stage."

"How long does she have?"

"I cannot say."

Amanda rose from her seat and paced about the parlor in a disorganized fashion.

"I want another doctor!" she cried, then ran upstairs to resume her vigil in the nursery.

He turned an awkward face to the surgeon. "I'm sorry."

The doctor shook his head to dismiss the remark. "There is no need to apologize, Mr. Randall I take no offense. In fact, I encourage you to seek another opinion. Allow me to write down the names of several of my colleagues who enjoy peerless credentials and reputations in this field." He pulled a piece of paper from his bag and a pen and ink as well. When he finished writing, he said, "I have known only too many who find themselves in the tragic circumstances of you and your dear wife. I understand your need to feel that you are doing all you can."

"Yes, I—" Emotion cause his voice to break. "Doctor, I can't bear to watch my daughter suffer day after day with no end in sight. Her screams of pain, you can't imagine it. The poor little thing. This is inhuman. How much longer can this possibly go on?"

"As I have told you, Mr. Randall, only heaven above knows the answer to that now. She may not last the night or she may hang on for weeks."

"Weeks?" The word felt like a physical blow, as though the doctor had knocked him so hard in the chest that he could no longer breathe.

As the physician made his exit, Randall looked upstairs to see Amanda standing on the landing outside the nursery. From her devastated expression, he knew she had overheard the doctor's remarks. He joined her on the landing and folded her into

his arms. They pressed their faces into each other's shoulders.
"My darling," he whispered, "whatever are we going to do?"
Before she could answer, if she even had an answer, all-too-
familiar sounds issued from the nursery door. Another seizure.

Randall rode through the Sand Hills, impressed by their rolling beauty. The undulating mounds of grass and sand bore a hypnotic quality, unexpectedly pleasing to the eye. The number of small, jewel-like lakes astonished him as well.

As he paused to water Night Sun he chanced to see a lone rider crest the top of a hill some two miles in the distance. He tensed. He did not expect company in so lonely a place.

He could only hope this traveler had friendly intentions in that he did not fancy the need to draw his misfiring Colt on anyone. His injured hand still pained him such that he could scarcely bear to hold his reins.

He raised his hand to the man in that age-old gesture of peace and felt relief when he not only returned the sign, but rode rapidly to meet him.

When Randall introduced himself and his destination, the rider returned the courtesy and informed him he was an army scout for Major Thornburgh who was leading a column of two hundred and fifty men seeking out the remaining Cheyennes who had not surrendered at Fort Robinson.

Randall invited the scout, who introduced himself as Potter Greer, to camp with him that night. As soon as the pair had seen to their horses and created a good fire, they shared a meal as well as the events of the previous month. Though the scout smelled like he did not believe in the concept of bathing, Randall found him enjoyable company as long as he stayed downwind.

"The Third Cavalry out of Robinson nearly bumped right into them," said Greer, a part-Crow half-blood who, from his speech and opinions seemed to have lived among the whites most of his life. "The snow was that heavy. Hard to say who was startled the worst. But they surrendered and came on in without a fight."

"When did Little Wolf and Dull Knife part company?"

"Don't know. Sometime after they left Kansas. That Little Wolf is a cagey one. I swear he sends out warriors all over creation to lay down false tracks. We've followed more bad trails than good in the last month."

The men finished their dinner of a roasted rabbit contributed by Potter Greer and settled in to talk and smoke.

"Dull Knife was making for the Red Cloud Agency," Greer opined as he drew on his long clay pipe. "They didn't know it had been moved north from Robinson to Pine Ridge. Did you know that?"

Randall nodded and tried not to smile. As the commissioner of Indian Affairs he presided over the entire reservation system and had personally authorized the move in question. He had thought it prudent not to disclose his true connection to the situation.

Greer spoke at length of the efforts to catch the elusive band. Admittedly, the country was rough and difficult for a large cavalry unit to traverse. Some of the canyons were so narrow, they permitted only a single file of men on horseback—a recipe for ambush that did not require a military tactics textbook to imagine.

Even the assistance of the Union Pacific Railroad, which had made available to Thornburgh a special train just for the use of his troops, had been of no help.

"They say there was hardly but seventy men in the whole band above the age of ten, but the strongest ones, I think they've gotta be with Little Wolf. Finding them'll be no easy trick."

———

After two full days of riding into the mouth of a relentless North wind, Randall reached the White River. The Unceded Territories lay only a few miles away.

Great white bluffs rose above Camp Robinson like a fortress wall. Sentries met his approach with rifles aimed. He identified himself and was ushered in to see the post commander, Caleb Carlton.

"I know that we at Camp Robinson have been the center of attention since the surrender of Dull Knife's followers, but I never expected a visit by the commissioner of Indian Affairs, himself."

"Frankly, Colonel, I am currently on a leave of absence from my duties at the Bureau. I am here solely as an observer and a private citizen. But I can offer my services as an interpreter, if you should need one."

"You speak Cheyenne? Well, I'll be bound. We've been waiting for them to send down an interpreter from Pine Ridge. This *is* fortunate."

Carlton invited Randall to dine with him and over a welcome meal of roasted beef and boiled potatoes, the young commander expounded on the perplexities of the Cheyenne situation. "The evening they arrived, we counted one hundred and forty-nine in all. About forty men and forty women, the rest, children. Their condition was shocking. Dressed in the barest rags, I have no idea how they have survived this cold."

"What orders have you been given so far?"

"Ones I cannot in good conscience obey, I swear to you. Neither the Indian Bureau nor the military seem inclined to take responsibility."

"I hope that the Bureau is justifiably embarrassed at having created this problem," Randall said.

"You are most refreshingly frank, sir. But the army is mightily chagrined at having been unable to solve the problem, either. Little Wolf's band remains at large and, between you and me, we stumbled on Dull Knife with the good grace of a blizzard, thank Providence. But for that spell of weather, who can say what would have happened?"

"I heard about the incident from one of Major Thornburgh's scouts."

"Since the murders on the Sappa River in Kansas, the matter has firmly been in the grip of the military, but I am faced with the various departments arguing among themselves as to the proper resolution. General Crook of the Department of the Platte is inclined to keep them here in the north, whereas General Sheridan, who commands the Department of the Missouri, complains that the Department of the Platte shows an unbecoming sympathy. Some use the word 'sympathetic,' where others might say, 'humanitarian.' "

Randall could not help but recall the parting words of the secretary of the Interior, "I hate to see you throw it all away over some misplaced sentimentality for a few Indians."

The commander saw Randall fumbling with his fork. "How did you hurt your hand, Captain?"

He reddened and shoved the bandaged hand under the table. "It's nothing. Just a trifle."

"You ought to get our post surgeon to take a look at it. Wouldn't do to let it turn septic. I know too many men who've ended up losing a limb for want of a clean bandage."

Randall thanked Carlton for his concern, but was far too embarrassed about how he came by the injury to seek medical care.

Caleb Carlton handed him the most recent telegram he had received from his old commander, Phil Sheridan. It read, in part:

THE CONDITION OF THESE INDIANS IS PITIABLE STOP IT IS MY
OPINION THEY BE SENT BACK TO WHERE THEY CAME FROM
STOP IF NOT THE WHOLE RESERVATION SYSTEM WILL RECEIVE A
SHOCK WHICH WILL ENDANGER ITS STABILITY

This missive did not surprise Randall in the least. He knew Phil Sheridan's opinions only too well, having once been directly un-

der his command during the controversial Winter Campaign of
1868–69.

Carlton sighed. "I am caught in a vise here, Captain Randall."

Carlton ushered Randall in to meet with the Cheyennes directly
after dinner. Though the captives were afforded the freedom of
the entire post during the daylight hours, they were required to
return to a single large room at night. Though ample enough to
contain them, the quarters were warmed by only one small stove.
He felt inclined to place his hands in his pockets, the room was
so cold and yet he was dressed far better for the chill than the
dormitory's residents.

The condition of the group was appalling. Carlton's description
did not begin to prepare Randall for the sight he beheld as he
was ushered in to begin the parlay. The Cheyennes' clothing hung
in ragged tatters upon their starved bodies. Many were barefoot—
how did they avoid frostbite in this miserable chill? He heard
much coughing and wheezing among the curious crowd who
gathered about him.

He found the sunken eyes of the children the hardest sight to
countenance. They shyly peeked at him as they clutched at their
mothers' skirts. Their bony little fingers resembled quail's feet.
He thought of his own son, sturdy and strong, well-fed to a fault.
How B.J. pouted whenever he was denied sweets in punishment
for some petty infraction.

Randall could not avoid the hateful thought that he, in great
measure, was responsible for this blighted and tragic circum-
stance. He, who had devoted his life to improving the situation
of the Indian people. How could he have failed so miserably?

Randall was introduced to all the head men—Dull Knife,
whom Randall quickly learned was called *Wo he hiv*, Morningstar,
by his own people. "Dull Knife" was a humorous nickname given
him by his friends among the Sioux. Next, he met Dull Knife's

son Buffalo Hump, then Wild Hog, Tangle Hair, and Strong Left Hand.

Dull Knife spoke with passion of their resolve not to return to the south. They had come north at all hazards and they would die here if need be.

They spoke long into the evening on the issues at hand. The Cheyennes were grateful for the rations that they had been given at Camp Robinson—which was to be redesignated a "fort" by year's end, but they remained so steadfast in their desire to remain in the north that Randall was forced to advise the anxious Colonel Carlton, "If the government insists that they be removed south, I think you had better deprive them of all their weapons, even their hunting knives."

"To prevent them from attacking us?" he asked.

"To prevent a mass suicide."

By the end of the week, he was welcomed among the prisoners. They no longer feared him and even invited him to dine with them one night when a dance was planned. That they could be hopeful and cheerful enough to plan a celebration in the midst of so much misfortune and privation, amazed Randall. He remained convinced they were truly a remarkable people, just as Eden Murdoch had always claimed. He wished he, too, could find joy despite loss and disappointment.

He was offered the place of honor next to the chief, a matter which pleased him greatly. He decided he would finally broach the subject nearest to his heart.

"Do you or any of your band know of a Cheyenne medicine man named Hanging Road? He would have originally come from the south, but I know he would be living somewhere in the north lands now. His wife was a white woman with auburn hair." Randall was not sure he had conveyed the term "auburn" correctly, but surely the rest of the description would narrow the field.

Morningstar frowned in concentration and seemed to remember something. "On our journey here, we came upon a white woman at the fork of the Solomon River, near the Sacred Spring, who spoke our language. This surprised us a great deal."

He called to another man named Standing Elk, who was seated in a different circle.

"Oh, yes," said Standing Elk. "That woman was the widow of Hanging Road."

Randall felt a surge of such unbridled joy flow over him, he could barely maintain his composure. "Was her name Seota?"

"I don't remember. It was an odd name. It might have been that. Or it might have been, *Maheo Mahpe.*"

Randall tried not to betray his excitement, "Medicine Waters?"

"Yes, they lived near there, you see. At the fork of the Solomon. It's a well known place. Sacred to all."

The Sacred Spring—Eden had described it to him years ago with a note of rapture in her voice.

Standing Elk thought a moment more, then shook his head. "No, Medicine Waters was the *daughter's* name. They both had white names, too, but I don't remember them."

"So she had a daughter, but her husband is deceased?"

"Yes, the extraordinary manner of her husband's death was the talk of many campfires."

Standing Elk went on to relate that Hanging Road, while on a vision quest, climbed to a high promontory in the Black Hills and was struck by lightning out of a clear blue sky. There were many witnesses to this phenomenal event and its interpretation was the subject of great speculation.

Randall had heard of clear sky lightning. They used to speak of it in the cavalry while out on a scout, but he had never actually heard of it striking someone.

He found it almost impossible to sleep that night, for thinking he might actually have found her. When he finally drifted off he dreamed of the silent lightning storm he had witnessed outside Fort Hays. She had been calling to him after all.

Thirteen

Eden rose from her cot when she saw the young man approach. She could not fathom why the slightly built, curly haired boy looked so familiar.

When he smiled, and a nervous smile it was, deep dimples appeared in his cheeks. Dimples so like Hadley's she could not help but stare.

He extended his hand through the bars. "Good day, ma'am."

"Are you a reporter? If so, the marshal likes to be present during interviews. I don't know why. He just seems to think he's entitled."

"No, ma'am, I'm not a reporter. My name is Christopher Randall. I've come on behalf of my uncle, Bradley Randall."

Eden could hardly believe her ears. For half a second, she feared the boy had come to retrieve the photograph she had stolen from Brad's house.

"I'm sorry. I didn't mean to scare you. My uncle is looking for you."

"Brad Randall is looking for *me*?"

"Yes, ma'am. He—"

"Where is he?" She glanced around him as though expecting Brad to walk in at any minute.

"He's in Nebraska. He's working. That Cheyenne situation. Did you know about that?"

"Yes, I do, as a matter of fact, but how is he involved? I was told he had taken a leave of absence from his post in the Indian Bureau."

"I think he got tired of dealing with the government and thought he could do something better on his own. He speaks Cheyenne, you know."

A smile of pride graced Eden's face. "I'm the one who taught him." She sat down on her sleeping cot, secretly thrilled that Brad Randall had remained true to the principles he had espoused the day they parted.

"Is that so?" The boy smiled broadly. "Hey, Marshal? You got an extra chair?"

"You want comfort, sonny, visit somebody at the Grand Hotel, not jail."

Marshal Bunch carried a straight chair down the short hall from his office, despite his remarks. He placed it next to Eden's cell door and Kit promptly seated himself with a brief word of thanks. He did not know quite what to do when the marshal continued to stand next to him. He looked up at the old man in confusion.

"Ain't it customary to tip your servants, where you come from, boy?"

Kit's jaw dropped open in surprise and he promptly reached into his pocket.

Eden tried not to giggle. "He's just teasing you, Mr. Randall."

The marshal grinned, curving his enormous white mustache in a sly curlicue, then he walked back to his office chuckling while his victim turned a reddened face to Eden.

"He pulls that on everyone who's visited me so far. Now tell me more about your uncle, Mr. Randall. Why is he looking for me?"

"You can call me Kit. I'm not sure, he's been a little bit secretive about it. I take it that you two were once . . ." He raised his black eyebrows suggestively, "close?"

"Did *he* say that?"

"Well, he didn't have to. I mean, what else would a body think when he packs his bags and comes all the way out here the minute his marriage folds up on him."

Now Amanda Randall's curious remarks and accusatory tone came into sharper focus.

"I wired him as soon as I read that story about you in the Hays newspaper. But he hasn't answered yet."

Eden brightened. "You read about me in the newspaper?"

"Yeah. It was a funny story, really. Like the reporter couldn't figure out what to make of it all. They compared you to Joan of Arc and said you heard voices."

"Voices? I never said any such thing."

"That some Indian maiden was talking to you and telling you to do this."

"That's absurd." She shook her head and groaned.

"Listen, the marshal told me that all I have to do is pay your ten-dollar fine and you're free to go, so I'll—"

"No, you don't understand. I'm committing an act of civil disobedience. Just like Mr. Thoreau. Are you familiar with his writings?"

"I don't think I could have gotten through Georgetown without reading his essays, Mrs. Murdoch."

Eden's amber green eyes widened with new respect for her young visitor. "You're a graduate of Georgetown University, just like your uncle? Then you must understand why I *want* to stay in jail."

"She wants to be a thorn in Phin Claypool's side and she's doing a fair job of it," said Marshal Bunch as he returned with a pot of coffee. He handed the tin cups round and began to pour. "He's been in here three times in the last week trying to pay her fine, just to get her out of the limelight, but I keep turning him down. Don't know if I have the legal right to or not, but it's fun watching him get mad."

"Marshal Bunch and I have become old chums during my confinement here," said Eden. "In fact, I've enjoyed the support of a lot of new friends. That Unitarian minister, he's a dear. I only wish more of the local clergy saw fit to support my cause. It's based on religious freedom, after all."

They finished their coffee and Kit rose to leave. "Is there anything I can do for you? I feel like my uncle will want me to do something. And I've got to stay around until he gets here."

"You're very kind, Mr. Randall." She thought for a moment. "I could certainly use some help on my farm. Someone just to go out there and check on the horses. My daughter, Hadley, is staying in town with a friend, but I hate to think of her riding out there all alone—"

"Say no more. It's done."

She gave him directions to her farm and they shook hands. "And do come visit me again."

"Twice a day, if you'll have me, ma'am." He made a sweeping bow, then replaced his hat.

She smiled as she watched him leave. She sat back down on her cot with one thought in mind: *Brad Randall is coming here.*

———

Kit rode straight out to Eden's farm, following her directions and was met by the startling sight of a tall child, her blond braids flying, running at him with a shotgun.

"Turn around and get out of here!"

"Whoa, young lady. Let's talk about this. I'm a friend."

"Prove it!" She stood in her little yard and aimed her gun straight up at him, just ten feet away.

"I'm a friend of Eden Murdoch's. This is her place, isn't it?"

"Who wants to know?"

"You're tough enough to grind pepper, you know that? Come on. Put down your piece and we can talk. See . . . I'm not armed." He pulled his jacket open wide to display his lack of a weapon.

"I'm going to climb down now. Don't shoot me."

The girl allowed him to dismount but kept her shotgun trained on him every second.

He held his hands up. "Can you at least point it away while we talk?"

She lowered the barrel slightly. "Who are you?"

"Christopher Randall, at your service, miss." He took a step nearer to her and she instantly leveled the shotgun at him again. He noticed then that her little face was swollen and wet with tears. "Why are you crying?"

Her face puckered up and threatened more tears. "Somebody shot him," she said in a tiny voice.

Kit looked around quickly. "Shot who?"

"Pink." She let the shotgun drop to her side and she began to sob.

"Who's Pink?"

"My dog."

"Ah . . . that's awful. Let me see." He tried to come closer, but she once again raised her gun.

"Come on, kid. This is getting old. Put your piece down. I just came from seeing your mother in jail and she asked me to ride out here and check on her horses. You must be Hadley."

She sniffled loudly and nodded. "And your name is Randall? Bradley Randall?"

"*Kit* Randall. Brad's my uncle."

"Where's he? My mother's been looking for him."

"Is that so?" He moved closer and she finally dropped her guard. "Why has she been looking for him?"

"She wrote him letters about the Indians and he never answered them, so she went all the way to Washington City just to see him—and we couldn't really afford it—and he wasn't there and she came back real mad."

"Well, it just so happens he came all the way out here to see her, too. It sounds like we've got two people crossing paths who want to get together pretty bad." He paused for a moment. "Where's this Pink?"

"I took him in the house. You want to see him? I'm afraid he's gonna die."

"Can we set aside your shotgun while we're at it? People pointing firearms at me tends to make me nervous."

She broke into a grin. "It's not loaded. I was just trying to scare you."

"You did well for yourself, little Miss Hadley." He could not help wondering about the strange, halting manner in which she spoke. It was not like a speech defect, yet it did not seem like a foreign accent, either. "Why do you talk like that?"

"I didn't learn English first. All the kids at school make fun of the way I talk." She led him into the little sod house built into the side of the hill.

He knelt down next to the bleeding, whimpering old mixed breed dog. A large wound covered his left hind leg. "Could you light that lantern so I can get a better look?"

She did as he asked, but started to cry again as she sat down on the earthen floor and pulled the dog's reddish-blond head into her lap. "Why would anybody hurt old Pink? He's such a good dog. I've had him all my life." She said this as though referring to one hundred years at least.

"Maybe he was trying to steal a neighbor's chicken. Or maybe it was just an accident. Somebody thought they were shooting at a coyote. Try and hold him still. I'm going to see if I can feel the bullet."

Kit half lay on the dog while Hadley held his head. Despite Pink's growling and howling protests, Kit managed to pull a little lead ball from his thigh muscle. He poured a cup of water over the wound to cleanse it, then pulled off the long wool scarf he wore around his neck to bind the dog's leg.

Kit washed his hands and arms in a basin and tried to sponge

134

some of the dog's blood out of his shirt as the girl stroked her pet and quietly sang a little song in a language Kit did not recognize. Some strange quality of her thin, reedy soprano gave Kit a chill.

She looked up to her guest. "It's nearly suppertime. Why don't you cook us some supper?"

Kit had not been planning to stay for a meal, but now he could not think about leaving the girl out here all alone, especially given the fact that somebody had shot her dog. He knew that it had probably been an accident, yet something made him uneasy about the situation.

"To tell you the honest truth, Missy, I don't know how to cook."

"Everybody knows how to cook."

"Everybody but me, I guess. How about this? You keep on petting old Pink there and you tell me what to do and I'll do it."

Thirty minutes later, Kit served his first-ever meal—fried corncakes. They were a little burned on one side, but Hadley politely told him they were delicious.

" 'Delicious' is a stretch, Peppermill, but I'll allow that they're edible." He raised a tin cup of water in mock toast. "Here's to my first cooked meal."

A gust of prairie wind filled with snow blew the door open and caused them both to start.

"We better get on back to town. I've still got to find a place to stay tonight."

"Why don't you sleep here with me, Mr. Randall?"

"Aren't you staying with someone in town?"

"Old Mrs. Redding. She sleeps all the time. She'll never even notice I'm not there and if she does, I'll just tell her she forgot."

"You got any blankets? I could camp out here on the floor, I guess."

"You can share my bed. It's big enough and we'll stay warmer."

Kit chuckled. "Now that wouldn't be considered proper. Men

135

and women are not supposed to share a bed unless they're married, Missy."

"Men and woman aren't supposed to have babies unless they're married, either."

Kit laughed out loud at this unexpected remark. "I guess that goes without saying."

"But my parents weren't married."

"Is that so?"

"When I was little I thought Hanging Road was my father, but he wasn't. He was just my mother's husband."

"A stepfather, eh? I've got one of those devils, myself." He added under his breath, "The son of a bitch."

After some considering, he got the nerve to ask, "Who might your father be?"

"I don't know. I don't even know what day my birthday is."

"Everybody knows that," he scoffed, playfully turning the tables on her.

"My mother didn't have a calendar. She just knows that I was born on the night after the fullest phase of the moon in late September or early October of 1869."

"Well, that means all we have to do is locate an old almanac for that year and that would tell us."

Hadley's blue eyes widened with delight. "Really? You could do that?"

"It's a promise."

By the time Kit had seen to the horses and walked around the place, satisfying himself that all was secure, he returned to find his little hostess already in bed and sound asleep. He stoked up the potbelly stove as best he could, but the cold dirt floor still did not look too inviting. He cast aside his platitudes about social propriety and climbed into bed with the little girl. She curled up next to the curve of his back while he lay awake listening to every rattle the prairie wind set off and each coyote howl and even the strange moans of animals he could not identify.

He pondered the possibility that his little bed partner might be his cousin. He wondered how he could discreetly find an answer to this question. His straight-laced uncle was not the type to expound upon his youthful indiscretions and it would certainly not be prudent to acknowledge any bastards just prior to suing one's wife for divorce. He finally drifted off to sleep without a clear course in mind.

Fourteen

Kit had taken up residence at Eden's homestead for a week before she found out, during a disturbing visit by the local Baptist minister and his wife, that he and Hadley were living there alone together.

The long and solemn man marched into the jailhouse with his plump and pompous spouse on his arm. They asked Marshal Bunch's permission to see the prisoner and informed him that he would be involved in what they had to say.

Eden rose from her cot to greet them, hoping they had come to lend the support of their congregation to her cause. When she saw their ruddy, unsmiling faces, she knew something else had occasioned their visit.

"Mrs. Murdoch, we wish to know why you would allow your daughter to live alone with a young man to whom she is not related in any way. I called upon your home today and found them completely unchaperoned. Such blatant disregard for your daughter's welfare, not to mention the morals of the community, reflect that you are not perhaps a fit parent for the child."

This announcement caught Eden wholly by surprise. She struggled to make a response. "First of all, my daughter is only nine years old, so I believe your implications are completely ill-founded. Mr. Randall has graciously offered to look after my farm for me during this unfortunate time and I am certain he would find your comments slanderous. Secondly, I believe you are mistaken about this situation, sir. My daughter is staying with Mrs. Lavergne Redding right here in town. I am certain of it."

"I am afraid you do not even know the whereabouts of your own child, madam. And her schoolmistress further informs us that she has not been in attendance at school for the last four days. Her inquiry is actually what prompted us to investigate. As you may or may not know, my wife and I head up the county child welfare committee."

Eden looked about her as her mind swirled with concern. Who was Kit Randall and what was going on with him and her daughter? He seemed like such a straightforward and amiable young man. He and Hadley came to visit her every day at about the time the Bluestem school would adjourn for the afternoon. They had given no hint that she was staying out at the farm alone with him.

"What did Mr. Randall say when you arrived at my home?"

"He was most rude," said the wife. She jerked her round chin out in a haughty manner, her prominent jowls giggling.

"I am at a loss here. I—" Eden's remark was cut short by the arrival of the two subjects of discussion.

"I knew you'd be here," said Kit to the minister. "You're a nosy son of a . . ." He curbed his oath in deference to the ladies. "Why do you think this is your business?"

"Young man, I do not like your tone," said the minister. "The welfare and well being of this child is my business."

"Says who?" Kit shouted.

"Whoa, now," said Marshal Bunch. "Sonny, you step outside this minute. I'll let you back in when you cool off."

Kit opened his mouth, but saw Eden gesture for him to comply with the marshal's demand. He replaced his hat with a growl and left the jail, though Eden could see him peeking through the front window once he was back out on the sidewalk.

The minister straightened his waistcoat. "We may well have to start proceedings to have the child placed in protective custody should the mother be declared unfit."

"No!" cried Eden.

"Everything's going to be all right, Mama. Calm down."

"Might I at least have a word with my daughter alone?"

"That's sounds like a good idea," said Bunch. He deftly ushered the steaming minister and his wife away from Eden's cell.

"Hadley, why haven't you been staying with Mrs. Redding?"

"Because Kit said he'd look after me. He's a lot more fun than Mrs. Redding. I like him, Mama. He tells jokes and we race our horses—"

"You know better than to disobey me."

"You never told me *not* to stay with Kit."

"It was also wrong for Mr. Randall to take you out of school without telling me."

"He thinks my school is no good," Hadley said. "He says he has lots more education than my teacher and he doesn't like the mean way she and the other kids treat me. He says we need a man around the house and then people wouldn't dare treat us bad."

Eden sat down on her little iron bed with a groan. The truth of Kit's words, however awkwardly repeated, caused her to despair. She hated to admit that the presence of a man in her life would ease so many burdens. It was all coming back to her now, why she left the world of her birth to begin with. But there was little use arguing with fate.

"The fact remains, darling, that we cannot allow a complete stranger to—"

"He's not a stranger, Mama. He's family."

"According to whom?" Eden rose in alarm and returned to her cell door.

"Kit says we're cousins. He has it all figured out. When I showed him that photograph of Brad Randall, he was certain. And he says I have the Randall family dimples." She pasted a false smile on her thin face to illustrate her point.

Eden placed her hands on her hips. "You got into my sewing notions? Hadley, haven't we discussed many times how we need to respect the privacy of—"

"Excuse me," said the minister, returning to the scene. "Did I correctly overhear the girl say that she and the young man were cousins?"

Eden caught her breath. She realized she saw a way to defuse this uncomfortable situation.

"Yes," said Hadley. She glanced up at Eden for confirmation of this.

Her anxious mother drew an uneasy breath and did not contradict the child.

The minister and his wife exchanged embarrassed glances.

"Why, I . . . I don't know what to say, madam. Why didn't you tell me the young man was a member of your family? I feel quite foolish at the moment."

Eden straightened herself, and raised her chin in an imitation of the minister's arrogant wife. "You did not give me the chance, sir."

"Well, I still do not understand why the girl was taken out of school."

"Let me deal with this in my own way. Please."

"Yes, well, I suppose so." The minister made a fumbling exit.

Before he and his wife turned to leave, Eden called, "Did Phineas Claypool put you up to this?"

The startled expression on the faces of both the couple hinted that her guess was correct, but they hurried out the door without a reply.

Kit entered the moment they left. Eden studied the young man with a critical eye. He seemed so good-natured and eager to be of help, yet she barely knew him at all, certainly not well enough to consign the care of her precious only child to him.

"I didn't mean to do anything wrong, Mrs. Murdoch. Honest. I was just trying to help."

"I'm sure you were, Kit. But—"

"I'm sorry I was rude to them, but they were saying all kinds of awful things. Implying that I couldn't be trusted around your little girl. What do they think I am—some kind of . . . I don't even want to say it."

"They were completely out of line, I'm sure."

"Some people sure have evil ways of looking at things."

"I believe a man with a very evil mind of his own actually placed the idea in their heads."

The outraged Kit began to calm down though his cheeks were still on fire with emotion. "Anyway, what made 'em back down?"

"She told them we were cousins, Kit," said Hadley. "See, you were right."

"I didn't actually say that," said Eden. "I just wanted them to stop harassing you."

Kit frowned in confusion.

Eden changed the subject. "We have much to talk about here."

Three days later, Kit and Hadley walked into the jailhouse wearing smiles as bright as the November sun.

"He's coming, Mama, he's coming today!"

"What? Why aren't you in school?"

"My uncle's coming today, ma'am."

Eden's eyes widened. "Oh, my."

"I'd like to stay and talk," said Kit, "but I've got to look out for him. He's supposed to arrive on the morning stage from Hays, due just any time now. His train got in there last night and he wired me here. I guess he must have found the note I left him. He had to take the stage because his horse got injured in the freight car of the train—which I warned him would happen, I'll have you know."

Kit was quickly out the door, so Eden returned to her first question. "Why aren't you in school?"

"Kit said today was special."

"And I told you that *I* am the one making the decisions, not Kit Randall."

The girl hung her head with a guilty look. "I guess you're not gonna like hearing about the lumber then."

"Lumber?"

"Kit had a load of lumber delivered the other day. He won one hundred and twelve dollars in a game of po-ker, but don't tell him I told you because he said it was a secret. If his uncle finds out he's been gambling again he says there will be hell to pay. How can someone pay for hell? Anyway, he's going to make our house bigger. Since that bossy minister came, he says he needs his own room. He says men and women are not supposed to sleep together unless they're married."

Eden shook her head at this barrage of information and struggled to sort it out, but was interrupted by the sound of the jail's front door swinging open. The voice she heard address Marshal Bunch was so familiar, ten years vanished in an instant. A feeling of delight splashed over her and next she saw the tall, lean form of Brad Randall himself.

He strode directly back to her cell. She opened her mouth to greet him, as breathless as a schoolgirl, but no words would come out.

He looked at her with an odd expression at first, smiled tentatively, then he broke into a broad grin.

"Eden, is it really you?"

"I'm afraid so." She took a few halting steps towards him and he thrust his arms through the iron bars that separated them. She grasped his offered hands and studied every detail of his bearded face.

He pulled her hands back towards him and kissed the backs and the palms of each one. "What in heaven's name are you doing in jail?"

The color rose in Eden's cheeks. "It's a long story."

"One that you'll have plenty of time to tell me. Now that I've found you, I plan to stay a while, I hope you know." He could not seem to stop smiling, no matter how hard he tried.

Kit appeared and said, "Come on, Peppermill. Let's get out of here."

Randall turned and for the first time seemed to notice the presence of Hadley. "Hello, young lady."

The girl turned uncharacteristically shy and merely nodded.

"Hadley," Eden whispered to remind her of her manners.

"How do you do, sir?" She dropped an awkward curtsy.

"Very well, indeed, Miss Hadley." He studied the girl's face and then cast Eden a curious frown.

"Let's go. We'll all meet later." Kit scooped up the girl and threw her over his shoulder, causing her to hoot with laughter. Kit walked out of the jail with his lively parcel waving good-bye backwards.

"Charming girl," Randall said to Eden. "Anything you'd care to tell me about her?" He arched one eyebrow.

Eden knew from his tone that Kit had already shared his conclusions on Hadley's paternity. "Not really."

"Well, anyway . . . I have some news for you. Some news so shocking you had better sit down to hear it. No, I'm serious. You really will be shocked."

"You're scaring me, Brad."

Randall laughed. "No, no, it's good news. Shocking, but good." He drew a deep breath. "Your son is alive."

She looked blank. "My son?"

"The child you named Samuel Murdoch. The babe you lost when your coach was attacked by Dog Soldiers. He's alive, Eden. I've met him. A fine, strapping fourteen-year-old boy. He lives not forty miles from here."

"Oh, my god, oh, my god." Eden's hands flew to cover her gaping mouth as she sat down hard on her little cot. She stared straight ahead, her eyes seeing only racing images in her mind. "How is this possible?"

"A farmer saw the attack on your coach. He arrived after it was over and heard a baby's cry. He picked up your son and carried him home to his wife. They assumed the child's parents were dead in the coach."

"The man and his wife—did they raise him well? Were they kind to him?"

"By all accounts, yes. They're both dead now, I'm afraid. The boy is quite alone, though they've left him well off, I'm told. They named your son Marcus Vandegaarde."

"Can I see him?"

"Of course! That's why I'm here. Now let's get you out of this cell, shall we?"

He called to Marshal Bunch, paid Eden's fine, and in a matter of minutes she left the jail a free woman.

They walked along the street, both shy and awkward. They struggled to make small talk after Randall had conveyed everything he knew about Marcus Vandegaarde.

"I'm anxious to hear about your life," she said, though she knew much of it from Kit. Still, Kit's version of events was probably not quite the same as Brad's.

"Not half so anxious as I am to hear about yours. And Hadley's."

"I don't know what that nephew of yours has said about my daughter, but he doesn't know as much as he thinks he does."

"That seldom stops him from saying whatever is in his head."

"I hope you don't mind that I've put him to work. I fear he suffers from too much energy."

Randall could not help but laugh at this. "Too much energy? I've never heard it put quite that way before."

"What would you call it?" Eden asked, all innocence.

He shook his head. "I don't think you want to know what I'd

call it. Is there a decent place to eat in this town? I think all four of us need to celebrate."

"There are several restaurants, but I've never eaten in any of them."

The unwelcome sight of Phineas Claypool came into view as he emerged from the bank and strode toward them on the sidewalk.

Eden took a deep breath, preparing for an unpleasant scene. Without thinking she slipped her arm through Brad's and pressed close to him.

"Good day, Mr. Claypool," she forced herself to say.

Whether Brad's presence deterred the man or he was not in the mood for a confrontation, he simply grunted in acknowledgment to her greeting and touched the brim of his hat to avoid the appearance of giving offense. He cut to the side of them and hurried on down the way.

"Who is that man?" Randall turned to look at him and saw that he was studying them as well. Claypool almost bumped into a woman pushing a baby carriage while walking backwards to stare.

She squeezed Brad's arm and forced him to resume walking. "He's no one. I'll tell you later."

"I don't like anyone treating you rudely."

"He's feels he's earned the right."

Before Eden could explain this curious remark, she saw Kit and Hadley outside the mercantile loading boxes onto the back of Eden's wagon.

"I must freshen up before we go to this restaurant, Brad. I need to wash my face and hands, at least. And smooth my hair."

"In ten years of marriage, I've learned that a lady must always keep a gentleman waiting for the pleasure of her company."

She smiled coquettishly. "It's one of those unwritten rules."

"Is it true you went all the way to Washington City to see me?"

"Yes, but you must not flatter yourself. I went there to complain of the job you were doing."

Her reproach did not stop his smile. "And you went to my house and met my wife?"

She nodded.

"Exactly how did Amanda receive you? Was she . . . civil?"

"Somewhat. She invited me to tea. Then matters took a strange turn."

Randall shook his head. "I'm trying to picture this."

"I don't think she liked me very much."

"That part I have no trouble imagining."

Hadley joined her mother while Randall helped Kit finish loading the wagon.

"I'm proud of all you've done to help Mrs. Murdoch, Nephew."

"Surprised?"

"What's got your back up? I was trying to compliment you."

"I'm tired of you treating me like a kid."

"I'll treat you like a man when you start acting like one. Consorting with whores doesn't make a man of you, despite what your school friends may have told you."

They both grunted to hoist up a wooden box containing four double hung windows.

"I'm done with all that. I've reformed completely. No more whoring. In fact . . ."

"In fact, what?"

"I had a recent amorous opportunity involving a very willing young lady in Hays and I declined it. I have some morals after all, you see."

"Don't tell me, let me guess—the little waitress, Solange. I feared that would happen."

"The very first night I was up in that attic of hers, she's sliding into bed next to me, as naked as the day she came into the world. But I told her 'no.' "

"Well, bully for you. If there were a medal for morals, I'd pin one on you directly."

"You never take me seriously! I'm just a big joke to you. You said we'd be partners on this trip. Friends, even. But I'm just your dead brother's son. A boring obligation, nothing more."

Randall sighed. He hated to admit the boy was right. "I'm sorry, Kit. I meant it when I said I wanted us to be friends. Sometimes, when you've known someone since they were born, it's hard to remember that time has passed and now they're adults. Someday, years from now, you'll look at B.J. or Jennetta's boys and find it hard to believe they're suddenly grown men."

Kit shrugged, still sulking.

"I'm proud of what you've accomplished here helping Mrs. Murdoch and her daughter. Truly, I thank you for it."

Kit grudgingly took his uncle's offered hand and shook it. He had not shared the full story of Solange's attempted seduction, it not being quite so tidy and sterile as he had intimated.

She had indeed slipped into his room in the attic that first night. He sat up with a start when he saw her approach his bed, carrying a single candle in a small brass holder, harkening back to an older time. Before he could utter a word from his astonished mouth, she had dropped her nightdress and climbed into his bed.

"Solange, you've got to leave here. What if your father—?"

"He sleeps like the dead." She tossed the quilt to the foot of the bed, apparently wishing him to enjoy a full view of her.

"Solange, your father outweighs me by about a hundred pounds at least. He could probably wring my neck with one hand and never stop scrambling eggs with the other."

"But I love you, Kit. I'm yours. You can do whatever you want." She stroked his face with a tender hand.

"You can't love me. We hardly know each other. You've fed me for a couple of weeks and we play checkers in the evening. That's not love. That's friendship. And I like you, I do, but—"

"You want me. I can tell." She pointedly glanced at the erection now making a tent in his long johns.

He grabbed the quilt to cover himself, then studied her lithe form in the flickering yellow candlelight. Something was not quite right about her shape.

She was a slender girl. Arms so lean her hands seemed too big for them. Her breasts barely swelled around dark nipples that stood out in stark contrast to her icy white skin. Her hips were boyishly slim, but her waist . . . her unusually hard, round little belly was the only thing about her that hinted at a womanly fullness.

"Solange, are you in a family way?"

Her little face twisted with a sudden rain of tears.

Kit folded her into his arms and tried to soothe her. "Come on now, don't cry. Tell me who did it. Who's responsible?"

She pulled away to sniff and wipe her eyes on the bed sheet. "A soldier. His name was Jimmy. He said he loved me. He said he wanted to marry me. But when I told him it was time to get married, he ran away."

"Son of a bitch. All men are sons-a-bitches, Solange. Just assume it, then you'll never get hurt."

She sniffed again. "I went to the fort and talked to his captain. He said they were looking for him and when they found him, they'd hang him for desertion." This caused her to cry again. "The captain told me that he'd see to it that he married me before they hanged him, so the baby would have a name at least."

"Small comfort, I guess."

"But I wouldn't get no widow's benefits because he was a deserter."

"I wish I could help you, but I don't want to get married. It's not you. I don't want to marry anybody just yet."

She said between sniffles, "Who'd want me now?"

"Don't talk like that. You're a beautiful girl."

She smiled through her tears and gave him a little kiss. He kissed her back, without thinking. One thing led to another and soon their kissing and caressing and rubbing against each other culminated in a shuddering groan from Kit.

He rolled onto his back to catch his breath then grimaced to notice a little wet stain now seeped through the waist of his long johns. He tried to cover it up before Solange saw it but he was not quick enough.

"I knew you liked me," she gloated.

"That doesn't mean anything. Men are like clockwork." His words were based on theory rather than experience. Prior to his week among the whores of Hays, he had never even kissed a girl, much less rubbed up against one to the point of orgasm. He hoped the hot blush rising in his face was not visible in the candlelight.

She tugged at the sleeve of his long johns. "I'll wash 'em out for you."

"You don't need to do that."

"I don't mind. Besides, I caused it."

"I'd love to hear you explain to your father why you're washing my underwear."

"Give me all your dirty clothes and I'll tell him you're paying me to do your laundry. He loves money better than anything."

"I've got some shirts and socks that could use a good wash. Would a dollar be enough?"

"Six bits is more than fair." She rose to leave and pulled her nightgown over her waterfall of cornsilk hair.

"Solange, are you sure your father can't hear us up here?"

When her head emerged from the neck of her gown, her smile hinted that this might not be her last visit.

———

As they all rode to the farm in the wagon, Eden finally got around to asking Brad a question that had been gnawing at her since he had made his stunning announcement. "Does Lawrence know?"

He drew an uneasy breath, hating to discuss the subject of Lawrence Murdoch, Eden's husband and Marcus Vandegaarde's real father. "The army is looking for him. I think we should assume . . ."

She nodded with a troubled expression.

"Don't worry. I won't let anything happen to you. He'll never get the chance to hurt you again."

As her homestead came into view, Eden strained to note all the changes.

"Are you surprised, Mama?"

"I don't know what to say. Kit, this is just . . . just—"

They all climbed down from the wagon and stood in awe of Kit's accomplishment. He had framed a large addition to the front of the little sod house, more than doubling its size.

They all walked among the skeleton walls, as Eden and Brad murmured in wonder. Eden was so thoroughly astonished she hated herself for ever doubting the young man's sincerity and motives. She hated even more the nasty implications tossed out by that Baptist minister and his wife, though she knew they had Hadley's best interests at heart, even if their actions had been occasioned by the odious Phin Claypool.

"Where on earth did you learn carpentry, Nephew?"

Kit shrugged. "I built that tree house in Aunt Jen's backyard for Lindal and Burt."

"My sister's children," Brad explained to Eden. He said to Kit, "B.J. adores that tree house. I always assumed Bob had built it."

"Bob *supervised*," Kit said with a wry wink. "I did all the work and he took all the credit."

Eden ushered Brad into her sod house with a shy awkwardness she seldom displayed. "This must look like such a wretched little place compared to what you're used to."

"I've spent the last couple of weeks in an army barracks. That is, when I wasn't traveling over land, riding all day, sleeping under the coldest stars imaginable."

"I meant your house on K Street. It's quite the most elegant and fashionable dwelling I've ever entered in my life."

"You mean my *wife's* house." His tone was dry and empty. "The only thing I own in there is the contents of the library. My father-in-law's only legacy to me."

"Oh, your books. I saw them. I must confess the sin of envy when I saw them."

"My wife took you on a tour of the place?"

"Oh, no, I just wandered in by accident when she was off preparing our tea. I suffer from bad manners in addition to envy, I guess."

He chuckled at this as he looked around.

She hurriedly tried to tidy up. Neither Kit nor Hadley was much acquainted with the housekeeping arts. "I know it may sound silly, but I'm proud of this little place. I don't actually own it. I'm just borrowing it, but it's the closest I've ever come to owning a house."

With a wistful smile, he said, "I know what you mean. I always wanted a house of my own."

———

Eden spent the evening preparing for her journey to Ellis County while the men strung up a large tarpaulin over much of the house framing to allow them their own bedroom separate from her and her daughter.

"Mama, why are the men sleeping outside?"

"Where should they sleep?"

"Kit told me that you and Mr. Randall would be taking the bed and he and I would sleep in a tent."

"Mr. Randall and I are not married, Hadley. Only *married* couples share sleeping quarters. Remember how you and Kit discussed this very point?"

152

"But Kit says it won't be long until you and Mr. Randall are married."

Eden let out an exasperated sigh. "Your Mr. Kit needs to mind his own business. For your information, Mr. Randall already has a wife."

"And a son. His name is B.J. which is short for Bradley James which is the same as Mr. Randall's name."

"You're just a walking authority on all things Randall tonight."

"They're our family, Mama. Our tribe."

"Hush now, time for sleep."

As Randall and his nephew shook out their bedrolls and chatted about the trip to Nebraska, Kit finally found a discreet moment to ask a more personal question. "Was I right about Hadley? Mrs. Murdoch as good as said so the other day."

"She refuses to confirm or deny it. I don't know her reasoning, but I suppose she'll say something if something needs to be said. She's had over nine years to come forward, after all."

"Women are complicated," the younger man said with an air of authority.

"That's an understatement and then some."

"But it *is* possible, isn't it?"

Randall hesitated to speak. Talking about matters closest to his heart did not come easy to him. He no longer cared about his own reputation, but there was still hers to consider. "I've never told this to anyone, Kit. Can I count on your discretion?"

"Absolutely." The boy propped himself up with an elbow, eager to listen.

"Yes, it's entirely possible I could be that little girl's father. But I'm not the only possibility. Eden's husband was also in the picture that year."

"She was married at the time?" The scandalous proposition that Brad Randall had once had an affair with a married woman resulting in an illegitimate child raised Kit's interest to the rafters. He could not quite imagine his all-too-proper uncle would be confessing such things—especially to him. Perhaps Brad was going to start treating him like an equal after all.

"I didn't know she was married at the time. Actually she had two husbands.

"*Two* husbands?"

"She thought her Cheyenne husband was dead, but she knew her white husband, Lawrence Murdoch, was very much alive. She lied to me and told me he was dead, though. She hated him, you see, and wanted to be quit of him. But, if I had known she was married, I would have kept my distance. I would never bed another man's wife, no matter what the provocation."

Randall heard a doubtful snort from his audience. "It's true, Kit. I respect the sanctity of marriage. I'm proud, in fact, to tell you that I've never been unfaithful to your aunt."

"Flawless Bradley J. Randall. A shrine to nobility and perfection."

"I'm far from perfect. I just set standards for myself. And when I fail to meet them . . . I hate myself."

Kit did not like the odd tone his uncle's voice had taken on and now regretted teasing him. He sensed the conversation straying into an uncomfortably darker place, so he changed the subject. "Well, anyway. Mrs. Murdoch must still have feelings for you or she wouldn't keep a photograph of you hidden in her sewing box."

Randall smiled into the darkness, pleased and flattered by this. "I wonder where she got a picture of me? I haven't had my likeness taken more than dozen times in my life. We'd best get some sleep. Mrs. Murdoch wants to leave at daybreak."

"Can I come with you to Hays?"

"I had hoped you would continue to look after the farm and the little girl a few more days."

"I want to check on a friend there."

"Solange? Kit, be smart. Keep your distance."

"She's in a world of trouble and I'm worried about her, that's all."

"What sort of trouble?"

"A soldier got her knocked up and then ran off and left her. She's scared to death of what her old man will do when he finds out."

"That's a common story, I'm afraid."

"At least my father did the right thing. He didn't run off."

Randall gasped. "You know about that? That's a deep, dark Randall family secret. Who told you?"

"My son-of-a-bitch stepfather. Who else? He said my dad didn't want me and my mother didn't want me either. I was just . . . a mistake."

"That's not true, Kit. Your father loved you. You're too young to remember, but I'm not. The day you were born was the happiest and proudest day of his life."

"Sure it was," the boy sulked.

"I'm serious, Kit. He dragged me into the nursery and showed you off to me. He said, 'This boy is destined for great things.' "

"He really said that?"

"Let's get some sleep." Randall turned over on his bedroll and tried to get comfortable—both with his bedding and with his fabrication. But was it a bad thing to lie to Kit about his father? Grant Randall was long dead . . . and Kit's loathsome stepfather had been entirely and cruelly truthful.

Fifteen

Randall did not tell Kit the real reason he hoped he would stay behind in Mitchell County: He wanted time alone with Eden. The long ride to Hays City, with Randall riding Kit's horse, afforded him much-needed private time to talk to Eden about so many things. Unfortunately, Eden had no interest in discussing anything or anyone other than her son.

"Do you suppose I will recognize him? I imagine I won't. I mean, how could I? But wouldn't it be amazing if I did?"

He chuckled at her fretful excitement. "I think I should warn you about something, Eden. All of this has come as quite a shock to the boy as well as you. He's only known since last summer that he was adopted. It may take him awhile to get used to the idea of a brand new mother."

Eden nodded and mulled this possibility over in her mind. "I guess I mustn't rush him. I'll go slowly. He will . . . love me, don't you think?"

"I'm sure he will in time. I'm just cautioning you not to expect too much all at once. Though he looks half-grown already, he's still a young boy and he's just recently lost the man who raised him, so he's probably still grieving."

"I know I should be grateful to that man for saving my son's life, but some part of me hates him for not coming forward. Ten years ago, when you found me, you could have reunited us then, but for that selfish man and his wife."

They rode south toward the Saline River and chatted about many things, but the conversation never took a truly personal turn. The weather was fine and fair for the lateness of the season, barely requiring a coat. They soaked up the winter sun and so did their horses.

They reached the river by early afternoon and headed east a few miles, following its course. The Vandegaarde Ranch came into sight and Randall bid them halt a moment.

"That's it."

Eden took a deep breath. "Oh, Brad, I'm scared."

"We can wait a little bit, if you wish. You've waited fourteen years for this day, a few more minutes won't hurt."

With a wild grin, she shouted, "Let's go now!" She dug her heels into her horse and he did likewise.

They raced at full speed onward to the farmhouse and arrived breathless and laughing. They tethered the horses to the fencepost of the corral and turned to the house. Eden surprised Randall by impulsively grabbing his hand as they marched forward.

Their noisy arrival was heard inside the house. Marcus Vandegaarde stepped out of the door and stood upon his porch to view his uninvited visitors.

"That's him," Brad whispered.

"Oh, dear God." Eden's voice trembled with emotion. "He's . . . beautiful. I mean, handsome."

"Marcus?" he called to the boy. "Do you remember me? Brad Randall. I told you I would find your mother for you and so I have."

The boy's wary gaze did not alter.

Eden advanced to within half a dozen paces of where her son stood. "Hello . . . Marcus."

She chewed her lower lip waiting for his reply. Before he could answer, he was joined on the porch by a slender man in his early forties. His black hair and startling green eyes closely mirrored the boy's.

"Well, if it isn't my wandering wife."

Randall instinctively wrapped a protective arm around Eden's shoulders.

"Hello, Lawrence," she said in a dull voice.

Lawrence Murdoch turned his attention to Randall, narrowing his eyes and obviously not pleased by his proximity to Eden. "Have we met? You look familiar to me, sir, but I can't place you."

Randall strode forward and tried to appear friendly. When he reached the porch, he extended his hand. "Brad Randall. We met once long ago in Reliance, Kansas."

"Oh, that's it. The soldier boy." He shook Randall's hand, but sneered, "Isn't she a bit old for you?"

Randall stiffened, but fought the urge to retort. He was only a few years Eden's junior, but was often mistaken to be more youthful than his years. This unintended deception often proved a handicap to his professional advancement. Even men of his own age sometimes refused to take his opinions seriously, thinking they could dismiss them as the views of a mere boy. He had learned to put such naysayers in their place, but he would not take such a harsh tact this day. For Eden's sake and the boy's, he refused to respond to Murdoch's baiting.

"Marcus, might we come in?"

The boy nodded and all entered the dwelling.

The Vandegaarde farmhouse was a spacious one by prairie standards. Though the parlor, kitchen, and dining area all shared the same space, the room was large and inviting. An enormous fireplace of native limestone graced the parlor end of the house. It looked as though it also rose to heat a bedroom above it on the second floor.

Eden removed her gloves and hat and glanced about for a place to put them. She saw a row of hooks behind the door and helped herself since the boy did not offer.

"You have a lovely home, Marcus," she said.

"Yes, I know. My pa built it when I was nine."

"Your *adopted* father," Murdoch corrected.

The boy gave his real father another one of his wary looks.

"Perhaps I could fix us all some coffee?" Eden offered, trying to sound cheerful.

The men nodded their approval, and as she entered the kitchen she called to her son for assistance. When he came close, she could not resist placing her hands on either side of his face, but he jerked away.

"Oh, Marcus, it's so good to see you. Do you know how much I love you?"

"You love me? Then why did you abandon me?"

"Who said that?"

"He did. He showed up here a few days ago and told me the whole story."

"What did he tell you?"

"That you ran away from him and you hated him and you hated me because I was his son and you dropped me on the prairie and ran off to live with the Indians. And when the army hauled you back, you didn't try and find me, but just ran off again."

Eden gasped. "That's not the truth, Marcus. That's a terrible lie."

"I guess you'll get the chance to tell it to a judge. Murdoch's bringing a court action to make himself legally my father. I suppose he's after my inheritance, just like you. My pa told me before he died to expect that."

She rushed out of the kitchen to where Murdoch and Randall stood in the parlor.

"Lawrence, what is the meaning of this? How could you have told him all these lies? And what is this court action?"

"I told him the truth as I saw it, my dear. I cannot be responsible for your shortcomings as a wife and mother. Soon the court will extinguish any claim you have to him along with ending our marriage."

"*What?* I thought you divorced me years ago."

"Divorces are expensive. I honestly thought I'd never see you again. But I'll soon have money enough."

"Eden," said Randall. "We had better get into town and find lodgings before it gets any later. We can sort all this out in the morning."

He grabbed her hat and gloves for her and guided her toward the door before she could protest. She managed to touch her son's sleeve before Randall succeeded in propelling her to the porch.

Once there, he whispered, "We need to get into town and find you a lawyer."

"But Brad, I don't have money for a lawyer. I barely have money for a hotel."

"Don't worry about that," he said as they mounted their horses.

"I can't take your money." She cast a longing look back at the farmhouse as they rode west into the early-setting winter sun.

"I'm not letting a matter of money keep you from your child."

She treated him to a heartfelt smile. "What did I ever do to deserve you?"

She watched him blush in answer to this, the edges of his ears turning scarlet just like she remembered from all those years before.

They rode along quietly for awhile, then he felt compelled to make conversation. "Kit says that a new hotel just opened in town. It's called the McClellan House and it's supposed to be very nice."

She glanced at him quickly to broach an awkward subject. "Is that where you'll be staying as well?"

"No, Kit's got a room rented over a cafe. It's paid for until the end of the month. I just hope the owner's daughter thinks I'm too old for her."

To amuse her and distract her from her worries, he related Kit's story of Solange's attempt to seduce him and thereby secure a much-needed husband.

"The poor girl," was Eden's only comment as she lapsed back into glum silence again.

They arrived in town and rode to the stables in back of the new hotel. Main Street held a number of hotels and restaurants in convenient proximity to the railway depot, though Eden wondered if she could tolerate the sounds of a city. Back home at her little homestead, the only noises she ever heard were the rushing of the prairie winds and, on still nights, the sound of the creek near her house.

Brad checked their horses at the stable, then escorted her into the hotel. The McClellan House was sparkling new and lavishly furnished. It's sign proclaimed, "Sixteen beds at the service of the weary public." Eden indeed felt weary after the emotional ordeal at her son's ranch.

"Did you see the way Lawrence looked at me?" she said as they waited at the front desk to secure a room for her. "There was such hatred in his eyes. I know I don't deserve anything better from him. I've deserted him twice after all."

"With good reason on both occasions."

"Many would not agree with you. Most would say a wife's duty is to stay by her husband no matter what."

"Don't be absurd. Please don't tell me you still have feelings for this man."

"You, of all people, know I don't. It's just upsetting to be so . . . despised. By anyone." She thought of Phineas Claypool as she said this.

He took her leather-gloved hand in his and squeezed it.

"Eden, you have *me* now. I'll see to it you never have to worry about Lawrence Murdoch again."

She declined Brad's invitation to dine, blaming a headache, and asked instead that the hotel send up a tray later in the evening. His disappointment showed so clearly on his face she promised to meet him for breakfast in the morning.

He left to stop in at another livery stable to check on Night Sun. He was pleased to see the horse much improved and probably could be ridden in a day or two. As he chatted with the stable owner, he chanced to ask if he knew any attorneys.

It turned out the man was an expert on the local bar. He was constantly suing people for overdue charges or filing liens against horses left unpaid for. He consulted with lawyers at least once a month.

He recommended a young attorney named Nick Wallace. "Still a little wet behind the ears, but as straight and honest as they come. A hard worker. He's still new in town and he needs the work, so you can count on him giving you his all."

Randall went directly to the young man's office and made an appointment for Eden to meet with him the following afternoon.

Eden waited for Brad the next morning at the Prairie Sunrise Cafe, the restaurant owned by Solange's father. She sat watching a staircase in the rear of the cafe, expecting him to descend from his room in the attic.

She jumped in surprise when a rap on the window glass near where she sat alerted her that he was on the sidewalk outside the restaurant. He waved with a smile and swept in to join her. He carried a large packet of papers under his arm and explained that he had risen early and ridden over to the fort to collect his mail.

Young Solange marched directly to their table the moment he sat down. She tossed her cornsilk braid back over her shoulder and asked, breathlessly, "Will your nephew be joining you soon here, Mr. Randall?"

"I'm sorry, not this trip. He sends his regards, though."

The girl's lower lip nudged forward in disappointment.

"Solange, I'd like to introduce my friend, Mrs. Murdoch. She's going to be staying here a few days and I'm sure you'll be seeing a lot of us both."

Eden smiled and politely dipped her chin. The girl dropped a little curtsy before taking their order for breakfast and retreating to the kitchen.

"I take it from the conversation, you were not *molested* last night?" Eden said.

"Alas, no. I had only attic mice for company. She doesn't look like the predatory creature Kit described, now does she?"

"After what you'd told me, I couldn't help but glance at her waistline. I feel terrible knowing secrets about someone."

"Me, too."

They stopped their conversation to allow their steaming breakfast plates to be laid before them by Solange's enormous father.

To try and keep Eden's spirits up, Brad read aloud from several of B.J.'s letters to him. He discreetly edited them to remove all references to Amanda.

Just as he hoped, she found his son's letters amusing and he watched with delight to see a smile replace the melancholy face she had worn since leaving the Vandegaarde Ranch the day before.

They ate their steak and eggs in silence as he perused the rest of his mail. She fell back into her own thoughts again, until he broke the quiet with an outraged snort.

"This is rich," he said without looking up from the offending letter. "If you don't mind hearing about someone else's custody battles, you'll find this interesting. My wife has just offered to *buy* my son from me."

"You can't be serious." She tried not to frown, but the level of contempt in his voice disturbed her. Sarcasm did not become him. "Unfortunately, I am. This is a letter from my attorney relating an offer he received from Amanda's attorney." He glanced up to explain, "We find it expedient to communicate only through our lawyers these days. She has offered to settle on me the sum of fifteen thousand dollars if I should relinquish all claim upon our son. Well, what do you think? Should I hold out for twenty?"

Eden blinked and repeated dumbly, "You can't be serious."

"No, this time I'm not serious. What the devil was she thinking? Does she imagine I am so hard up for money I would actually contemplate such an offer? She's a madwoman in addition to being a slut."

"Brad, don't use words like that. You're speaking of your son's mother, after all."

"I think I'm entitled to the occasional outburst of righteous anger. Surely my talkative nephew filled you in on why."

Eden looked down at her plate. This told Randall that Kit had indeed shared the tawdry tale of Amanda's infidelity.

She reached across the table and placed her hand on his. He took it and held it. When she finally dared to meet his eyes, they shared a quiet smile.

Sixteen

"Are you saying that there is no hope?" Eden asked the lawyer, Nicholas Wallace. At the edge of her eye, she caught Brad making a strange expression as she said these words, but turned her attention back to the lawyer.

"Mrs. Murdoch, I would love to tell you anything else, but the plain fact is—you are facing an uphill battle here. I spoke with Mr. Brindle, your husband's attorney, this morning and from what he told me, your husband simply can present a much stronger case for sole custody over the boy, once the marriage is dissolved. Of course, Mr. Brindle was surprised to learn that you had also arrived in Hays. He was planning to initiate an *ex parte* divorce action until I informed him you were indeed alive and well."

She twisted the fabric of her blue traveling frock, the one she had made for the trip to see Brad in Washington City. "This is so unfair."

Randall placed a comforting hand on her shoulder and she touched it and tried to smile.

Wallace, a young man in his middle twenties, adjusted his spectacles and noted the familiarity between the two persons who sat before him. To have a married woman as a client and a gentleman to whom she was not married offering to pay for his representation was not going to help their case at all.

"Does he really have the right to alienate my son's affections from me?"

"His suit seeks to establish his parental rights over the boy. Once that occurs, he can essentially do anything he likes."

"Does the child have any say in this?" she asked.

"Not really. He's underage. I think I should mention there is a substantial sum of money at stake. The young man stands to inherit both money and property from his adopted father's estate."

"No doubt Murdoch's primary motive," Randall said with a bitter smirk.

"Hush," Eden said in a low voice. "What if I challenged my husband's divorce action?"

"Eden, you can't be serious." Randall turned to her in disbelief.

She raised a hand to silence him. "Can he divorce me against my will?"

"If you fought the action, it would complicate his case." Wallace looked perplexed by her question. "I was under the impression you had no interest in continuing your marriage."

"If that's what it takes to get my son back. . . ."

"Eden, think about what you are saying, for God's sake."

"Brad, calm down. Let us discuss this when we are alone."

"I must remark," said Wallace, "and please do not take offense—that the two of you must avoid even the slightest hint of impropriety if you are to pursue this course. I know that one of the charges your husband plans to make against you is that of adultery."

Eden blushed at this; she saw Brad direct his gaze at the floor. The three sat in an uncomfortable silence for several seconds.

Randall was the first to speak. "If Murdoch is convinced his wife is an adulteress, what proof does he have that he is the boy's father?"

"He doesn't need proof, Mr. Randall. The husband of a married woman is legally the father of her children, regardless of the true paternity, unless he challenges it and can present some sort of tangible proof."

Randall pressed on. "That's a rule? A law?"

"More or less."

"So that means that Lawrence Murdoch is the *legal* father of Hadley." He turned to view Eden's reaction to this. She was appalled, just as he suspected she would be.

"Hadley?" the lawyer asked in confusion.

"Mrs. Murdoch's nine-year-old daughter."

"You have a daughter as well, Mrs. Murdoch?"

Eden nodded, unable to speak.

"I don't know quite how to ask this delicately, but is Mr. Murdoch the child's father?"

She stared into her lap and slowly shook her head no.

Randall felt a calming wave splash over him to see her admit—to his satisfaction at least—that the little girl was indeed his. What a remarkable turn of events. In meeting her again, she had gained a son and he a daughter. But would either of them ever enjoy this new-found family?

"Well, if there is no chance your daughter is his, and he knows this, his case will be made, I am sorry to say."

"But . . . he doesn't know I have a daughter." She looked for some hint of reprieve in the young lawyer's face.

He only sighed.

———

Eden spent a long and miserable dinner listening to Brad's relentless verbal assault on why she should not try to derail Murdoch's divorce action. She agreed with every point he made. That was the problem. She wanted to get her son back so badly, she was willing to do anything and she hated that fact most of all.

He felt such passion on the issue of her divorce he refused to let the matter rest, no matter how many times she repeated that she was finished discussing it. Finally, she left the table and walked to the hotel unescorted. Before she reached the etched glass doors of the McClellan House, she heard hurried footsteps behind her.

He's come after me to apologize, she thought with relief. She could not bear for Brad to be upset with her. She cared about him so deeply and she respected his opinions too much to feel good about ignoring them.

She turned around with a grateful smile, ready to speak, but the man behind her on the sidewalk was not Brad Randall at all. If fact, no one could have been further from Brad Randall than the short, scruffy-looking young man who now halted and stared back at her in the semi-darkness.

He was no taller than she, herself, and wore a heavy, dirty buffalo coat. His age was hard to place, probably older than Kit but not by much. He appeared to be trying to grow a beard, but the haphazard results only served to make his face look dirty, at least in the low light cast by the windows of the hotel onto the wooden sidewalk.

"Sorry, ma'am," he said. "Didn't mean to startle you. A fine lady like yourself shouldn't be out and about after dark all alone."

She said nothing, but rushed into the small lobby of the McCelland House. She watched through the double glass doors to see that the man kept on walking.

"Is everything all right, Mrs. Murdoch?" asked the desk clerk.

She nodded and quickly retired to her room, but found sleep hard to come by. When she finally ceased her tossing and turning long enough to drift off, she woke up with a start, convinced she had heard someone try the knob of her hotel room door.

She sat up in bed, alarmed but too groggy to think clearly. The room was utterly dark, so she concluded she must have dreamed it. She remembered turning the key in the lock and if her door had even been slightly cracked, she would have been able to see the light from the hallway. A lamp was kept lit all night to allow guests to tread the stairs in safety.

After such an unpleasant awakening, she had even more trouble returning to sleep. She was actually glad to see dawn creep in at the shade so that she could simply give up and rise for the day.

She dressed and headed straight to the Prairie Sunrise, hoping to meet Brad. She only had to wait a quarter of an hour until he descended the stairs. She rose from her seat and waved to him and was gratified to see him break into a large smile the moment he saw her.

His words gushed out as he sat down. "I'm sorry we had an argument last night."

"I am, too. I can't bear for you to disapprove of me."

"It's not that. I just care about you so much and I can't stand the idea that you might make a terrible mistake here. I'll hold my tongue from now on. We've hired an attorney, after all. You should take your advice from him, not me. I'm too personally involved to be objective."

They tried to keep their topics of conversation light and inconsequential through their meal, neither wishing to plunge into the darker waters in the bright light of day.

"How would you like to come with me to Fort Hays this morning? I'm taking Night Sun over to be looked at by one of the army vets. I think he's going to be all right, but I want a professional to tell me so before I actually start riding him again."

She stirred cream into her coffee. "I don't think so, Brad. I have too many bad memories of the last time I visited that place to want to go there again."

He cast her a sympathetic gaze. He knew she spoke of the awful last encounter she had with his commanding officer,

George Armstrong Custer. She had ventured to Fort Hays to try to secure the release of Hanging Road, who was being held prisoner there.

"Were any charges ever brought against you? I worried about you so much."

"None. Custer guessed what happened, but no one else did. We reached an understanding that doesn't bear close scrutiny."

"Then I won't ask any questions." She smiled at him above her raised coffee mug. She savored its rich flavor. Coffee with cream in it was a luxury she could seldom allow herself. "I prayed for your recovery. I hope that's some small comfort. We left Fort Hays and rode straight to the Sacred Spring, in fact. The very place I'm working now to save."

"You must have been carrying Hadley by that time. Kit told me she was born in the early fall."

Eden frowned and set down her coffee mug with such a clatter it sloshed its contents on the table. She angrily mopped up the mess she had made. "I truly wish your nephew would stop trying to play amateur detective with my personal life."

"He *is* something of a busybody, I'm afraid. For the life of me, I don't know how he'll turn out. He's a bright one, but a tad wayward. Sometimes I think it's not his fault. He was so spoiled— and by my *own* mother."

"You grew up together?"

Brad nodded. "Kit and his mother always lived with us. My brother was killed in '62 when Kit was just a tyke. From that moment on, my mother and his seemed to wage a war for his affections. He's never had to struggle for much. The only bad turn he's ever had was his mother's remarriage a few years back. He didn't get along with his stepfather for some reason and pretty much got the boot. He went to live with my sister, Jennetta. Yet another female intent on spoiling him."

"Oh, but I like him, I really do."

Randall grinned and glanced at Solange who was busily clearing tables nearby. "I know somebody else who likes him. She's been pestering me for information about him since the moment we arrived."

"Poor thing." She watched the young girl bustle about the busy dining room, filling cups, taking orders, placing tables. Her slender waist showed no hint yet of pregnancy. Eden wondered how far along she was. If early enough, she knew of certain herbs that could induce a miscarriage. She had mixed feelings about their use. Her white heritage preached against such measures, but her years among the Indians exposed her to a more pragmatic philosophy. Overpopulating their fragile world was viewed as a threat to all. Giving birth to more children than one could care for was thought to be a dangerous form of self-indulgence, contemptuous of the common good, in fact.

She decided it was time to speak of Hadley and her life with Hanging Road. "He was a good father to her. He couldn't have loved her more if—" She paused, knowing now she had perhaps said too much.

"You had no children together?"

Eden shook her head sadly. "I felt like I failed him. But, maybe, given his early death . . . I don't know."

"A man named Standing Elk knew him. At least, knew *of* him. He told me about how he died."

"Yes, I think everyone talked about that. Clear sky lightning. A strange phenomenon. A supernatural death for a supernatural man. Somehow fitting. I tried to tell myself that, at least."

"Were you happy all those years?"

"As happy as one could be given the circumstances, I suppose. Living in a constant state of war creates some very hard times. Still, there were a few years of quiet. In the early seventies. Those were good years."

She looked across the table with a pleasing serenity. He wanted to kiss her, she looked so beautiful. To his loving eyes, she had hardly aged at all.

171

"But after his death," she continued, "I knew I had to leave the band. I knew the reservation days were only a whisper away. I chose to come to the Sacred Spring because it was the most peaceful place I could think of." She shook her head. "I see now I was wrong."

He decided to change the subject for fear she would grow melancholy again.

"So how will you occupy your day, if I can't persuade you to come riding with me?"

"Shopping! What else? I'm a normal woman after all. I want to find some nice cloth and notions to make Hadley some new school clothes. I fear she's not nearly so nicely dressed as some of the other little girls."

She had left strict instructions with Kit that Hadley was to return to school. Though she had to admit Kit was a superior teacher to the local Bluestem schoolmistress, she wanted her daughter to get more used to mixing with other children. Kit had argued against this. He had witnessed, as she had, the other children's cruelty to the girl.

Eden had refused to be swayed. Hadley was no stranger to child bullies and grew up bearing the taunts of the Cheyenne children who did not accept her white skin.

Kit proved as stubborn as he was brash, but they had finally reached a compromise. Kit would continue to tutor her in the evenings and would pick her up every day after school. He said he would not let on that he was "protecting" her but rather that he simply wanted her company.

This offer pleased Eden, especially given the dog shooting incident that concerned her just as much as it had him.

With the mention of buying clothes for Hadley, Brad pulled out his wallet. "Let me buy—"

"No." She held up her hand. "You're already doing too much. I'm embarrassed that you're paying for my attorney and my hotel and all my meals." She tilted her chin in a provocative fashion. "Who knows what you'll expect in return?"

He laughed out loud. "Who knows—indeed! I could make suggestions. . . ."

He left her to see to his horse's care while she stayed to finish another cup of delicious coffee. While she sat perusing the local paper, the *Hays Sentinel*, she became aware of only a single diner left from the morning service besides herself.

Every time she glanced at him, he pretended to look elsewhere. When once he could not avoid her gaze, he smiled and nodded as though to say hello. That was when she recognized him to be the man who spoke to her on the sidewalk the night before. He looked even more unpleasant in the morning light that now cut a high angle through the cafe's large windows. Elaborate dark red braiding and fringe decorated the glass and caused intricate shadows to fall across the dining room.

Eden signaled to Solange, who immediately brought a coffeepot to her table. As she allowed the girl to refill her mug she whispered, "Who is that man over there? Do you know him?"

Solange made a sour face. "That's Harry Knapp. He thinks he's a big shot now that Sheriff Streeter decided to hire him as a deputy. He's nobody. Just ignore him."

Eden felt immediate relief that the man was an officer of the law. Surely that meant he was no danger, as she had first imagined. He certainly represented a poor specimen of lawman though. His dark hair looked greasier than the dripping strips of bacon on his plate.

She left to start her shopping and enjoyably entertained herself for a couple of hours buying things for Hadley. She wandered into the market, hoping to pick up some of the peppermint candies her daughter loved when she caught sight of Marcus Vandegaarde paying for a purchase at the counter near the door.

Her pulse doubled its pace as she made her way toward the front of the store.

"Hello, Marcus." She spoke in a quiet voice, hoping she did not startle him.

"Hello." He did not look enthusiastic about their meeting. He picked up his purchase, a bag of apples, and headed for the door.

She followed him out onto the sidewalk. "May I walk with you?"

"I don't suppose I can prevent it."

She tried not to betray her disappointment at his attitude, remembering Brad's admonition that she must not expect too much too soon. Brad was so wise in these matters. "I named you Samuel, after my father."

"So?"

She had to quicken her pace to keep up with him. "I would like to get to know you. Learn all about you."

He shrugged without looking at her. "There's not much to tell."

"I can't imagine that's true."

He stopped walking and finally turned to face her. She noticed he was nearly her height. "Look, I don't have anything to say to you. He's told me all about you."

"Who has? Your father? Lawrence Murdoch? What has he said?"

"That you're basically no better than a common harlot, like in the Bible. That you're that fellow Randall's whore and that you even bed down with *Indians*. I'm not pleased to be speaking with you on the street, much less claiming you as kin."

Tears of outrage filled her eyes. She tried to control her anger toward Lawrence. She would not complicate her dealings with her son by a show of temper.

"Marcus, you know that Mr. Murdoch doesn't like me and he hopes that you won't like me either. That's why he's told you lies about me. You are a nearly grown boy, so I am going to talk to you like you were an adult. I'm asking you to give me a chance. Listen to *my* side of the story before you make up your mind."

"I don't think much of him either, if that pleases you. I don't want to claim either of you as parents and if a court says I've got to, I'll . . . I don't know, I'll run away or something."

He dashed off down the street and Eden tried to hide her tears from passersby as she hurried back to the privacy of her lodgings.

Brad was furious when she told him at dinner what her son had said.

"Damn that Murdoch." He turned the handles of his knife and fork round and round in his hands. "If he wants a fight, by God, he'll get one from me."

"I never imagined—" Tears choked out the rest of her sentence.

"Don't cry, Eden. This is somehow going to turn out all right. I'll make it turn out right. I can't stand to see you so unhappy. Let's go visit Lawyer Wallace again tomorrow and try to find out what is happening on your case."

———

They spent the following morning sitting in the lawyer's office, waiting for him to return from court. He arrived at just after noon and advised them he needed to be back in court at one. He sent his clerk to fetch them all a tray of food.

"I filed the papers yesterday," he said. "I've not yet received a response, of course. Mr. Brindle has probably not had a chance to talk with his client on the matter, so I have little new to report."

"How long until my case comes to court?" Eden asked.

"It could take weeks, Mrs. Murdoch."

"Weeks! But I have to return to Bluestem and my daughter and my farm."

"I'm sorry. The law moves but slowly, I'm afraid."

Eden and Brad exchanged unhappy glances.

"In filing your answer to his suit for divorce, I did not mention the existence of your daughter. If they ask the question, we will be forced to answer it, but I felt we were under no obligation to divulge extraneous information . . . yet."

Randall let out an disapproving sigh. He was still violently opposed to Eden's decision to fight Murdoch's divorce action.

"I have to warn you, Mrs. Murdoch, when the court date arrives, they will mercilessly cross-examine you. They will do everything in their power to present you as a terrible wife, a terrible mother. Mr. Brindle advised me that this would be most unpleasant for you. And I know that it will."

———

They left the lawyer's office feeling glum and hopeless. Brad offered to send a telegram to Kit, telling him they were delayed and would come home for a brief visit on the weekend.

She left him standing in line at the express office, needing some time alone to walk in the chill air and try to sort out her thoughts.

She stared at the wooden sidewalk beneath her feet as she walked and did not see Lawrence Murdoch until she was about to collide with him.

"I have just come from my lawyer's office, Eden," he said. "What in hell do you think you are doing? He said you had retained an attorney and that you planned to fight my divorce action. Isn't that just a little inconsistent with your behavior of the last fifteen years?"

"I think it awfully strange that you now wish to claim custody of a child you refused to acknowledge as your own all those years ago."

"Don't be absurd. He looks exactly like me. No one would question it."

"You questioned it virtually every day I carried him. Remember all those filthy names you called me? And all those outrageous acts you accused me of? According to you, I must have bedded every man in the Army of the Potomac!"

"I don't know what you're talking about."

"You had better watch out, Lawrence. If you try too hard to

make me out a poor mother, I shall have to tell them about you."

"There's nothing to tell, you despicable—"

"Our marriage was short, but dramatic, Lawrence. Don't claim you were so drunk on those occasions that you don't remember."

"Shut up!"

"I know many men beat their wives and the law tolerates it, but few go to the lengths of cruelty you devised."

"Close your mouth, woman. You're making a spectacle. People are starting to stare."

"What's the matter, Lawrence? Don't you want everyone to know why I left you? Why I never wanted your son to see your face?"

"Shut up. I'm warning you." Despite the cold air, beads of sweat glistened on Murdoch's forehead.

"The judge will be interested to hear the story of the day I knew I had to leave you. I was carrying him at the time, seven months gone. Do you recall what you did to me? Do you recall why the landlady at my boarding house called the police? Remember the looks on those policemen's faces? And we all just assume they are hardened to such matters. I'm going to give details, Lawrence. Every single—"

He cuffed her with the back of his hand across the face, knocking her backward onto the wooden sidewalk. Passersby who had been observing the altercation from a discreet distance now rushed up.

A young woman with three small children clutching at her skirts cried, "Are you all right?"

Murdoch made a quiet exit and walked off down the sidewalk as though nothing had happened.

Eden tried to recover her dignity as well as her breath. She nodded to the concerned woman and pulled herself into a sitting position, straightening her skirts to cover her exposed legs. Radiating pain from her cheek made it feel ten times its normal size.

The waiflike blond waitress from the Prairie Sunrise Cafe also rushed up and whispered to Eden, "I'll go fetch the sheriff, Mrs. Murdoch."

"No, no, that's not necessary," Eden said, but Solange hurried off anyway.

She stood up with the assistance of a young soldier, though she still felt shaky from the blow. She did not at first see the tall figure shoving through the small crowd that had gathered about her.

Brad Randall's long arms wrapped around her and she gazed up into his worried face. She hugged him with a grateful relief and did not want to let go.

"Eden, what happened?"

She had only to speak the word, "Lawrence," and he reacted with instant fury. He pulled off his heavy jacket and thrust it into her arms and was off in pursuit of her tormentor before she could stop him.

She ran after him down the wooden sidewalk, as did numerous others who knew what would happen next and wanted a front row seat.

Randall caught up with his prey in a matter of seconds. He tackled Murdoch from behind and both tumbled into the frozen mud of the street. Randall pummeled Murdoch with powerful fists. The smaller man quickly realized his only hope was to try to escape. He managed to pull away a couple of times, but his liberty was always short-lived. Randall fought like a man possessed by demons. Eden could not imagine such violence spilling from such a gentle soul.

Soon, Murdoch could no longer even present a token show of defense. He cowered and tried to shield himself from Randall's relentless blows.

"Brad, stop it! You're killing him," she said, but he seemed beyond hearing her.

The crowd, which had been shouting encouragement and cheering and booing as though attending an entertainment staged for their benefit, now fell silent and watched in a mixture of curiosity and horror. As Murdoch's blood began to splatter, they understood they might soon be witnesses to a killing.

Eden saw in the crowd three young soldiers from Fort Hays, each sturdy and healthy looking, easily capable of breaking up a fight.

"Please make them stop," she implored.

They glanced at each other. "We can't help you, ma'am. There's strict new orders. If we get into any kind of trouble in town, they slap us in irons."

"Please, somebody help," she called out to the crowd, but no one came forward.

Frightened tears rolled down her wind-burned cheeks until she heard a man's deep voice shout, "*Stand aside.*"

The crowd parted like the Red Sea for Moses and Sheriff Plum Streeter arrived on the scene with the questionable little deputy, Harry Knapp, in tow. Between the two of them, they succeeded in dragging Randall off the nearly lifeless form of Lawrence Murdoch. They shoved Randall into a sitting position on the edge of the wooden sidewalk.

"Stay put!" the sheriff warned as he shook a threatening finger in Randall's face. He placed his other hand on his sidearm as an unspoken threat.

Streeter and his deputy pulled the unconscious Murdoch up from the mud of the street. Murdoch did not open his eyes, but began to groan and mumble, blood issuing from his lips like drool. He was able to spit out a couple of broken teeth to keep from choking on them. The sheriff called for someone to fetch the doctor, but was told he was already on the way.

Eden crouched next to Brad on the sidewalk to see if he was hurt. He did not display a single mark on his handsome face. His only noticeable injury appeared to be badly torn knuckles, though he did hold his side. Murdoch had managed a strong kick in the ribs before he gave up the fight.

Randall leaned his head back against the post that held up the roof of the covered sidewalk and drew deep, long breaths. He reached for Eden and gently touched the mark on her cheek. She offered him back his jacket, but not before noting that it was unusually heavy. She slipped her hand into the large pocket to find a revolver. She gave silent thanks that he had not carried this weapon into the bloody fray.

She then looked down in the street at her husband. Not only did his nose and mouth gush blood, his left earlobe was torn and he carried a deep gash over his left eyebrow. Judging from the damage to Lawrence Murdoch's face, his rival threw a powerful right hook.

"I saw the whole thing, Sheriff," offered a chubby young butcher from an adjacent shop. He wiped his hands on his bloodied white apron and stepped forward with a pompous air. "That fella started it." He pointed to Murdoch. "He hit this lady and knocked her right off her feet."

Eden turned her face slightly so that the sheriff might see the swollen red mark on her cheek. She even sported a tiny cut where Murdoch's school ring had bitten into her flesh. Streeter nodded to her.

"Then this gentleman came to her defense," continued the butcher. "I would have done the same, but I was engaged with a customer at the time."

The doctor arrived with his medical bag and took a quick visual inventory of the damage to Lawrence Murdoch. He declared the patient would need stitches in several locations. Two men from the crowd volunteered to help Murdoch walk around the corner to the doctor's surgery.

When they departed, Sheriff Streeter turned his full attention on Randall. The lawman made an imposing figure when he drew himself up to his full height.

Eden looked up nervously into the sheriff's solemn face. He was a middle-aged man of dignified bearing, far more impressive than his smarmy little deputy. He wore a full, graying beard and a well-cut black frock coat.

"I'm not going to arrest you, given the provocation for the fight," he began. "But I want to tell you that a fight is not a fight when one man keeps hitting another long after the other one's given up. At some point it turns into an assault and then a killing and I'm pretty certain that's what I would have witnessed if I'd come on this five minutes later."

Brad sat back against the post, still breathing hard.

Before leaving, Streeter warned, "I'll be keeping my eye on you."

The crowd of onlookers gradually dispersed until all that remained was a fourteen-year-old boy. He made a plaintive figure alone in the gathering whims of dusk. He did not brace against the cold prairie winds even as their dry, icy snows swirled around him.

"Marcus?" Eden rose to go to him. "I'm sorry you had to see all that."

"Stay away from me!"

"Please let me explain."

"Go away from here. I don't need you or want you. Nor him neither. I already had a father and a mother. I don't need any more now. I wish you both were the ones who'd died!"

"But Marcus . . . give me a chance . . ."

He turned and ran down the street.

Eden started after him, but Brad caught hold of her skirt's hem. She turned back with an angry frown, but when he shook his head, she realized he was right. Chasing after the boy with the mood he was in now would accomplish little. Brad pulled himself to his feet and wrapped his arm around her shoulder. They walked the short distance back to the McClellan House Hotel.

Seventeen

Brad led Eden into her hotel room, ignoring the disapproving scrutiny of the desk clerk. She sat down on the edge of the bed in dejected silence. He hesitated for a moment, then thought, *To hell with the desk clerk*, and closed the door. If the hotel manager wanted to complain about this small assault on public morals, he would break *his* face, too.

He tried to turn the key in the lock, but it would not move. He gave up and sat down next to Eden on the bed. He took her hand. "Darling, are you all right?"

She nodded with a sad smile, though she touched her reddened cheek as a reflex. "Shouldn't I be asking you that question?"

"I'm sorry about what happened. I don't know what came over me. When I found out he had struck you . . . I just lost control. I came . . . unraveled. I wanted to kill him. I confess it. I've never wanted to kill anyone so much, not during the war, not even the man who . . . well, you know about Amanda and all."

"Why are you carrying a gun?"

"How did you—? Oh, I gave you my coat before the fight." He forced a bitter smile. "Glad I did now, given my mood. Please forgive me."

"I just wish Marcus hadn't seen this all happen."

"I'm more sorry for that than anything. I'm sure he'll come round. He was just shocked and upset. He didn't know what he was saying."

She looked down at his hand in her lap and examined his skinned knuckles. She was as shocked as her son by what she had just witnessed. The intensity of Brad's violence against her husband seemed so out of character. But she did not want to talk about the fight. Her son's hard words were the only thing that had strong meaning for her now.

"I don't know. I feel like I've lost him twice." She stared at the floor, as though studying its shiny oak planks and a simple, colorful rag rug.

Brad pulled her close. "At least your son is alive. Won't that give you a little comfort? No matter how things turn out?"

"Yes. I guess I'm being selfish to want more."

"Your feelings are the most natural in the world. Don't apologize for them." He kissed the top of her head. She lifted her face to his and he could not resist kissing her mouth.

She did not taste pity in his kiss; at that moment, she had no use for pity. She let him push her back onto the bed for a sweet and wild barrage of kisses. His hard, hungry body pressing against hers felt like a blessed balm to the pain that threatened to swallow her.

He finally paused, somewhat breathless. "If you want me to stop, you need to tell me."

She looked up into his earnest, loving face. "Is the door locked?"

"Yes," he lied.

———

She opened her eyes to the orange glow of the winter sun against the window shades. The fluid light filled the room with a false warmth. She turned to look at Brad's sleeping form next to her. He seemed to her the most perfect man on earth.

She gently pulled the bedsheet down and studied him more fully, pleased to have this private moment into which even he did not intrude. She blushed like a virgin to recall all that they had done last night. He had been so eager to make love to her he had not allowed them time to even remove their shoes, much less their clothing. She smiled at how startled he had been when he first ran his hand over her starched cotton blouse and felt her soft breast beneath it.

"No corset?" he had whispered in surprised delight.

"No drawers either."

He quickly ran his hand up under her skirts to verify her claim. "Well, I'll be damned. You're making this too easy for me."

She had been so happy to have him back in her arms she had wept.

"Eden, did I hurt you? God, I'm sorry."

"No, no, that's not it." She had tried to smile through her tears.

After they had recovered from that first, frantic coupling, the night turned into one long, erotic dream so filled with love her heart ached to contain it all. Other parts of her ached as well. They had nearly worn each other out with love.

After Hanging Road's death she had felt so certain she had no more need for a man in her life. Now she realized how wrong she had been. If only Brad could be hers. *If only*. What dangerous, hopeless words.

She examined the large, shiny white scar on the pale skin of his chest, the reminder of his stabbing at Fort Hays all those years ago. She recalled trying to staunch the flow of blood from that terrible wound. She could not resist lightly tracing her fingertips over the scar. She felt responsible for it. He had risked the wound for her sake.

Her touch caused him to stir.

"Good morning," she whispered with a kiss. She allowed her hand to drift down his torso and under the covers to play with his nakedness.

He murmured and stretched. "Is it morning already?"

"The sun's up."

He opened his eyes and grinned. "The sun's not the only thing that's up."

"So I noticed."

He rolled on top of her and pinned her to the mattress, then kissed the tip of her nose. She wrapped her arms and legs around him. She could not remember feeling this happy in so long.

"My darling, darling, Eden," he murmured, nuzzling her neck. "You know what they say, don't you? 'Make love before breakfast and your whole day will go right.' "

She giggled. "I've actually never heard that before."

"That's probably because I just made it up."

She laughed with delight. She adored him being so silly and light-hearted, for a change. "I suppose we'd better test your theory then."

He stopped kissing her suddenly and looked serious. "I feel a bit guilty about last night. You were in such a state. I took advantage of you, didn't I?"

"I don't recall resisting."

"And I committed adultery. I'll probably roast in Hell for this."

"Since Lawrence claims we're still married, I guess I committed adultery, too. If there is a Hell, at least we'll roast there together."

"Remember our first night in old Hugh Christie's bed? Did you know I thought for the longest time that I only dreamed that night? Did you put a spell on me?"

Eden provocatively arched one eyebrow. "Maybe. Is that why you never mentioned it? I thought you were just being a gentleman."

"I don't know." He laughed again. His dark and light moods seemed to change quicker than the prairie weather. "I still can't imagine you and Amanda in the same room together. Oh, to be a fly on that wall. The only two women I've ever loved. The only two women I've ever bedded."

"Liar. Even I know that's not true."

He bit his lower lip and raised his eyebrows in a comical attempt to appear innocent. "It's *nearly* true. Unlike my nephew, I prefer *quality* over quantity."

"Then I'm honored to be in such an exclusive sorority."

He laughed and kissed her again. "You can't imagine how long I've waited to talk to you just like this."

"About ten years, I'd guess."

"Must you always be so literal?"

"You know me."

He flipped her over on top of him. Her long curly auburn hair fell down around his face, curtaining it. "Before we go any further, we have to talk about something important."

The playful smile fell from her lips and she tensed.

"Why don't you wear underclothes like a decent woman?"

She laughed out loud in relief. "Corsets aren't the fashion under doeskin. I got so used to being able to take deep breaths, I didn't want to give it up."

He laughed, too. "Well, I've got just one thing to say about that: I like it! How wonderful to put my arm around a woman and feel *her* ribs instead of the bones of some long-dead whale."

"Is that really the important matter we needed to talk about?"

"No." He took a deep breath. "Eden Elizabeth Clanton Murdoch, are you going to let me make an honest woman of you? As soon as we legally can, that is."

"Oh, Brad . . . I—"

In the fatal half-second of her hesitation, his smile grew less certain. "You're going to say 'yes,' of course . . . aren't you?"

"But this is so sudden. I can't think about the future just yet."

All the happiness melted from his face. "You told me you loved me."

"I do. But I'm not ready to—"

He pushed her away and sat up in bed, completely stunned.

"What was last night about then? I can't imagine you're the type of woman who—"

"Don't you dare finish that sentence. All I'm saying is we've only just met again after ten years. And I have so much trouble right now to cope with—Marcus and Lawrence and—"

"Murdoch . . . Murdoch—that son of a bitch," he muttered. "I wish I'd killed him when I had the chance."

"Brad, that's a terrible thing to say. I never thought—" She stopped and began again. "We need to take our time, go slow."

He got out of bed and strode over to the window. He pulled back the edge of the shade to peek around it and view the street below. His widely veering moods frightened her. Kit had warned her that his uncle "wasn't himself," but what did that mean?

He turned back to her with cynical smile. "This is rich. Just when I thought there was nothing left to go wrong in my life . . ."

"Brad, all I meant was—"

"Don't." He raised his hand to silence her, then gave a mirthless little laugh. "Don't make it worse by explaining. I already feel enough like a fool. Forgive me for playing the ruined virgin. I *misinterpreted* last night. Let's just leave it at that."

"No, you don't understand anything. So much has happened to me in the last week that I—"

"Eden, stop. Just let me get dressed and I'll leave you in peace." He stomped around the room in his bare feet, collecting the clothing he had discarded in the heat of last night's passion.

"Why are you so angry?" she asked.

He threw his clothes back on the floor. "Why am I so angry? Maybe because the woman I love does not return my feelings in equal measure. Maybe because you went off and left me to bleed to death on the floor of that stockade ten years ago. Maybe I'm angry that you never bothered to tell me we had a daughter." He pointed an accusing finger at her. "You said he couldn't have been a better father to her . . . well, he couldn't have been a better father to her *than me!*"

She meekly pulled the bedsheet up to her throat as though it could shield her from his harsh words. She found his sarcasm even more disturbing than his anger. How dare he think himself the wounded one. "I did what I thought was best for both of us all those years ago. I did what I thought was best for *you!*"

"To hell with your good intentions! I followed your wishes to the letter and look what they've gotten me—a failed marriage and a failed career. Does that make you happy? On some level, I could say that your *good intentions* have ruined my life."

Her lips trembled and her eyes filled with tears. "That's not true, Brad. You know that's not true."

He slumped into a nearby chair. "No, it's not altogether true."

"And I'm not the only one who needs to go slow here. You're so anxious to abandon your marriage, but you shouldn't rush that either. Think of your son. How he'll suffer."

"*My wife* ended our marriage, Eden. Not that that's any of your business."

"I want you to be certain of *your* feelings. I don't want you running into my arms just to spite her. Just to salve your wounded pride."

He narrowed his eyes. "You really think my feelings for you are that shallow?"

"I don't know what to think! We're practically strangers." She did not dare say what she really felt, that she feared his feelings for her were based on fantasy, not fact, concocted of memories collected in a scrapbook. The passion was still there, but what else? They needed time to get to know each other, time to learn to love again.

The room grew quiet.

"Rest assured, Amanda and I will never reconcile."

His morose tone chilled her so thoroughly she wanted the cover of more blankets. He made a strange sight, sitting sprawled, completely naked, across the hard wooden chair that was too small to contain his long-limbed body. His legs splayed in opposite directions and his arms hung down, his fingers nearly grazing the floor.

"Is your heart so cold you can't imagine ever forgiving her? I don't defend what she did, you understand, but let's not forget you did the same to her ten years ago. And she knows it."

"No, she doesn't. I never told her about us."

"Maybe you didn't have to. In any case, she knows."

With a sad smile, Brad said, "That foolish affair she had—I would give anything if that were the only problem between us."

"There's more?"

"Much more. My wife and I both happen to be monsters. Guilty of such sins as you cannot imagine. If you knew the truth of it, you wouldn't love me either."

She had no idea what he meant, but the utter resignation she heard frightened her.

He stared at the ceiling and began to speak in a distant, detached voice. "Have you ever imagined being shipwrecked? Clinging to the wreckage on an endless sea with no rescue in sight? The question would become, at what point do you simply let go?"

She got out of bed and walked over to stand before him, baring her own scarred body. She longed to draw him back from the far, dark place to which he had retreated, but when she reached forward to caress his face, he pushed her hands away.

He got up and dressed and left the room without a word to her, without even a glance. She curled up in the middle of the bed and tried to cry, but no tears would come.

Eighteen

After wasting a long time lying in bed, Eden decided to get dressed and go out looking for Brad. He would have to cool down eventually so that they could have a reasonable talk about the future.

Her first stop was the Prairie Sunrise Cafe. Solange informed her that Mr. Randall had dashed over and cleared out his personal belongings from their attic. He did not stop to talk, just hurriedly bid Solange's father farewell and thanks for the use of the lodgings.

His horse had been removed from the stable where he had it boarded. The liveryman had not spoken to him, but rather had found money and a note left in the stall when he came to work.

Eden resolved to return home to Mitchell County as quickly as possible. She did not care to be in this wild town all alone. Perhaps she might catch up with Brad on the road. He might be headed to her homestead. After all, his nephew was still there. If she left immediately, she might still overtake him.

On her way to the McClellan House, she noticed a large crowd gathered in an alley next to the Hays National Bank, but she rushed on by, too preoccupied with her own problems to care about those of others at the moment.

She hated to face the desk clerk at the hotel for fear he might remark upon her male visitor. She had no choice however and stepped up to the desk. Before he could say a word, she said, "I'm checking out immediately, sir. If you could please total my bill."

"Will you require assistance with your luggage, Madam?"

She shook her head, then darted up the stairs to her room. Some of her clothing, lovingly removed last night by Brad, still lay strewn about the floor. But the bitter morning had now soured the sweet, erotic memories of that night. She knelt down and gathered up the stockings and yesterday's blouse and tossed them into her open valise.

She got down on her knees to hunt for a stray garter and saw Brad's revolver under the bed. It had probably fallen from his coat pocket last night. He must have forgotten it in his hurry to dress and be quit of her this morning.

She picked it up, dangling it by its walnut handle. Sidearms made her uneasy, plus it was all dirty with black power. What to do with it?

She thought to place it in her valise. She could give it back to its owner, if and when she found him, or she would give it to his nephew and let him figure out what to do with it.

She grimaced to think it would get the contents of her bag all dirty. She plucked the towel that hung behind the basin and pitcher, wrapped the gun in it, and placed it in her bag after making sure the safety latch was fastened.

She glanced around the room one last time, still heartsick to recall her parting from Brad. She returned to the front desk to brave the next encounter with the management.

"I needed one of your towels," she told the man. "Might I charge that to my room?"

"Why, yes," said the clerk, "but it seems we will still owe you money. Mr. Randall paid for an entire week in advance. You still have two days to go."

"I must leave today."

The man looked slightly annoyed. "Deducting the cost of the

towel will leave a credit of seven dollars and seventy-five cents. I shall have to seek my superior as I do not have authority to pay out monies."

Eden made a sigh of exasperation. "How long will that take?"

"Not long. Please be patient."

She waited, chafing at every minute she stood there and longing to be on the wagon road back to her home and her daughter, hopefully seeing Brad on the way. Still, nearly eight dollars was a large sum, even if the money was not hers.

After ten minutes, she gave up and marched around back to the hotel's stable yard. She told the attendant she needed her horse immediately, but he was busy mucking out stalls. She gritted her teeth and said nothing, resolving to saddle the horse herself.

She had not even finished a quick grooming of the animal when she met with yet another setback—one of her horse's shoes was loose.

"I know you are busy, sir, but could you fix my horse's shoe right away? I'm in a great hurry."

He glanced up. "Yeah, I'll get to it."

"I need to leave now."

He frowned. "I said I'd get to it, lady, and I will. I charge six bits to fix a shoe, by the way. That ain't covered in your stable fee."

"I'll double your charge if you do it right now."

He debated her offer.

"I'll triple it."

He shrugged. "Pay me in advance and it's a deal."

She handed him the money, then decided she might as well walk back to the front desk of the McClellan House and collect her refund. "I'm going to see to some other business. How long will you be?"

"Fifteen, maybe twenty minutes. No more. Feel free to leave your poke. I'll keep an eye on it."

She hung her valise up by its handles on the end of a tack rail and headed out.

She stopped short of opening the etched glass hotel doors when she saw the tall sheriff of Ellis County and his deputy in the lobby talking with the desk clerk.

She winced with the thought of crossing his path again after what had happened the afternoon before. She reversed her direction and entered the Prairie Sunrise Cafe yet again. This time she ordered a quick bite to eat.

As she dined on cold biscuits and gravy—the leftovers from the morning's breakfast shift—she brooded on how she might have answered Brad differently, to have prevented the awful scene that followed.

She now worried that she knew even less about him than she feared. His talk, his actions were so unpredictable, so unlike the man she once knew and fell in love with. What was wrong with him?

And what was this "sin" Brad alluded to? She knew from Kit that the couple had lost their little daughter to a painful illness, but how was "sin" involved? She recalled the remarks of the gossipy young clerk at the Bureau of Indian Affairs. He had said that Brad had suffered a personal tragedy and was much altered by the experience, so much so that his superior had ordered him to take a leave of absence to recover. The daughter's death was a tragedy, to be sure, but one countless parents had faced before. How was Brad's case different?

A commotion in the restaurant caused her to look up from her meditations. Plum Streeter, the well-groomed sheriff whom she had just seen at the hotel, now entered the room. He cut a dashing figure with his understated air of authority. She watched uneasily as he asked a question of Solange, who nodded in response and then pointed directly at Eden.

She felt a chill as the man strode decisively to her table. Scurrying behind him was the greasy young deputy who had stared a hole in her at breakfast the other day.

193

The sheriff removed his hat and stood before her. "You are Mrs. Lawrence Murdoch?"

"Yes."

By way of gesture, he asked to seat himself at her table. She indicated her assent. The deputy sat himself at a nearby table instead.

"How may I help you, Sheriff?"

"I need to ask you some questions, ma'am. When was the last time you saw Mr. Bradley Randall?"

"Are you going to press charges about yesterday? Because the fight was provoked by Mr. Murdoch." She pointed to the cut on her cheek from Murdoch's ring.

"Please just answer my question."

"I saw him last night. After the incident."

"Excuse me for speaking plain, here, but what is the nature of the relationship between yourself and Mr. Randall?"

The room had no extra heat to spare on this cold late November day, but Eden suddenly felt herself start to perspire. "He is a family friend. I've known him for nearly ten years."

"Just a friend? Nothing more?"

Eden felt the eyes of every diner in the room upon her. Even Solange and her enormous father had halted their work to view the proceedings. She swallowed the quaver in her voice. "What are you implying?"

"The desk clerk at the McClellen House saw Mr. Randall enter your room last evening. He says that he did not emerge from that room until early this morning. So I'll ask you again, when and where did you see Mr. Randall last?"

Eden held her breath with the sudden urge to cry, both from humiliation that her indiscretion was now common knowledge and from fear—she did not even know what she feared, but she knew something was terribly wrong. "Why are you asking me these questions?"

"I have some very bad news to deliver, Mrs. Murdoch."

Oh, God no. Don't say it. He's not dead. He can't be dead. He was angry and disappointed but he wasn't suicidal, surely not. And yet Brad's sister had feared him so unstable she had insisted Kit accompany him West. Please don't say it, please don't say it.

"I regret to tell you that . . ."

Eden fainted before he could finish his sentence.

Despite the swimming sensation in her head she recognized Solange's thin, pretty face floating above her. With her wispy blond tendrils creating a silvery halo, Eden though for a moment she might be an angel.

She next realized her head lay in Solange's lap and a dozen anxious faces hovered around her. She sat up and recovered her breath. The tall sheriff extended his hand and pulled her back into her seat while Solange's father brought her a glass of water.

Sheriff Streeter waved back the onlookers. "Did you hear what I said, ma'am? I'm not certain you did."

Eden stared dumbly at the man and tried to brace herself for the terrible, unspeakable announcement.

"Your husband is dead."

She did not react at all. Husband? Husband?

"Your husband, Lawrence Murdoch, is dead. Do you understand me now?"

Lawrence? Not Brad? A torrent of relief broke over her so potently she almost shouted, *Thank God*, but managed to control herself.

"My husband is dead? How? When?"

"Your husband's body was found in an alleyway this morning by the employees of the Hays National Bank. He was shot in the back of the head. The surgeon is determining the details right this minute. Now he had plenty of money on him, so robbery doesn't seem to be the motive. I must ask you again, do you know the whereabouts of Mr. Randall and can you account for your own time this morning?"

"Lawrence . . . shot to death?"

"His lawyer, Mr. Brindle, identified the body. He told me the pair of you was suing each other for divorce and for custody of the Vandegaarde boy. I still don't understand what that is all about, but the fact that disturbs me the most is that you have already lied to me this morning and I think that makes you and your so-called 'friend,' Mr. Randall, both suspects."

She raised a trembling hand to her bosom and tried to speak, but could not think of what to say. The sheriff and his deputy escorted her to the town jail where she was told she would have to wait until the sheriff had time to question her further.

Solange whispered to her before they left the restaurant, "I'll send a wire to Mr. Kit. He'll know what to do."

Eden vaguely recalled nodding, but now sat on a plain wooden bench in the front office of Plum Streeter's jail. She felt so upset her breath came in short bursts. She loosened her collar button as though this would help, but it did not.

The little deputy, Harry Knapp, paced around the room, apparently not knowing quite what to do with himself. He stole glances at her periodically.

Peering outside the window she saw the lawyer, Nick Wallace, hurrying across the street at such a pace he held his small brimmed hat to his head.

He burst in the sheriff's office, breathless and agitated.

"Mrs. Murdoch, I just heard the news. I . . . I don't know what to say."

Eden did not know what to say either, so she said nothing.

He sat down next to her on the bench, took her hand in his, and announced earnestly, "If you are charged in this matter, I will represent you to the utmost of my ability."

"Mr. Wallace, I appreciate your offer, but I must point out I have no money to pay you."

He waved off this comment. "Mr. Randall presented me with a fully adequate retainer to represent you in your divorce and custody action . . . which is now moot, I guess."

"Dead, I'd say," allowed Harry Knapp with a snicker.

Wallace jerked his head in the direction of the deputy. "Mr. Knapp, when we require your opinion, we shall ask for it!"

The little man slunk toward the pot-bellied stove and made the actions of preparing some coffee, though Eden could tell he wished only to eavesdrop.

"Mrs. Murdoch, I simply had no idea that this matter would arrive at such a terrible conclusion."

"We don't know what has happened, Mr. Wallace. I certainly don't know at least."

"I shall contact Mr. Brindle at once and see what I can learn, in addition to speaking directly with the sheriff. Mr. Knapp, where is Sheriff Streeter at the moment?"

"Oh, now I'm good enough to talk to, huh?" The deputy walked over to where they sat and assumed a superior manner. "He's gonna be pretty busy all day. After he's done talking to people in town, he's riding out to see the Vandegaarde boy. If he's not out at the ranch then he's a suspect, too."

"That's absurd. He's just a child," said Eden.

"Lawyer Brindle said that Murdoch and the boy quarreled last night," the self-important deputy continued. "The boy ordered him off his place at gunpoint. That's why Murdoch was in town this morning seeing his lawyer to find out if he could get back on the ranch. He'd been staying there, you see, and he thought he was gonna own it soon."

"Where is Mr. Randall?" Wallace asked his client.

This question brought her near to tears. She could only whisper, "I don't know."

———

An hour passed as Eden continued her wait for the sheriff's return. When he arrived, he carried her carpetbag under his arm and when she saw it and remembered its contents, her head swam with the implications.

"I just came back from another enlightening chat with the folks at the McClellan House. The stable man came looking for you when you didn't claim the horse you were so anxious to have shod that you offered him three times his price. Look what he presented me with."

Streeter sat the valise at Eden's feet, opened it, and unwrapped the .44 caliber army Colt revolver with the letters "BJR" carved into the walnut handle.

"Is this your gun, Mrs. Murdoch?"

"No."

"Do you know who it belongs to?"

"I . . . don't know," she stammered, unable to think of a nonin-criminating reply.

"Damn it, woman, you need to stop lying to me!"

She blanched at this, but said nothing. She wished Mr. Wallace had not left. He might at least have provided some protection.

The sheriff ran his hand over his forehead and down his face as though to calm himself. "So just who might 'BJR' be, do you reckon?"

When she did not respond, he answered his own question. "Your friend Mr. Randall paid for your room at the hotel with a bank draft that he signed, 'Bradley J. Randall.' I think that's a pretty big coincidence, don't you? Do you want to try again to tell me whose gun this is?"

"Mr. Randall gave it to me for my protection." She was not an experienced liar and wondered if this showed in her delivery.

"This gun has been fired recently. There's black powder all over it."

"I have nothing more to say."

"You may as well be prepared: If the doctor pulls a .44 caliber slug out of your husband's body, I'm arresting you and your good friend, Mr. Randall, for the murder of Lawrence Murdoch."

The doctor arrived in half an hour's time and announced that he had removed a .44 caliber lead ball from Lawrence Murdoch's skull. He unwrapped it from a wad of bloody gauze and held it up to the light for Streeter's examination.

"I couldn't tell if there had been a struggle, Plum," said the doctor. "He was so beat up from the day before and all, but it didn't look like any new bleeding or damage to indicate a fight this morning. The sutures I put in yesterday would have probably given way if he'd been hit much."

"The folks in the bank come to work at ten and he stopped in at Lawyer Brindle's office at eight," said the sheriff. "In fact, was waiting for him to arrive there, so we would have to say the crime occurred sometime between eight and ten, right?"

"My findings would be consistent with that analysis. Do you need anything else, or can I release the body to Mr. Fry for burial?"

To hear her husband referred to as "the body" sounded strange to Eden's ears, like a minor chord struck in an enormous, empty room. "Might I see my husband?"

The two middle-aged men turned to her as though they had momentarily forgotten her presence.

The doctor looked to the sheriff for guidance and the sheriff nodded his consent. "Allow me to do a little cleanup first, ma'am. I will reclothe the person of your husband and sew up . . . let's just say you would not wish to view him in his current state. About an hour, Plum?"

The sheriff and the doctor spoke in whispers, then the doctor departed.

Streeter stood before her. "This is how I see it: The clerk at the McClellan House saw Mr. Randall leave your room about seven-thirty. You left the room yourself about nine or so. Came back an hour later, in a real big hurry to check out. Such a hurry, in fact, you wouldn't even wait a few minutes to let them refund eight dollars you had coming to you. Then you go try to get your horse and offer to pay the stable hand three times his charge to fix a loose shoe extra quick. Excuse me for saying so, ma'am, but you don't appear to be the type who can afford to throw around money like that without a good reason."

"You actually believe I could kill my own husband?"

"I think you and your friend had all manner of reason to see him dead. Randall tried to do it right out in front of everybody yesterday afternoon. Lord, how I wish I'd arrested him when I had the chance. I might've put a stop to all this. Anyway, I think the pair of you split up to get out of town, to meet up somewheres else, only he got luckier than you."

She felt as though all the oxygen had once again been sucked out of the room as she listened to his perfectly logical, though completely erroneous, theory of her husband's murder.

"Are you looking for Mr. Randall?" Eden asked.

"Of course, but I think he's long gone by now. I went over to the Kansas Pacific depot. The K.P. clerk remembers a tall, well-dressed gentleman buying a ticket for himself and cargo passage for his horse some time this morning. There was a nine o'clock and a ten-twelve. We think that was Mr. Randall."

"To where? The train, I mean."

"All the clerk can remember was some point West. I've wired the sheriff in Denver, Cheyenne, and several other stops to look out for him. I'm also asking the marshal over in Bluestem to place a watch on your house to see if he shows up there." Streeter resumed his writing.

"Don't you find it strange that the desk clerk at the McClellan can account for the comings and goings of every single guest, every minute?" she said.

"They were real certain of Mr. Randall's departure. That much, I know. They were waiting for him to leave your room. They saw him go in the night before and did not like the looks of it one bit. They were going to confront him about it. They are a new hotel and want to protect their reputation, you see. But when he came out of your room this morning, they said he looked ready to spit fire. He shoved the manager out of the way with a strong oath and that was the last they saw of him."

Eden sighed with the effort of inventing some plausible explanation for Brad's behavior. She could think of none.

"They were planning to ask you to leave the premises as well," Streeter went on. "They were waiting until you were up and about. That manager is a little bit the squeamish sort about matters of . . . well, he didn't want to be in the middle of anything awkward. Now do you honestly have anything to say in your own defense? You asked what I think—well, I think that man of yours did the deed, but that you helped him out, that you were getting the murder weapon out of town for him. I'll ask you for the last time, do you have anyone who can account for your time between eight and ten in the morning?"

She shook her head.

"I'm filing charges against you whether we locate Mr. Randall or not."

She struggled to comprehend it all. How could Brad's gun be the murder weapon if it had lain on the floor of her room all night? If he had killed Lawrence, did he actually use the gun, then return it to her room? What would be the sense of that?

"Sheriff, did anyone else enter my hotel room this morning? The desk clerk seems to have nothing to do but spy on people."

"I asked him that question, all right. He said not a single soul entered or left the hotel between the time you left in the morning and the time you came back to check out. Except for Harry Knapp. He's my deputy. He said he was just running an errand. He does what he can to pick up extra cash. He's no suspect here, I'm sure you'll agree."

Eden slumped against the wall behind her bench, more confused and dejected than ever.

Nineteen

The sheriff led Eden to the doctor's surgery to view her husband's body. Everyone on the street stared at her. Some called taunting remarks and names. She tried to shut out the humiliation and focus her thoughts on what really might have happened. She could not sort it out. The world had gone mad.

She was so numbed by the shock of the morning's events she felt no emotion at all when she viewed the remains of Lawrence Murdoch. She knew that her apparent stoicism would make her look even guiltier, but she could not help it.

As they returned to the jail, a troubling new issue arose in her mind.

"Where is my son? Where is Marcus Vandegaarde?"

Streeter sighed uneasily. "I don't know. I rode out to his place and couldn't find him. Of course that doesn't mean much. The Vandegaarde spread is big. There's no telling where he might be, but I'm going to send some volunteers out to look for him tomorrow."

"Can't you do something sooner? Perhaps he's hurt, or in danger. There is a killer still on the loose—whether you believe me or not."

He made an indifferent motion before he led her to the cell she was to occupy. She grimaced when she saw it. The Ellis

County jail was not nearly as new as the jail in Bluestem which had opened for "business" only three months prior to her taking up residence there.

Ellis County's lockup had seen considerably more action. The cell was small and dark, lit only by a single high, barred window with a wooden shutter to cover it. The floor was brick and the only furnishings consisted of an iron cot with a thin mattress and a threadbare wool blanket. The sheriff brought her some clean, muslin bed linens from upstairs. She guessed that the stairway at the back of the building led to his living quarters.

The sheets were a nice touch. He also removed a tin bucket from the corner of the cell which Eden realized must have served as a slops jar when he replaced it with a traditional porcelain chamber pot. She assumed he provided these niceties from his own home solely because she was a woman. Whatever the reason, she was grateful.

"I'll need you to undress and remove your corset, ma'am. Just call out to me when you're done dressing again afterwards."

Eden frowned. "Corset?"

"I'm not so much interested in the corset as the laces. I had a prisoner once manage to hang himself and I won't let that happen again if I can help it. I treat the men the same. I take their suspenders and belts. Shoelaces and neckties, too, if they've got 'em. I run a tight operation here."

"Well, rest easy then. I'm not wearing a corset."

He eyed her figure critically. A cursory glance over the soft lines of her torso confirmed that she lacked the structured underpinnings in question.

She sat down on the hard cot and tried to concentrate on something other than the smell of the place. Countless drunks had probably emptied their poisoned stomachs on this floor and more than a few had missed on their aim at the slops jar, if they had bothered to aim at all. The unpleasant mixture of odors burned her nostrils. The mopping the deputy had been required to give the floor a few moments earlier has served to intensify the nasty smells rather than remove them. She pulled her skirts up enough to protect them from skimming the wet floor.

Eden caught a glimpse of the sheriff's wife as she descended the back stairs and hurried past the cell on her way to her husband's office.

The woman did not speak or even glance at Eden as she passed. Streeter and his wife conversed in low tones that she could just barely hear as she eavesdropped. Apparently female prisoners were so rare an occurrence as to necessitate a careful rearrangement of routine. The sheriff assured his wife that, though he expected few arrests now that the cattle drive season was over and the town had returned to its quieter days, he would house what male prisoners he did have in the shed out back. He did not anticipate anyone other than the occasional drunk-and-disorderly who needed a place to sleep it off, or perhaps the odd soldier taken into custody only for the time it took a military escort to retrieve him and return him to the fort for army discipline.

This eased Eden's mind as much as that of Mrs. Streeter. The woman returned to her dwelling upstairs, once again hurrying past the cell and carefully avoiding eye contact.

———

Kit arrived the following day. "Mrs. Murdoch, excuse my language, but *what in hell is going on?*"

"Where's Hadley?"

"Don't worry, she's gonna stay the night in town with that old lady friend of yours."

She breathed a sigh of relief and then tried to tell him all that had happened in the last week. He listened carefully but was so agitated he could barely stand still.

"But where is he? Where did he go?"

"I don't know. He was angry with me when we parted. He didn't even say good-bye."

"I think he's lost his mind, plain and simple. Aunt Jen warned me about this."

"Jen—that's his sister?"

"Yeah, I used to live with her and her husband, Bob. Uncle Brad's been acting odd ever since little Sarah died. Jen and Bob have been worried about them both. Sometimes they'd seem as normal as daylight and then other times—" Kit shook his head.

"You mean he and his wife?"

"Right, my Aunt Amanda. She's been doing crazy things that don't make sense. Running after fellows hardly older than me. She was never like that before. I didn't think it would come to this though. *Murder.*"

"Don't tell the sheriff this, but," she pulled him close to whisper in his ear, "your uncle asked me to marry him yesterday morning and I turned him down. That's why he got so angry and left."

"Why don't you want the sheriff to know that?"

She turned a tormented face away from him.

"Because it makes him look guiltier," Kit answered for her. "If he's guilty, why protect him? You've got to look out for yourself. You've got to think about Hadley."

"How is she? How much have you told her?"

"Just a little. I promised her I'd bring her here on the weekend. Is that all right?"

She nodded. "Let me tell her most of it."

After dinner, Kit retired to his attic bed over the Prairie Sunrise and, just as he expected, Solange slipped in around midnight.

"Miss me?" she whispered with a kiss. She slid her hand into his underwear, having become proficient in the art of milking his lust from him during their many quasi-chaste nights together.

He pushed her hand away. "I'm not in the mood."

She sat up, insulted. "Fine, then!"

He caught hold of her wrist before she could leave the bed. "Don't go. I need somebody to talk to, a powerful lot."

Somewhat mollified, she slid back in next to him. He put his grateful arms around her and nestled his face into the curve of her neck.

"Solange, why is all this happening? I just can't believe it. I always looked up to him."

"Your uncle?"

"Yeah. I grew up thinking he was just about perfect. I wanted to grow up and *be* him. He had everything. A big job, a beautiful wife, a fancy house, plenty of money. He's eaten dinner with the goddamned *president of the United States*, for christssake."

"No need to curse," she scolded.

"I'm sorry, but just look what it's all come down to."

"Maybe *she* did it. That man of hers was no good. I saw him hit her, right in broad daylight. Knocked her off her feet."

"But my uncle was the one who ran off. I've learned so much about him on this trip. So much I didn't like finding out. Did you know that because of him Mrs. Murdoch was once in the same fix you're in now?"

"She was?"

"Yep. The son of a bitch." He gently ran his hand over the hard round swell of her belly. It had grown in size since the last time he saw her, but was still small enough to conceal under a careful arrangement of petticoats. "How have you been doing? How's our little friend?"

"Fine, I guess." There was no enthusiasm in her voice. "I think I've been feeling him move lately."

"Kicking?"

"Not exactly. More like little flutters."

"If I kept my hand here, would I be able to feel it?"

"I don't know. Doubt it."

"How come you didn't answer the letter I sent you? Didn't you get it?" He felt her stiffen when he asked this.

"Yes, I got it."

"Well?"

He heard her sniffle. With Solange, tears were always an eyelash away. "I can't read very much or write worth spit. I didn't want you to find out. I know you're real educated and you'd think less of me."

"Then you don't know me very well."

"It's not my fault, though. It's just that when my mother died, my dad needed me to work in the restaurant full time, so I had to quit school real young."

"Don't worry about it. You know how much I like you."

She kissed the top of his curly head. "You're always so sweet to me. You don't even hold this against me." She placed her hand on top of his where it still lay waiting to feel the baby kick.

"If I held that against you, I'd be the biggest hypocrite on earth. I'm not exactly a virgin either."

"There's been another girl?"

"More than one."

"Were you in love?"

He chuckled. "No, far from it. I was just looking for a good time."

"Like Jimmy," she said, referring to the young soldier who had gotten her pregnant.

He sat up angrily. "I'm not like Jimmy! I would never lie to a girl like that. I would never tell her I loved her and wanted to marry her if I didn't mean it."

She pulled him back into her arms. "You're such a good man. I wish every man were as good as you."

"My uncle once said we can all be heroes if we try. He was wrong though. I think the days of heroes are long gone."

Twenty

Lawyer Wallace, excited by his first capital murder case, could not stay away from the jail. He visited his client almost daily, though he seldom had any new information to impart.

Eden had not been impressed with his first court appearance on her behalf. After she stood before the judge and pleaded not guilty to the charges, Wallace asked that his client be released upon posting the appropriate bail. He cited her lack of a criminal record and her need to care for her daughter and farm.

Judge Blackmore, a man with wild, white eyebrows that resembled a pair of bird's wings ready to take flight from his broad, ruddy forehead, exploded on the young lawyer. He stated that he never allowed bail in capital cases and implied that the honorable Mr. Wallace should have known this. The prosecuting attorney openly smirked throughout this dressing-down.

As young Wallace walked her back to the jail, he apologized for the incident. "I must confess I have little experience in criminal matters. Mine is mostly an office practice—real estate, wills, liens, debt collections."

This revelation did not hearten her, but she had no choice, given her lack of funds.

"The prosecution seeks a six week postponement," Wallace

told her the following afternoon. "I did not challenge it. I thought it best to wait. They hope Mr. Randall can be located in that time. I hope so, too."

"Six weeks," Eden groaned. "That will be after the New Year." The thought of being separated from Hadley all that time horrified her worse then the possibility of hanging for a crime she did not commit. The former was far more tangible to her than the latter. "I can't bear to stay in this jail month after month! I have a daughter, I have a farm. I—"

"The longer we wait the better."

"I don't understand."

"The better to prepare our case, ma'am. On second thought, it might be better to go to trial without Mr. Randall's presence. That way we can shift blame to him without rebuttal and create the necessary doubt in the jury's mind."

"Mr. Randall did not kill my husband."

"Then who did?"

"I don't know!" She was so upset, she wanted to tear her hair.

"Mrs. Murdoch, calm yourself. I know this is distressing, but I will try my best to see you through it."

After he departed, the sheriff returned with a new suspect to interrogate, one Eden took intense interest in—Marcus Vandegaarde.

She strained to see him, though the angle down the short hall was difficult. She could hear them well enough.

"Now look, son, I'm going to ask you straight—where have you been for the last four days?"

"I told you," came the belligerent voice of the boy, "I was staying with the minister and his family."

"Even though you had to know I was looking for you?"

"I didn't feel safe."

"I want you to account for your time the morning Mr. Murdoch was killed."

Eden was outraged by the sheriff's harsh treatment of her son. "Answer me, boy! Now this isn't the first time we've locked horns and I've got a feeling it won't be the last."

"I thought you arrested her. Everybody says she did it. If you ask me, neither one of them were my real parents. They're just a couple of grifters after my inheritance."

"That's not for us to decide today. Now account for your time or I'll put you in jail, too. Don't think I won't. You're plenty old enough to know how to obey the law and know the consequences for breaking it."

Eden bit her lip at this awful exchange. She had to shake her head at all the foolish dreams she had entertained about her reunion with her lost son. She had actually imagined bringing Marcus home to Bluestem, introducing him to his half-sister, with the three of them living happily ever after, just like in fairy tales. She felt like a fool.

"I decided after I saw that fight between Mr. Murdoch and Mr. Randall that I didn't want to have anything to do with him anymore. He was a lousy coward, didn't even try to defend himself. I was ashamed to think we might be related. Well, he showed up out at my house that night after the doctor got done sewing him up and he'd had plenty to drink. That's another reason I don't like him. I don't have any respect for boozers."

At least we agree on something, Eden thought. She blamed Lawrence's drinking for most of his mistreatment of her. He was a different man when sober, or at least she had once thought so. She now had different ideas.

"I told him to get off my property," the boy continued. "When he started to argue and threatened to whip me—which was a pretty big laugh, given the shape he was in—I got out my shotgun and fired it into the air over his head."

"You shot at Murdoch?"

"Not to hit him, just to scare him. Anyway, the next morning, I felt sort of worried. He said he was gonna get some legal paper against me and bring you into it, forcing me to let him stay there. I didn't know what to do so I went to see Mr. Parker and his wife. They were my pa's best friends and all and I knew they'd help."

"Mr. Parker is in trouble with me for hiding you."

"They thought it would all just blow over, but then Murdoch got killed and I was twice as scared."

"I'm not going to file any charges against you or Mr. Parker today, but you watch yourself and the next time I need to talk to you, I want to know where to find you. I guess we're done for now. You can go."

Eden saw Marcus peek around the corner of the sheriff's office. As soon as their eyes met, he withdrew and asked the sheriff, "Is she gonna hang?"

"Don't know yet, son."

"I hope she does."

"That's a mighty harsh thing to say." The boy made no response to this and the sheriff continued. "I know you've had a hard time of it. Losing both your folks in the same year, then all this trouble starts with two strangers coming to town and claiming you. That's got to be confusing for anybody."

Still Marcus said nothing.

"Circumstances are forcing you to grow up pretty fast. Don't be afraid to ask for help. I know the Parkers want to do what they can for you."

"Their house is too small, they said. I gotta go back home."

"Don't go around assuming everybody's your enemy."

"But how can you ever tell?" said the boy. Eden thought she could hear a childlike, confused pleading in his voice, as it quavered in timbre between boyhood and manhood. "For the life of me, I don't know how to tell."

———

Eden's most unexpected visitor arrived the week before Christmas: Clyde Summerfield, the assistant to her old nemesis, Phineas Claypool.

"Why Mr. Summerfield, this is a surprise." She rose from her cot to greet him and tried to smooth her hair a bit. She did not know why she felt the need to make herself presentable for his benefit. Perhaps it was because he represented her only visitor from Bluestem, save for the weekly visits from Hadley and Kit.

Old Mrs. Redding was not in proper health to make the trip though she wrote often to try and keep Eden's spirits up. Eden's neighbors, the Layton family, sent their regards through Kit, but did not have the time to visit, or so they said.

"Hello, Mrs. Murdoch." Clyde Summerfield courteously removed his hat. "I just had to come and see if it were really true, all those stories in the paper about you."

"This has made the papers in Bluestem?" Kit had not bothered to tell her this, though he undoubtedly knew. She shuddered to think how Hadley was coping. All of the children she went to school with were undoubtedly talking about it. She ached to imagine what her daughter must be enduring. As if matters were not bad enough already.

"Yes, ma'am, on account of how . . . famous . . . you are."

"I think 'notorious' is the word you were looking for." She tried to smile. "Have they been kind to me?"

Summerfield looked at the floor. "Not exactly."

"No more Joan of Arc?"

He shook his head, still feeling too awkward to face her.

"I suppose this pleases your employer, Mr. Claypool."

He nodded sadly. "He went out and bought lots of copies of the papers and cut out all the articles on you and sent them to his investors to show them you were a . . ."

"Madwoman?"

Summerfield ducked his head. "Let's just say he wants them to see that they shouldn't pay your opinions too much attention."

"Very diplomatically put, Mr. Summerfield. At least someone is benefiting from this nightmare."

He finally dared to look her in the eye and said with noticeable emotion, "I'm not like Phin. I don't think you're crazy . . . or a killer."

"Thank you, Mr. Summerfield. At least someone is on my side."

"Can I do anything for you, ma'am? It kills me to think you're in this place. I am sure it is all a big mistake."

"It's nice to hear that someone believes in my innocence."

"Those two men, Murdoch and Randall. You're better off without either of them, if you'll permit me to say so. They didn't deserve someone so fine as you. Truly, I'm certain they didn't."

She disliked such a personal remark from a man she felt she barely knew. His implied intimacy made her uncomfortable.

The arrival of Lawyer Wallace rescued her from a longer interview with Mr. Summerfield, who politely withdrew.

"I have *three* new ideas," Wallace announced, somewhat breathless as always. He smoothed his light brown hair, which was already thinning on top despite his youth.

Eden wondered if he did anything with his day besides sit in his office and think up new theories for her defense. She had to admit the liveryman had been correct in assessing him as a hard worker.

"You're not going to like them," he said, raising a cautioning finger in the air, "but here they are. We could raise the suggestion of Marcus Vandegaarde."

"No." She folded her arms across her bosom and turned her back on him.

"Hear me out first. He had a motive."

"He's a child!"

"He didn't like Murdoch, and from all accounts, he didn't like you either. He was hell-bent on keeping his property to himself, so why not kill Murdoch and make it look like you did it?"

Eden turned back to face him, with chin thrust out. "He's just a little boy. You can't lay such sophisticated, adult motives onto him."

"You don't really know him at all, Mrs. Murdoch. Whether he's your son or not, he's a stranger to you. I've talked to lots of people including his former schoolteacher. She expelled him for being a bully."

"The world is full of schoolyard bullies, Mr. Wallace. They don't commit murder at the age of fourteen."

"He brought a gun to school once, determined to get even with some boy who'd made fun of him. The sheriff was called and everything. Of course, he claimed he just wanted to scare his tormentor, but who knows what he really had on his mind?"

Eden sat down on her cot to digest this unpleasant revelation. "All right, even if we assume for a moment that this theory had any merit—which I'm not—how would he have gotten Mr. Randall's revolver?"

Wallace sighed. "That's the one hole in my theory. I haven't come up with an answer to that yet. Well, I have another question I must ask and this may yield more productive results. Do you have any other—how shall I put this?—suitors?"

Eden almost laughed at the absurdity of his question. "None that I'm aware of, Mr. Wallace. Why?"

"It is obvious to me that whoever killed Mr. Murdoch wished to implicate Mr. Randall as well. Someone seeking your attention, romantic attention, that is, would view these two men as impediments, would they not? Rivals?"

Eden's thoughts shot straight to Clyde Summerfield. He had only moments before declared that neither Murdoch nor Randall was good enough for her. "Now that you mention it . . . that man who left as you came in, Mr. Summerfield. He said a strange thing to me. Telling me I was better off without either of those gentlemen in my life."

Wallace's eyes widened at this new possibility. "We must have this man questioned."

"He lives in Bluestem. He is no doubt returning there as we speak."

"I will try to find him before he leaves town, but if I miss him, I will request that the marshal in Bluestem question him. We'll see if he has a good alibi for the morning in question."

"Don't you think it odd that a murderer would come to pay a call on me?"

The young lawyer shrugged. "I have no special insight into the criminal mind. Does anyone? It is a terrible shame that the murder weapon was not examined for fingerprints."

"Fingerprints? What do you mean?" She glanced at her own hands.

"Fingerprints can be used to identify people. It's thought that each and every human being has a unique pattern of skin furrows on their fingertips. When someone leaves that pattern behind on some smooth object like a glass or a smooth piece of metal like a gun trigger, it can be matched to that person at a later date."

"How interesting." She thought about this, but concluded it might work against Brad. His fingerprints would certainly be on the weapon in addition to whomever else fired the trigger.

"I just read an article in a scientific journal by a Dr. Henry Faulds. He's British, but he works in Japan. He has made a scientific study of the issue and has positively identified *nine* separate patterns of these skin furrows. I'm going to give this article to the sheriff as soon as I am done with it in hopes that he will consider using such evidence in future investigations."

Eden tired of the topic before her counselor did. "What was your other theory for my defense, Mr. Wallace? You said you had three."

"Oh . . . self-defense."

"What?"

"Half the town saw Murdoch hit you, in broad daylight. You could say that he attacked you again and you were forced to defend yourself."

"Mr. Wallace, I did not kill my husband. If you think so—"

"It doesn't matter what I think."

"It matters to me!"

"I'm sorry, I'm sorry. Every time I come here I seem to upset you. I'll come again tomorrow," he mumbled as he backed his way down the hall to leave.

―――

Christmas came and went and a dreary time it was. Kit and Hadley tried to make it as merry as they could given the dismal circumstances.

Solange brought delicious treats to Eden every day. Often much more than Eden could hope to finish so Solange's visits were welcomed by the sheriff and his various deputies as well. Eden enjoyed the young waitress's calls because they afforded her the opportunity to talk about something other than her own desperate situation. Solange had only one topic that interested her: Kit Randall. The girl's daily stops allowed Eden to engage in the kind of silly girl talk she had not experienced since her own school days when she was Solange's age.

Solange confided her "problem" to Eden early on. She mentioned how Kit had told her they had this "difficulty" in common. Eden gritted her teeth at how Kit felt free to tell whomever he pleased about Hadley's illegitimacy. Though she was indebted to him for his generosity in helping her and her daughter, his lack of discretion was maddening at times.

She was grateful she could at least lend Solange a sympathetic ear. She wished she could help her somehow. Solange had learned of a school for girls in her "situation" that sounded ideal. The place provided room and board and offered classes to train the unfortunate young women in all sorts of skills and trades so that they might earn their own living if their families would not take them back. When the time came, suitable and loving families

were sought to adopt the girls' babies—or so the school's literature promised.

The only drawback was the expense. The school required a
tuition of $250, an enormous sum. Neither Solange nor Eden
could imagine where to get that kind of money.

Eden helped the girl write letters to Kit and assisted her limited
abilities to read his missives to her. Kit's letters betrayed no hint
that he felt anything but friendship for Solange.

The sheriff's night watchman, an elderly man who guarded the
bank during the daytime hours, suffered a stroke just after the
new year and Streeter replaced him with the deputy Harry
Knapp. Eden did not like this development at all. She felt his eyes
upon her at strange times and more than once awoke in the middle of the night convinced he was watching her though the room
was fully dark. She thought she heard breathing. She was certain
she could smell him.

Twenty-One

An icy, unrelenting wind greeted the early weeks of 1879. Eden's cell was so cold she could see her breath. The sheriff took pity on her and let her sit in his office near the stove as long as he was there during the day.

"It's a slow afternoon in the peacekeeping business, Mrs. Murdoch," he called. "How about another game of chess?"

He had been teaching her to play since before Christmas. She found the game frustrating, but welcomed any opportunity to leave her cell. "I think you like playing me because you know you will win. What sport is there in that?"

He chuckled. "Now you're improving with every game. That last one took me seventeen moves."

"You're keeping track?" She threw him a doubtful smile, but had to watch such actions: She sensed that his stern wife did not approve of their familiarity on any level. She noticed that he only invited her to play chess on afternoons when Rosemary Streeter either did her marketing or made her weekly round of social calls.

"What is your opinion of fingerprints, Sheriff?" She moved a pawn and immediately lost it to her opponent's knight. She wrinkled her nose in disappointment.

"How would you have cause to know about fingerprints?"

"Mr. Wallace is keen on them. He told me all about them."

"I've done some reading on the subject. It's promising, but there are a lot of practical problems in it. Once you've caught your man, they'd be of some use tying him to the crime, but I don't see much else you could do with them. Wouldn't help you find the culprit. Not like you could file away the fingerprints of the whole world and look 'em up like words in a dictionary."

She nodded, impressed with his knowledge and attention to his profession, but was forced to frown again when he relieved her of a bishop. "Might I ask you something personal?"

"We've been living under the same roof for more than a month. I suppose that gives you the right."

She smiled. "In some Indian tribes, that means we're as good as married."

"Don't tell that to Rosemary. She's jealous enough already."

"Why are you called Plum? I know that your real name is David. I saw you sign legal papers with it."

Streeter looked embarrassed. She had never observed him sheepish about anything before. "When I was a youngster in Nebraska, my family lived near Plum Creek. There were Streeters all up and down the Platte. My dad had lots of brothers and they all went into the same business of selling goods to the wagon trains from the earliest days on. Anyway, we were always referred to as the Plum Creek Streeters. As opposed to the Buffalo Creek Streeters or the Blue River Falls Streeters. When I was just learning to talk, I got it into my head that my name must be Plum Creek Streeter. Everybody thought that was real funny and the fool name stuck. Forty years later, I'm still hung with 'Plum Streeter.' Now Rose called me David when we were courting, but once we were married, she joined the crowd. It's embarrassing. Not a name for a grown man at all."

"You should think of it as endearing. No one nicknames someone they don't like."

"I'll try to keep that in mind." He contemplated his next move, both on the board and in their conversation. "I'd like to ask you a personal question as well, Mrs. Murdoch."

She frowned at the chessmen. She had never been generous with information about her strange history and did not feel inclined to change, yet she wanted to appear civil. The sheriff wielded too much power over her current situation to allow otherwise.

"How is it that you and the Vandegaarde boy are mother and son? I've heard stories from various parties, but I'm curious to hear your side."

"In December of 1864, when my son was a baby, I was traveling West to visit my father." Her story already contained a fabrication: She was not on a visit at all, but was in flight from her husband, Lawrence Murdoch, and hoped her father would take her in permanently. "He was with the Corps of Engineers and was working out of Fort Lyon at the time. The Cheyennes were on the warpath in retaliation for Sand Creek. You know about Sand Creek, Sheriff?"

"I imagine just about everybody in these parts has heard of that sorry affair."

"I had the misfortune to cross that warpath. Cheyenne Dog Soldiers attacked my coach and I tried to run, but I fell and dropped my baby. I was told this man, Avel Vandegaarde, found my son and took him home."

"You actually lived among the Indians all those years? I never heard of a captive—a woman captive, especially—surviving any length of time."

"Mine was not a typical story. The first few months were dreadful, but one fateful night my life was saved by a young medicine man. He took me into his family and eventually made me his wife. As the years passed my old life gradually faded. I lost my desire to return to my own people. With my son presumed dead, I felt I had little to go back to."

"Except your husband."

The eyes of both Eden and Streeter rose from the chessboard and met for a moment.

"I don't feel I should say anything more, given that I'm now accused of his murder."

The sheriff grinned and shook his head. "Just when I thought I had you in checkmate."

Though Streeter had never quite warmed up enough to be thought a jovial sort like old Marshal Bunch, Eden found him compassionate. He knew she was painfully bored and he loaned her reading material from time to time when he could not engage her in a round of chess or cards.

His tastes in literature were far from hers—he enjoyed military histories and biographies of famous generals—but she was so desperate for amusement, she read them without complaint.

He also passed on all his newspapers when he finished with them. He subscribed to several in addition to the local weekly. She followed the continuing saga of the Northern Cheyennes with interest. Their sojourn at Fort Robinson had turned into an ugly standoff when the army, under orders of General Sheridan, was told to return them to the reservation in the Indian Territory—the place they had left at all hazards and to which they swore never to return.

That morning the *Dodge City Times* had reported:

Slaughter of Savages

FORT ROBINSON, NEB.—JAN. 10, 1879—Hostile Indians imprisoned here since last October, having been informed by the commanding officer a few days ago that they were to be taken back to the Indian Territory, determined to die rather than consent to such movement. Last night at about 11 o'clock while nearly everyone was in bed except the guard, the savages jumped through the windows of the prison room and made for the prairie, which is thickly coated with frozen snow, firing on the guard from revolvers they had concealed since their capture, dangerously wounding four of the guard, of whom one has died and another is not expected to survive the day. The main guard rushed out of the guard house upon hearing the firing, and upon ascertaining the cause and seeing the hostiles running for the bluffs, immediately followed and opened fire, and killed over forty savages. Over one hundred and sixty cavalry, mounted and dismounted are still in pursuit, and the sharp bang of carbines in the hands of our men can be heard from the hills three miles distant, where the savages have evidently made for, it is thought that not one of them will escape.

Knowing Brad's previous involvement in the conflict, Eden had to wonder if he might have gone back there. Confirmation unexpectedly blew in on this dark and snowy day in the form of Major John Simon.

He burst in the sheriff's door and slammed it behind him to close out the hardy north wind. As he brushed snowflakes from the short cape of his blue overcoat, he approached the sheriff's desk and extended his hand.

"What can I do for you, Major?" Streeter rose with a cordial smile and shook the young man's hand. "Go warm yourself by the stove, sir. Your hands are like ice."

"Thank you, I will. I've come to talk to you and . . ." he paused to catch his breath, "to see your prisoner."

"She's sitting right behind you."

He turned and faced Eden with surprise. "You are Mrs. Murdoch?"

"I am." She shook his cold hand also.

"Mrs. Murdoch, I feel somehow responsible for all of this."

She frowned. "In what way?"

"It was I who asked Captain Randall to find you, ma'am. I had no idea it would ever come to this." He turned to address the sheriff as well. "I've just come back from a month's furlough and when I learned what had happened, I was so heartily shocked—"

"You said you needed to talk with me?" urged Streeter. "Do you have information on this case?"

"Well, yes. I know where Captain Randall is."

Eden gasped and even Plum Streeter betrayed a startled growl like a sleeping dog that has been bumped.

"He's at Fort Robinson. Or at least he was. My commanding officer had a letter from him in this morning's mail."

"A letter?" cried Eden. Both she and the sheriff stood up.

"I'm afraid he's not there anymore though. We wired the post commander as soon as we received this letter. They replied immediately that he had left Robinson four days ago. They don't know where he was headed. I think it may be important to point out that he . . . has been dismissed from his post as the commissioner of Indian Affairs over what happened there. His letter was written before this occurred and he may not yet have been informed of it."

"He was the *commissioner of Indian Affairs?*" Streeter was clearly astounded by this fact.

"Why, yes, sir," said John Simon. "He was only one level below a cabinet officer as I understand it. He oversees a branch of the government with a budget of many millions and countless employees. Though he was on a leave of absence from his duties."

Eden had kept this information concealed. Neither she nor Brad had informed Lawyer Wallace of Brad's prominence and Eden had sworn Kit to stay quiet as well in hopes of keeping publicity to a minimum. That no one at Fort Hays had leaked the information to the press remained an answer to Eden's prayers.

"I'll be damned," the sheriff mumbled. "And to think I debated whether to arrest him one afternoon for public fighting, like he was a common thug."

"Please don't tell the newspapers," Eden said. "He has a family back home. They would be so dreadfully shocked."

"They oughta be," said Streeter. "He committed a terrible crime."

"That's not proven!"

"Let me see this letter," he said to the major.

Major Simon pulled the folded paper from his breast pocket. He handed it to the sheriff, then sat down with Eden on her bench by the window.

"I'm just so sorry about all of this," said the major. "I feel I caused it, somehow. But I thought I was doing a good thing, a compassionate, humanitarian thing."

"You did nothing wrong, sir. Truly, I'm grateful to you for asking Mr. Randall to find me. You can't know how happy it made me to find out my son is alive after all this time."

"My dear Mrs. Murdoch. Meeting you in person now—it is so hard to reconcile all that is being said about you."

"I'm not a murderer, Major Simon. Please believe that."

"And Captain Randall—he seemed like such a decent fellow. We corresponded a bit. I liked him straight away. I guess I'm no judge of character. I don't have a deuce of an idea what to make of it all now."

"Do you know the circumstances of Mr. Randall's dismissal?"

"My commander knew a little of it from dispatches. The matter has not yet been publicly announced. During the escape attempt by the savages, Mr. Randall refused to be of help to the post commander. He had been translating, you see, and was useful in negotiations, but he refused after the breakout when the troops were in pursuit and had a group of the reds at a standoff. Captain Wessels ordered him at gunpoint to translate his words to the savages in order to facilitate their recapture or surrender or something. Randall flatly refused though a gun was placed directly at his head. The captain didn't shoot of course. Mr. Randall being a civilian, after all, as well as a high-ranking public official. But the captain complained of his actions quite loudly to General Sheridan, who relayed the situation to the secretary of the Interior and demanded action. The secretary promptly discharged Mr. Randall for acting in direct contravention to the policies the secretary had specifically set out. He had no choice, ma'am."

"Knowing Mr. Randall as I do, I doubt *he* felt he had a choice, either."

The major shrugged, then bid them farewell. The sheriff allowed Eden to read Brad's letter.

My Dear Colonel Ryan:

You asked me to keep you informed on the developments at Fort Robinson as I witnessed them and I am happy to oblige, though I wish I had more positive news to report.

When I arrived back at the fort in December, I was dismayed to learn that your friend Colonel Carlton had been ordered to pursue the missing Cheyenne band led by Little Wolf. He was replaced with a decidedly less compassionate Captain Henry Wessells.

The presence of this overly excitable man worsened the relations with the prisoners considerably. Upon assuming command, he immediately doubled the guard upon the Cheyennes and reduced their liberty about the grounds. He further saw fit to barge into their barracks room at all hours of the day and night to constantly keep them in a state of unease.

To his credit, he wired General Crook almost daily, pleading for additional food and clothing for his charges. How the government expects these people to travel in the dead of winter with only rags and worn-through moccasins was a continual source of consternation.

On New Year's Day, the acting head at the Bureau of Indian Affairs sent orders for the removal of the Cheyenne men accused in the depredations along the Sappa Valley in Kansas last fall. They are to be sent to Fort Leavenworth to stand trial for their crimes.

Then word arrived that the remainder of the Cheyennes were to be removed to the Indian Territory, despite the fact no food or clothing had ever been provided. On the following Friday, Dull Knife and the other leaders flatly refused to return. Dull Knife essentially said, "If you are going to kill me, do it now. I will die here in my own country. Nowhere else."

Captain Wessels's response to this defiance was to board up the windows to the prison room and remove all source of food or heat. He did invite the prisoners to send out their children to be fed. This started a controversy among them, with Dull Knife willing to allow the children out and his younger men refusing.

Troop strength was increased at Robinson to five companies. On Wednesday, Wessels cut off water to the prisoners. A young Cheyenne said to me that day, "I will not see you again. We are all going to die."

By the following evening, the Cheyennes were painting their faces and preparing their escape. They had disassembled numerous firearms prior to their capture and cleverly concealed them in plain sight by sewing the bits and pieces to their clothing like adornments, or wearing them as necklaces and bracelets, even braiding them into their children's hair. That evening they reassembled their arsenal.

The temperature dropped to more than twenty-five below zero that night, so cold it was said that gun metal could freeze to a man's hand. At ten, the first shots rang out and the Cheyennes poured from the window of their prison room and headed for the bluffs beyond Soldier Creek.

For the next five bitterly cold days, the soldiers pursued the escapees. In the end, thirty-two Cheyennes were dead and seventy-one recaptured. Dull Knife and a few others remain at large. I wish them well. They deserve their liberty after all they have suffered. With a heavy and bitter heart, I have decided to leave this place.

Eden carefully folded Brad's letter and thought to place it in the pocket of her jacket, but the sheriff insisted on keeping it as possible evidence.

"Do you really believe a murderer would be writing long letters to the commander of a large army post informing him of his whereabouts and his activities?" Eden asked.

"I don't know why people do anything," the sheriff said without looking up from his paperwork.

Twenty-Two

When Kit arrived unexpectedly on a Tuesday, Eden jumped up from her cot, fearful he had brought bad news. He usually came to visit only on the weekends when he could bring Hadley.

"Is something wrong?" she asked, further worried by his unusually downcast expression.

"I was just talking to the sheriff. He says that you'll be going to trial soon."

"Yes, this has been the longest six weeks of my life."

"Mrs. Murdoch, we need to talk." He sighed and paced back and forth in front of her cell door. "There's just no easy way to say this."

"Is something wrong with Hadley?"

"No, no, it's not that, but it does involve her. Your neighbors, the Laytons . . . they invited us to supper last Sunday night."

"How nice."

"Yeah, they're both real nice. Anyway, after dinner, Mr. Layton asked me if I wanted to go for a walk, which was about the last thing I wanted to do given the miserable weather, but anyway, it turns out he just wanted to get me out of the house so we could talk alone. You see, he and his wife . . . they said they'd be inclined to adopt Hadley, should the time come."

"Adopt Hadley?"

"And, well, I thought about the matter all night and all day and all the long ride over here and . . . if anyone adopts her, I think it should be me. I'm her blood kin. And since it doesn't look like my uncle is going to show up anytime soon. . . ."

"Oh, my God," Eden murmured in a tiny voice.

"When my father was killed, the whole Randall family stepped in to help raise me. I can do the same. Now it's my turn."

Eden wandered over to the little barred window and opened the shutter to let the icy breeze cool her distraught face. Until that moment she had not fully accepted the gravity of her situation. While she had ignored the obvious, others had not. They were making plans for her daughter, plans for the future . . . after she was executed for the murder of Lawrence Murdoch. After she was hanged by the neck until dead.

She tried to speak in an ordinary tone. "What about your plans? You told me you wanted to go to Colorado and look for gold."

"Silver," he corrected. "I can do that later. When Hadley's grown up and on her own. I'll stay here until she gets done with school. And don't worry, I'll make sure she doesn't quit. If she tries to run away, I'll haul her back. I'll do a good job, you can be sure of that."

She turned back to him and tried to smile. "You're awfully certain I'll be found guilty."

He did not smile back. The Randall dimples would not make an appearance this sorry day. "I think we need to be practical."

Eden did not hear the deputy, Harry Knapp, open her cell door. The light from an oil lamp faintly shone through her eyelids, but before she could even open them, the entire weight of a man's body crushed her into the mattress. He smelled so atrocious, it made her gag.

She kicked and fought wildly as she realized her arms had been yanked over her head and the cold metal of handcuffs were being snapped around her wrists. She tried to scream, but her attacker's weight crushed all the breath out of her lungs. The man's vest buttons dug into her cheek. All that issued from her mouth was a muffled growl.

"Shut her up, Klell!" came the deputy's voice in a frantic whisper. "Stuff this in her mouth. We don't want him to hear us."

The man pinning her to her iron cot now rose and knelt one knee on her chest. He attempted to stuff a dirty handkerchief between her clenched teeth. When she refused to open them, he slapped her hard across the face, once, then twice. The blows made her dizzy and he shoved the cloth into her mouth the moment her lips parted.

"Ouch!" the man named Klell cried.

"Shut up, for chrissakes," hissed Knapp.

"The bitch bit me." He slapped her again.

"Stop hittin' her," Knapp said. "We don't want to leave any bruises that show."

Klell succeeded in stuffing the handkerchief into her mouth, her jaws stretched so wide she could not swallow and barely could breathe. Her hands were cuffed around the bar behind the head of her cot and now each man took hold of her struggling legs. The deputy, his long, greasy black hair hanging down to obscure his face, tied her right ankle to the foot of the cot.

He stood back to admire his handiwork while his accomplice, Klell, a young man with straw-colored hair that stuck out straight from his head in bizarre directions, continued to hold her other leg in the air. Both men reeked of whiskey, along with the stench of sweat and something worse.

The deputy drunkenly smiled down upon his victim. A large build-up of food seemed wedged between each of his teeth. "Stop your fighting, honey. We're not gonna hurt you. In fact, we're gonna show you a real good time. The county don't pay me shit for this lousy job, so I figure I'm entitled to a little bonus now and then."

He pulled up her skirts and petticoats. "Well, look at that, will ya? No drawers! She was all ready and waitin' for us. Oh, honey, that sweet little cunny of yours is gonna get fed some nice juicy meat tonight. Right, Klell?"

Klell giggled in a silly, high-pitched way, displaying his yellow-brown teeth, several of which were missing. He held her leg by the ankle in one hand and leaned over to pick up the oil lantern with the other.

"I been wantin' to do this ever since I started followin' her," said Knapp as he slipped his suspenders off his shoulders and began to unfasten his trousers.

"You've been followin' her?" asked Klell.

"Yep. And been paid right well to do so, too."

"By who? The sheriff?"

"Hell, no, some gent from out of town. Wanted to know everything he could about her—who she talked to, where she went, and most important of all, who she shared a bed with. That was the fun part. I fixed the doorknob on her hotel room one night so it wouldn't lock. I got a real eyeful. I saw her fancy man going after it like he was tryin' to saw her in half. Now that old Plum Sobersides has put me on night duty, I can do this every night if I want."

"Hot damn!" The straw-haired man practically drooled at this possibility. "Wait a minute, Harry. Take her top off. I wanna see her tits."

"We don't got time."

"I wanna see her titties!"

"Shut up, you fool! The sheriff's sleepin' just over our heads."

Eden shut her eyes as the little deputy climbed on top of her. Tears oozed from her lashes and she silently screamed into the gag in her mouth.

"Ride her, Harry. Ride her hard," Klell said as he gazed, transfixed by the sight of his friend on top of her.

She prayed to an unknown god for deliverance and when she

opened her eyes she saw Klell still holding both her ankle and the lantern. She knew what to do. She stopped struggling and went utterly limp. Just as she hoped, Klell relaxed his grip on her ankle. She then kicked with all her might and knocked the lantern from his drunken hand.

The glass shattered and spewed flaming lamp oil across the stone floor.

"Sweet Jesus!" Klell screamed. He sidestepped the fire as the deputy jumped off his victim and yanked at his trousers.

"Holy shit You idiot!"

The two men stared frantically at the dancing flames, then bumped into each other in their drunken attempt to flee.

Oh, my God, they're leaving me here to burn to death, thought Eden in horror. Acrid smoke seared her nostrils as she thrashed against her manacles and tried to spit out her gag.

Klell headed out the front door of the jail, but the deputy was not so fortunate. Sheriff Plum Streeter, looking very un-sheriff-like in his long white night shirt, appeared in the doorway that led to his upstairs apartment.

"Dammit all Harry, what in hell is going on?" He ran to his office and returned with a rug. He dashed into Eden's cell and beat the flames with it.

Knapp stood by looking scared and penitent, as the sheriff extinguished the small blaze that had burned only the spilled oil. The room was momentarily plunged into a smoky darkness until the sheriff's wife appeared with a lamp in hand.

The lamplight illuminated Eden's cell and both the sheriff and his wife gasped when they saw her tied to the bed with her skirts thrown up, displaying her nakedness.

"You go back upstairs now, dear," said the sheriff as he took the lamp from her.

The wife stole one more glance at Eden, a look of both pity and disgust on her sharp face. She rapidly exited as her husband hastened to cover Eden up with her skirts and petticoats. He knelt at Eden's side and removed the gag from her mouth. Her aching jaws snapped shut and she began to cough from the smoke.

"I can explain," said the deputy, whiskey still slurring his voice.

"Hand me the keys, Harry, then get out."

"I didn't hurt her none. I swear it. I was just givin' her something she's had plenty of before. Where's the harm?"

"My female prisoners are not here for your entertainment, Harry, nor any of your friends. Who was he—the other one who ran out of here?"

"Nobody. It don't matter. We was just havin' a little fun. She wanted us to do it."

"And that's why you had to bind and gag her?" Sheriff Streeter finished releasing Eden's arms and bound ankle and helped her into a sitting position. "Leave your pistol and your rifle on my desk, along with your badge when you leave."

"You're firin' me for this?" Harry Knapp seemed genuinely shocked. "Over *her*?"

"Get out or I'll do worse!"

When the deputy slammed the door behind him, the sheriff said, "Should I get the doctor?"

Eden shook her head. "If I could just have some water . . . to wash with."

"Of course." The sheriff rose and left the cell door open behind him.

Eden stared for a long time at that open cell door. She could walk right out, run away perhaps. Was that his intention?

The air still swirled with smoke, yet it masked the stench of those two horrible men. She rose from the cot but her legs felt like rubber and she sat down again with a thump. She could feel the sticky, disgusting remnants of the deputy between her legs and she felt light-headed and sick.

The sheriff returned, fully dressed and carrying a wooden bucket and a towel. He sat them down at her feet and began to pick up the pieces of broken glass from the lamp.

"I'm sorry about this. I run a good jail and this kind of thing isn't supposed to happen. It's so hard to hire decent help. You can't imagine. Well, anyway, the thing is done and I'm sorry for it. I just hope that—"

"May I have some privacy, please?"

"Oh, yes, I'm sorry. If you change your mind about the doctor, let me know."

He left the lamp just outside her cell to allow her some light to wash by. As she pulled up her skirts to sponge away the deputy's filth from her body, she felt another wave of nausea.

Her jaws still hurt from the gag and her head throbbed with a headache, but she felt something else, some odd sensation she could not identify.

She lay back down on the cot to wait for the dizziness to pass and stared up at the cobwebs on the ceiling of her cell. She felt so upset she could not even summon tears. Soon her exhaustion swamped her tormented thoughts and she fell into a dreamless sleep.

Just after dawn, a strong cramping in her lower abdomen and back awakened her. The cramps intensified and had a rhythmic quality almost like the pains of childbirth.

She felt a warm wetness between her legs. She could not see the sheriff, though she heard sounds of him snoring lightly out in his front office. There was just enough light filtering in around the wooden shutter to see about the cell. She pulled up her skirts to find bright red blood staining her muslin petticoat.

She untied the drawstring at her waist and slipped the underskirt off to bunch the muslin between her thighs. She pulled her skirt back down and lay on her side, doubled up to fight the pains as the muscle contractions grew stronger. She rocked back and forth on the cot and silently cried.

At eight o'clock, the sheriff brought in her breakfast—toast, fried grits, and coffee, the same as every morning. He set the tray on the floor next to her cot and then he saw it—blood dripping through the thin mattress onto the stone floor beneath.

"Oh, damn," he whispered. "I knew I should have gone for the doctor. I'm going to send my wife down to help you."

Eden heard the sharp tap of the woman's heels descending the stairs. Mrs. Rosemary Streeter appeared, dressed in her wrapper and carrying an armload of towels and sheets along with a disdainful frown.

"I'll go get the doctor," said the sheriff.

"I don't need a doctor," Eden said in a hoarse voice. Her throat was raw, seared by the smoke from the fire.

"Are you sure, Mrs. Murdoch?" He looked relieved.

The sheriff's wife injected her own curt opinion. "A woman doesn't need a doctor for a simple miscarriage, Plum."

Eden's parched lips opened in shock. She could not believe it. She had not even guessed she was pregnant. Never had she even thought about it once. She should have known, as she was many weeks late. Usually her cycles were as predictable as the moon. Too many other thoughts had filled her mind in the last month and a half.

Six weeks gone. Six weeks since she had lain in Brad's arms. She at least had the luxury of knowing the date of conception, not that it made any difference now. She wondered if the baby she lost was large enough to see. It was probably no bigger than the head of a pin. Or was it as big as a pea? Or the tip of her little finger? So strange to think she had lost something she had not even known she had until it was too late.

"Let me clean you up," Mrs. Streeter announced brusquely.

Eden turned slowly, painfully onto her back as the woman lifted her skirts and found the wadded, blood-soaked petticoat between her thighs.

"Good heavens, what a mess." She twisted her lips as she pulled away the stained muslin and handed Eden a clean towel. "How far along were you? Do you know?"

Eden did not feel like talking about it.

"If you can turn onto your side, I will try to put some clean sheeting under you. We have no other mattress. You'll just have to get by with this one. A terrible thing, what happened last night, but maybe you're grateful for it, in a way. It solved your problem, didn't it? A woman in your situation has no business having a baby, now does she? A fine world that lets common riff-raff breed like rats, but a decent and honorable couple are unable to conceive a child."

Eden's back was turned to the sheriff's wife as she said these words or she would have been tempted to spit in her face. Mrs. Streeter efficiently replaced the sheets beneath her and Eden curled up into her original position.

A brittle smile pinched Rosemary Streeter's thin face. "On the other hand, being in a family way would have postponed your date with the gallows. We taxpayers really shouldn't have to feed you all those extra months just because you couldn't keep your legs together."

Eden shut her eyes as though this could close out the woman's contemptuous barrage.

"My doctor recommends this for pain. I'll leave it here for you." Mrs. Streeter set a small glass bottle on the stone floor along with a teaspoon. After she left the cell, Eden picked up the bottle. Laudanum. *It will make me sleep, if nothing else,* she reasoned and dosed herself.

Before she drifted into her drugged sleep, she heard the couple conversing in terse tones.

"What if they talk around town?" the wife demanded.

"They better not *stay* around town. I'll run 'em out if they do."

"We're lucky she didn't demand to see a doctor."

"Stop fretting, dear. I'm handling this."

By the afternoon, Eden's cramping had reduced to a dull ache and her bleeding had slowed. More like her normal monthly episodes.

The sheriff summoned his wife as soon as he noticed she was

up and about again. Mrs. Streeter brought more towels and a little cotton belt and rags to allow her to deal with her "female" situation. In the preceding weeks, the woman had not so much as uttered a word to her. Why was she now being so helpful?

"I've got your petticoat soaking in cold water. I'll try to get the bloodstains out of your skirt, too, if you wish. Here's a house frock to put on."

The sheriff stepped near and whispered to his wife, "You're not sending it to the laundry, are you?"

"Of course not," she hissed. "Do you think I'm stupid? I'll launder it myself." He nodded and left them alone so his prisoner could change into the clean clothing.

"Where, in heaven's name, are your drawers?" asked Rosemary Streeter.

Eden sighed as she handed the woman her skirt. She resolved at that moment to henceforth wear drawers, just to shut everyone up about it. She dressed herself in the calico house frock. Though it was too big for her, just having clean, fresh cotton against her skin soothed her. She would have happily burned the clothing the sheriff's wife took away to launder. She doubted any laundry soap could possibly remove the memory of those two men and their stench.

She decided she felt well enough to eat and called to the sheriff to request some dinner.

He brought back the tray with an awkward, sheepish look.

"Feeling better, ma'am?"

"Somewhat." She picked over the cold slab of ham and then buttered the two large slices of dark bread. She enjoyed this rare pleasure. He only allowed her to use a knife when he was standing by, watching.

"You know, there's no real reason anyone needs to know about what happened here last night, Mrs. Murdoch. I can't afford a scandal."

She glanced up to study his worried features and now understood why his sharp-tongued wife had been so generous. He was running for re-election. She had seen the posters up at various locations around town. RE-ELECT STREETER FOR SHERIFF.

"It wouldn't reflect very well on me and . . . I would think you wouldn't want the news about. Most women don't fancy such things being common knowledge."

"I've been accused of murdering my husband, Sheriff. Exactly how much more reputation do you think I have to lose?"

He chuckled uncomfortably. "I see your point."

She set down her coffee cup in a businesslike manner. "Let's talk plainly. I'll do you a favor and say nothing about what happened, if you will likewise do me a favor."

He raised his hands. "I can't turn you loose. I can't afford that either, though there's a part of me that says I owe it to you."

"You're damned right you owe it to me."

"I said I was sorry about what happened."

"I not only suffered an unspeakable outrage because of you, I lost a child. And don't bore me like your wife did with high-hat moral platitudes about how I'm better off without it. My baby is dead because of you. Dead. You definitely *owe it* to me."

"You're real fancy with words, aren't you? No wonder all those reporters love talking to you. Still, I can't let a murderess loose on the streets."

"I didn't kill Lawrence Murdoch and you know it."

"I don't know a thing for certain. That's for a jury to say. Still, my theory is that your lover—that baby's daddy, I assume—is the true one who did it. A shame he feels free to not only get a bastard on you but let you take the noose for him, as well. A fine fellow, indeed."

The possible truth of these words burned and shamed Eden deeply, but she tried to maintain a facade of composure; always the first rule of successful negotiation. "When my trial begins, you will have no means of keeping me from talking to reporters. . . ."

Sheriff Streeter let out a painful sigh. "Let me think about this awhile."

He left her alone. She sank back into her darkest thoughts. *A shame he feels free not only to get a bastard on you but let you take the noose for him, as well.* Is that what he had done?

Men understood men in a different way than women ever could. Perhaps the sheriff read Brad's motives more objectively than she did.

Brad could not kill a man in cold blood, could he? And yet he had plainly said, *I wish I had killed him when I had the chance.* Those words had chased her through countless troubled nights. Yet why would he kill Lawrence *after* he abandoned her? That did not make sense—unless Lawrence provoked him, a talent Lawrence had in abundance.

And Brad had been more upset than she had ever seen him that morning, a month and a half ago. Telling her she had ruined his life. Saying if she knew the truth about him she wouldn't love him. What was this horrible truth he kept alluding to? What awful secret had managed to rend his life, leaving both his marriage and his career in shambles?

She picked up her hairbrush and stroked it through her long auburn hair. She glanced at the bristles of the brush and noticed several gray strands.

———

Kit Randall had just finished his morning chores and was preparing to start work on the roof of his construction when he saw a lone horseman riding straight for the house.

The rider apparently saw him too and kicked his horse into a full gallop. Soon the rider was close enough for Kit to recognize. He dropped his hammer and roofing nails and ran full speed at his uncle.

"Hello!" Brad called in a cheery voice.

"Get down off that horse!"

The smile fell from Brad's face. "What's the matter?"

"Get off that horse this minute, you son of a bitch!"

Totally nonplussed by his nephew's rage, he did as Kit requested. The moment his feet hit the ground, Kit ran at him and shoved him in the chest with all his might.

Brad fell backwards into the dry prairie grasses and looked up to see Kit standing over him, fists clenched, anxious to hit him again.

"For the love of God, Kit—what in hell is wrong with you?"

Twenty-Three

Eden pinned up her hair and adjusted her borrowed frock as best she could while she waited the final word from Sheriff Streeter on how her "escape" would be orchestrated.

She heard muffled voices of two men talking in the front office of the jail. They spoke in such low tones she could not identify them, but she prayed that whoever had stopped by would leave so that she could be on her way before any more of the chilly January day could slip by.

Footsteps in the corridor leading from the office to her cell caused her to rise and wait with a strange apprehension. She knew the sound of Streeter's step too well to think it was he who approached.

The tall man who appeared before her was an utter surprise.

"Hello, Eden," said Brad Randall in a somewhat shaky voice. "I wish we could arrange our reunions in some place other than a jail for once." He stood before her collarless in his shirtsleeves, with his coat and vest draped over his arm. His other hand grasped the waistband of his trousers. With an awkward smile, he added, "I don't know how they expect me to keep my pants up if they're going to deprive me of my suspenders."

She was too stunned to speak.

Streeter followed Brad and cut in front of him to unlock Eden's cell. "You're free to go, Mrs. Murdoch."

He held the door open wide. Brad entered her cell and made a low bow to invite her to exit.

"I don't understand, Sheriff."

"Your friend, here, has just confessed to the murder of Lawrence Murdoch. Now come along. I've got all your belongings in a box in my front office. I'll need you to sign a paper verifying that everything is there."

He gently tugged at her elbow to lead her out. She could not close her gaping mouth. In her last sight of Brad, he had solved the problem of his trousers by simply sitting down on the cot, a cot still stained with the dried blood of the child she had lost. Their child.

"Sheriff, I demand to know what is going on here." She sat before his desk as he pulled out the box containing her personal property.

"It's pretty much as I told you. He walked in here and confessed to the murder. Said you were completely innocent, didn't know anything about it. Said he and Murdoch met up that morning and got into it again over you and he just pulled out his gun and ended the matter. Couldn't help himself, or so he claims."

"What else did he say?"

"We haven't gotten into too many details yet. He . . . I don't know—"

"What?"

Plum Streeter sighed. "He seemed kinda hazy on the details of the murder. Didn't even know which alley, for example. But every time I spotted a snag in his story, he was quick to come up with an explanation. He can think on his feet. I'll give him that much."

"So you believe he's lying?"

"No, not really. I've still got him pegged as the one. Sometimes people get so angry, they don't know where they are or hardly what they're doing. Lots of times, they forget the details. Or they just black 'em out. The mind works in funny ways."

"Did he say how his gun ended up in my room?"

"We didn't get that far. I was anxious to turn you loose. You know how sorry I am about what happened the other night. As soon as I locate the county clerk, I'm going to have him come over and record Randall's sworn statement. I warned him that what he said was going to put a noose around his neck and he just said, 'Sooner, the better.' "

"I want to talk to him."

"I don't think that's a good idea."

She responded to this with a fierce threat of a look and he instantly changed his tune. She knew she still had power over him with her ability to damage his reputation and his re-election bid.

She walked back to the cell and found Brad with his elbows braced against his knees and his face in his hands. He looked up with a mournful expression.

"I don't believe you," she said before she had even reached his cell door.

"I don't think that matters."

"It doesn't matter that you'll hang for killing my husband?"

His strange, sad un-Brad-like smile returned. "Eden, go home to your daughter. She needs you."

"She needs *you*, too."

"Oh, so you are finally going to admit I'm her father? Better late than never—isn't that what they say?"

"Don't talk to me like that!"

He rose from the cot and walked over to her. He hitched up his trousers as he walked and mumbled, "Damn, this is annoying." He looked her in the face. "Don't be angry. I'm sorry about the things I said the last time I saw you. I've wished a hundred times I could take them back. And I'm sorry I left so abruptly. You see, when I realized the depth of your feelings . . . weren't what I had hoped, I just . . . I needed to get away and be alone with my thoughts. And then I got that wire from Robinson. They needed me to return. All hell had broken loose and—"

"I don't want to hear about Fort Robinson!" She drew a breath to still her anger. "Brad, you didn't kill Lawrence. I know you didn't."

"It doesn't matter."

The soft and dispassionate tone of his voice chilled her. Perhaps he *had* lost his mind. "It doesn't matter that you'll hang?"

"Murderers should hang." He looked at the stone floor.

"Tell me the truth, damn you! I deserve the truth."

"My wife and I killed our daughter," he said as he returned to his cot.

Her blood froze in her veins and her ears seemed to ring in the icy stillness left after his words.

He set his eyes on some unknown point only he could see and shook his head as one amazed. When he spoke again, he appeared to address himself as if she were no longer there. "I finally said it out loud."

"What?"

Her question returned him to the present. "I think you heard me. Now you know the truth. Has it 'set you free'?"

"How dare you take that rough pitch with me. Yes, I heard you, but I don't understand you."

"There's not much to understand. My wife and I killed our daughter."

"What do you mean by 'killed'?"

With a bitter smile, he said, "You sound like a prosecutor, Eden. I suppose this is good practice. I'll have to talk to a real one soon." He returned to the little window and once again turned his face from side to side, luxuriating in the cold breeze. He drew a deep breath and said in a rush, "Amanda poisoned her with laudanum. The deed was hers, but the blame falls to me as well."

"Oh, my God," Eden whispered. She closed her eyes and pressed her forehead against an iron bar. "It's time for you to tell me the story, Brad."

It began with a simple head cold. Sarah caught it from B.J. who had brought it home from school. He recovered in a few days' time, but no sooner had he returned to his classes than Sarah began sniffling and complaining of a sore throat. At two, she was a precocious talker and could easily communicate her distress.

"Hurts to swallow," she told her mother who felt her forehead and decided the child had a fever.

In a week's time she complained of an earache, so the doctor was summoned.

"We must sweat the contagion out of her," the doctor decreed. "Cover her with heavy blankets until the fever subsides."

Neither Brad nor Amanda liked this prescription. It seemed to cause the child much more discomfort, yet they felt obligated to yield to the doctor's medical expertise and followed his instructions.

He told them to dose her with laudanum to ease the pain. At least the drug quieted her crying and caused her to get much-needed sleep. Brad and Amanda were able to catch a little sleep as well. They took turns sitting up with the child each night.

By the third week of Sarah's illness, Brad began to fear for his wife's health. Day after day, she tended to her daughter's needs, allowing no one but Brad to enter the nursery, not even Dora, their housekeeper.

Each day Sarah seemed to worsen rather than improve. The infection had spread to both ears. At first, they took heart that the contagion had not afflicted her lungs. They worried about pneumonia every time one of the children caught cold. Amanda's mother had died from the disease so they both feared it greatly.

Brad and Amanda began to argue over how much laudanum

to give the child and how often to call the doctor and whether or not to send B.J. to stay with Jennetta. As each day passed, their tempers grew shorter.

Then came the worst night of Brad's life. He had fallen asleep at the desk in his study. He planned to catch a few hours of rest before relieving Amanda from her vigil around two.

Just after midnight, the screaming of his name sent him running to the nursery. Amanda stood next to Sarah's bed. Her face was distorted with fear to behold their little girl's body jerking uncontrollably.

"What is it? What is it?" Amanda shouted at her husband. "She's so hot, it's like she's on fire!"

Brad rushed to the bedside and picked Sarah up. Her face was so red she did not look like herself and her beautiful blue eyes had rolled back in her head. He tried to quiet the spasms of her tiny body and was shocked to realize how violent they were. He laid her back down again.

"We must do something to cool her off," he said frantically. "Let's take her nightgown off and pull away the covers."

"But the doctor said—"

"To hell with the doctor!" They both struggled to pull the nightclothes from the child's convulsing form. When they succeeded, both gasped to observe the red flush that covered her entire body.

Then, suddenly, she relaxed. She looked calm, as though asleep, but a stain of urine spread out upon the sheets.

"Darling? Darling?" Amanda said in sweetly mothering tones. She shook her daughter's lifeless arm, then looked up at Brad in terror and whispered, "Is she dead?"

"No, she's breathing. Look at the rise and fall of her chest."

"Why doesn't she hear me, then?"

"I don't know. I'll hold her. You replace the sheets with fresh ones."

He carried his daughter around the nursery, cooing endearments into her ear and praying she would respond.

Finally, she did.

"Papa?" she whispered groggily. "Head hurts."

"Papa will make it better. I promise."

He carried her back to the remade bed, but before he could lay her upon it, she began to scream—a strange, high-pitched screeching. It was the most bizarre, horrible noise he had ever heard issue from a human being.

He announced he was leaving to fetch the doctor. He spoke in a quiet voice. He did not dare let Amanda see how frightened he was for fear she would lose control herself. He had never felt a human body radiate such heat nor make such a savage wail. This was no ordinary fever.

He hurried down the hallway and nearly tripped over his son in the process.

"Dad, what's all the noise?" B.J. sleepily rubbed his eyes.

"Go back to bed, son. Sister's just ill and needs the doctor again. Now back to bed with you. Be a good boy."

Brad ran from the house, forgetting both hat and coat despite the fact the March rain descended in sheets. No hack could be found at such an hour so he ended up running the eight blocks to the doctor's home. The rain slapped against him in such torrents he constantly had to wipe his face to see. At one point he became disoriented, thinking he had made a wrong turn. Some of the street lamps had been put out by the storm. He thought he would go mad until he recognized the doctor's street.

He dashed up the wet stone steps to the doctor's door and rang the bell until a light shone from the upstairs window. The doctor, no doubt used to being awakened at all hours, was already half-dressed as he answered the door.

A servant helped them harness the doctor's carriage and soon he drove Brad through the dark, empty streets of slashing rain.

"It sounds like a febrile seizure," the doctor said as he whipped the horses into a faster clip.

"What does that mean?"

"When the fever goes too high, it produces seizures . . . convulsions."

"But what does that mean?"

"It means we have a very sick child here. You're shivering, Mr. Randall. You're soaked to the bone, man. Cover yourself with the blanket I have behind the seat. No need for us to end up with two patients."

"That night was not the end of the nightmare. It was the beginning," Brad said. "Her suffering grew worse each day. The very next morning all her hair fell out. It was such a lovely reddish color. This bothered Amanda a great deal more than me. I was convinced that when she regained her health, her hair would grow back." His voice halted with emotion.

Eden had begun to weep. Though her nursing work had hardened her to many aspects of the human body's frailties, her mother's heart could not let her bear the suffering of a child lightly.

"We had to stay with her every hour of the day. Occasionally, she seemed to be conscious and we would try to get her to eat or drink something. The seizures became more and more frequent. They were always frightening. We felt so helpless. And the work was unending. The sheets needed constant laundering because—"

Eden interrupted to spare Brad more discomfort. "Yes, I know what happens after a seizure."

"The days grew longer and the nights . . . the nights were unrelenting. I suppose, in retrospect, our fatigue caused our judgments to be faulty at times. Amanda and I . . . we could have been kinder to each other. Well, anyway, the turning point arrived the night we realized Sarah was blind. The high fevers, you see, had damaged her brain and taken her sight."

Eden wiped her wet face on the sleeve of the sheriff's wife's house dress.

"The doctor made us sit together in the parlor and gave us a frank and forthright evaluation . . . to prepare us. He told us there was no hope—a fact we probably already knew but didn't want to admit, yet he also said her suffering could last days, even weeks, before the end finally came. When we heard that . . . you can't imagine how—" Brad buried his face in his hands again. He began to cry, no longer able to hold it in.

Eden ached to cradle him in her arms, but he could only be alone in his terrible memories. Finally, he calmed enough to resume his story.

"I went to work the next morning. I shouldn't have after the night we'd had, but I did. I *wanted* to get away. That's the horrible truth of it. I wanted a few hours of respite. But Amanda needed respite as well. And there was only one way that could happen."

"Oh, God," Eden whispered as she understood where his story was headed.

"No one blames a man for going to work. That's what men are supposed to do. Right? But I knew I shouldn't have left her alone with Sarah that day. I went home at midday to check on them both. I found Amanda sitting in the nursery. Sarah was lying in her crib and before I was halfway across the room, I knew she was gone. And I didn't have to see the empty laudanum bottle to know what had happened."

"Did you ask her about it?"

Brad shook his head. "How could I? How do you speak the unspeakable? But she knew I knew."

"And you couldn't forgive her?"

"She wouldn't let me. I don't think she can forgive herself. She began to push me away from almost the very first day. That pathetic affair she had with my associate, I think it was just another step in the process. My presence will always be a reminder to her of what happened. That's why we cannot live together anymore."

"But Brad, why must you blame yourself?"

"Looking back now, I realize that it was *I* who put the thought in her mind. After the doctor left, we sat in the nursery and talked all night. We were both so weary and distraught, not thinking clearly. I rambled on about the curious paradox that allows us to treat our animals with more compassion than we do our loved ones. If I owned a horse or even a dog that was suffering, I would not hesitate a moment to end its torment. Indeed, others would think less of me if I did not. Wouldn't they?"

Eden nodded.

Brad raked his fingers through his hair in a despairing gesture. "And yet decency and the law required that our darling daughter suffer unholy agony day after day with no end in sight. Where is the humanity in that? But I was speaking in *theories*, idle talk. Everyone's a philosopher at four in the morning."

"Anyone can understand how you felt."

"But then I went off to work and left her alone to cope with it all. Did I leave knowing, in some dark corner of my soul, that she would act on my words? Did I leave *hoping* she would do it?"

He turned his face away from her. She could tell he was crying again from the sound of his breathing, though he would not show her the tears.

"Brad, come here." She held her arms out to him and he rose from the cot and wiped his wet face on his sleeve. They embraced as best they could with the cold iron bars between them.

"I can't believe you want to look at me, much less hold me after what I just told you."

At last she realized why he insisted there was nothing left to reconcile when it came to his marriage. "I'm glad you've told me all this, but why do you now pretend you killed Lawrence?"

"I wanted you free of this jail cell. At least I've accomplished one thing I set out to do in this miserable life of mine."

"If you think you are protecting me, then why did you put your gun in my hotel room?"

His mouth dropped open in utter shock. "My gun? In your room? How could that possibly be? *My gun was stolen from me.*"

Twenty-Four

"Sheriff Streeter, he didn't do it."

"Sorry, Mrs. Murdoch, but he told me he did and I'm not in the mood to argue with him."

"Sit down and hear me out."

Plum Streeter's face bore the expression of a parent indulging a petulant child.

"Someone *stole* his gun! The very morning my husband was shot."

The sheriff frowned in disbelief. "That's a very convenient story."

She grabbed his arm and tugged until he agreed to follow her back to Brad's cell. She said to Brad, "Tell him what happened that morning."

Streeter gave Randall a severe look. "Are you recanting or not?"

"Not exactly," Randall said. "I'll tell you what I know as long as you agree not to arrest her again."

"I'll make no promises at all, but let's hear your version. I guess I don't have anything better to do this morning."

"I left Mrs. Murdoch at the hotel that morning after we . . . had a misunderstanding. I decided to leave and return to Nebraska. I had business at Fort Robinson, so I bought a train ticket to Jules-burg."

"Julesburg, Colorado?" Streeter interrupted, confused.

"You have to backtrack from Denver—"

"Just go on with your story, Brad," said Eden, impatient with both men.

"I bought a ticket on the next train west and I didn't have much time, so I rounded up my gear and was headed to the livery to pick up my horse. It's awfully time-consuming getting the horse loaded into the livestock car—"

"Stay on the story, for heaven's sake, Brad!"

"Mrs. Murduch, calm down and let the man speak."

"I passed an alley—"

"Which alley?" asked Streeter.

"I don't know. I'd know it if I saw it again. Anyway, a man stepped out in front of me, blocking my path. He stuck a revolver in my belly and jerked his head for us to go into the alleyway. I assumed he was going to rob me, but he just said, 'Give me your gun.' Now I wasn't even carrying it where it could be seen, so I played dumb and acted like I didn't know what he was talking about, but then he said, 'It's in your pocket.' That's the strange part. How did he know I kept a revolver in my jacket pocket?"

"How, indeed?" Eden repeated, like a character in a melo-drama.

"That's all he took, just the gun?" asked Streeter.

Randall nodded. "He ran off and left me standing in the alley wondering what the devil had happened. I would have reported the theft, but I was going to miss my train if I didn't move to get my horse settled out. I was planning on buying a new gun any-way. That old army Colt was in bad condition. I didn't care for it properly over the years. It was misfiring lately and nearly took my hand off the last time I shot it."

Brad showed Streeter the remnants of the injury to his hand. The skin was still dark pink from the two-month-old wound.

"Why would that man have wanted my gun? He had a fancy

little Remington double-barreled derringer. All shiny—it looked brand new."

"A derringer? Small caliber then, right?" said the sheriff.

"No more than a thirty-two, I'm certain of that."

"Describe the man," Eden said.

"Would you mind letting me ask the questions, Mrs. Murdoch?"

"Sorry."

Randall shrugged. "I honestly didn't memorize his appearance. It all happened so fast. I spent more time with my eyes on his gun than his face."

"How tall, how old?" prompted the sheriff.

Randall shut his eyes in an attempt to bring back the image to his mind. "He was shorter than me."

"That narrows it down to ninety-five percent of the town," said Streeter. Few men were tall enough to look Brad Randall straight in the eye.

"I'm sorry. I'm trying. Let's say middle height."

"Stout or lean?" Eden asked, thinking about plump Clyde Summerfield.

"I don't know, really. He wore a large buffalo coat, the type frontiersmen wear."

"What about his age?" said Streeter.

"I don't have any idea. He had a big beard and gray hair, but he didn't look like an old man. He looked odd. Almost like the beard didn't really belong to him."

"A disguise?" Eden suggested.

"Maybe."

"That doesn't help us much," said the sheriff.

The three stood in silence as each considered the information and tried to decide what to make of it.

"I just remembered something else," Randall continued. "The door to Mrs. Murdoch's hotel room would not lock properly. I tried the night before." He cast Eden a sheepish glance. "So anyone could have had access to her room. Anyone could have planted that gun there."

"Including you," said the sheriff.

Brad sighed and shrugged.

Streeter frowned and shook his head. "Assuming any of this were true—which I'm not—*why* would somebody do all this?"

Eden drew an uneasy breath and spoke up. "I don't know the answer to your question, Sheriff, but I think I know somebody who might."

She pushed Phim Streeter back toward his office. She did not want to talk in front of Brad, given the subject matter: Harry Knapp. When Eden heard Brad's remark about her hotel room door, a nasty and unspeakable memory was triggered—and she now knew it might prove their salvation.

"Harry Knapp told his partner in crime that he was the one who did something to my hotel room door so that he could spy on me."

"Why didn't you tell me this before?"

"I don't know. I guess I wanted to blot out all memories of that night."

"Can't blame you for that."

"Someone *hired* him to follow me, Sheriff. He admitted it. He boasted about it to his friend. I thought that Lawrence hired him. I just assumed that."

"To dig up dirt on you for the divorce and the custody suit? That's pretty typical, I guess."

She nodded. "But now that I think back on his actual words— he never mentioned it was my husband. I'm sure he would have, given the context and the timing of the conversation. He called him, 'some gent from out of town.' "

"Your husband was from out of town."

"Why wouldn't he have just said, 'Her husband hired me to follow her'?"

Another thought sprung to her anxious mind. "Harry Knapp was lurking about the McClellan House Hotel the morning of the murder. You told me so yourself, Sheriff. He had access to my room, if the lock wasn't working. He could have planted Brad's gun."

Streeter mulled this over and could not come up with a satisfactory rebuttal. "Why on earth would Harry Knapp want to kill your husband?"

"I don't know," she said, ready to cry with frustration. "I just know that you have to question Harry Knapp."

"I don't *have* to do anything. I've got the fellow I thought was guilty all along behind bars and ready to sign a confession. All I *have* to do is escort him into court and then on to the gallows and my job is done."

"Not quite. There is still the matter of the outrage you allowed to occur in your jail and your failure to prosecute the attacker *and* your attempts to cover up the crime, including *bribing* the victim!"

The color rose in Streeter's face. "You wouldn't dare."

"Oh, but I would."

"It's your word against mine."

"Will your wife lie for you? She was a witness to the crime. She saw what they did to me. And I think a doctor's examination will support my story all the more."

"All right! I'll look for Knapp. I don't know where in creation he is. I told him if I ever saw him around here again, there'd be hell to pay. He could be in Texas or California, or Timbuktu, for all I know."

Eden's heart sank at the possible truth of this. Still, she would not let the probability of failure stop her or even slow her down. "I am going home right now to see my daughter and get some fresh clothing. I'll return your wife's dress tomorrow."

"How are you feeling? Are you sure you're up to that much travel, Mrs. Murdoch?"

"I'll be fine."

She dashed back to tell Brad she would return tomorrow and asked if she could bring him anything.

"I told the sheriff to give you all the money in my wallet, Eden. There's a little over eighty dollars there. I want you and Hadley to have it. I wish there was more."

"Thank you, Brad."

"Why did the sheriff ask you how you were feeling just now? Have you been ill?"

"It's nothing." She stood on tiptoe to give him a quick kiss through the bars.

Twenty-Five

Eden had nearly been forced to wrestle Kit into staying behind in Bluestem. Though she could tell he still thought his uncle was as guilty as the sheriff did, he was excited by her theories and was definitely up for some adventure. The extreme quiet of farm life did not appeal to him now that his construction project was nearly complete.

She had another mission for him though and it allowed him to play detective. "There's a man in town that has me worried. His name is Clyde Summerfield. He works for Phineas Claypool, but I think he may be involved in all of this. He's made certain advances toward me . . . almost flirtatious."

"And why shouldn't he? You're a looker."

Eden rolled her eyes. "And you're such a flirt. Anyway, my lawyer, Mr. Wallace, suggested that the murderer might be someone who wanted to . . . attract my attentions and decided to remove the competition by killing my husband and trying to plant evidence to implicate your uncle."

"Sounds like a reasonable theory. I'll do what I can."

"Don't let on to anyone about our suspicions. And don't take matters into your own hands, no matter what."

Kit made a noncommittal shrug.

"I also want to tell you how wonderful your friend Solange has been to me throughout this ordeal." They sat at Eden's little kitchen table sharing a late night cup of coffee after sending Hadley to bed.

"She's nice, isn't she?" He looked pensive. "What's your honest opinion of her? I'm just curious."

"She seems to have a tender heart and a generous nature."

"Too generous perhaps."

"She's a young girl who fell in love with the wrong man. I did the same myself once. I even married the fool. You won't catch me judging her too harshly for that. I'm afraid the world will, though. She's going to pay a heavy price for her mistake."

"I want to help her, somehow." He propped his chin by his elbows and shoved his lower lip out ever so slightly.

He looked impossibly young to Eden at that moment, a mere boy confounded by life, not a young man trying to sort out his future.

"Don't confuse pity with love, Kit. It's easy to do. Pity is like lust, in that regard. Both like to masquerade as love and it's powerfully hard to know the difference when you're in the throes of it."

He looked even more dejected, though he did not take offense at her words as she feared he might. She decided to add, "On the other hand, the first step toward truly loving someone is forgiving them for not being perfect. That's real love, not foolish, superficial feelings you can read about in romantic novels. I'm talking about the kind of bedrock emotion that can bind two people together for a lifetime."

He glanced up at her with a certain challenge. "Have you felt that?"

She smiled. "Not only once, but twice in my life."

He raised his black eyebrows with a challenging smile. "Twice?"

"I know what you're wondering and, yes, your uncle was—is— one of the two."

"Who was the other?"

"My Cheyenne husband. I cared about him very deeply, but when I met your uncle I had been led to believe my husband was dead. By the time I learned the truth I was already deeply in love with Brad. In fact, I was already. . . ." She stopped, realizing she was about to say too much.

"Carrying Hadley?"

"I heard my name," came Hadley's voice from under the covers.

Eden glanced over her shoulder to the dark corner where her daughter's bed sat. "Go to sleep, Little Eavesdropper."

"What's an eavesdropper?"

"Just go to sleep." She leaned in close to Kit, their faces mere inches apart. "Leaving your uncle all those years ago was about the hardest thing I ever had to do."

He took her hand in his and squeezed it. "I feel like we're already related."

"That's a compliment I'll treasure, Kit. Let's hope it can some-day come true."

Before Eden left to return to Hays the following morning, she rode into Bluestem to chat with Mrs. Redding. She liked to check on her, to make sure her health continued. When she left the boarding house and walked to the market to buy a few food items for her long ride, she passed Phineas Claypool on the wooden sidewalk.

He stood nailing a playbill to the post supporting the awning above. No doubt it advertised the next production of the Bluestem Players, starring himself, she assumed.

When he saw her, his narrow jaw dropped open as though it had come unhinged.

"Good day, Mr. Claypool." She passed by with a superior smile and could not resist adding, "You look as though you've seen a ghost."

She arrived in Hays in the late afternoon dressed in her own comfortable work clothes, attire that finally made her feel like herself again—a serviceable canvas riding skirt and a heavy wool sweater that Mrs. Redding had knitted for her. Over it all, she wore her favorite coat that she had made for herself from a colorful old horse blanket. After dropping off another letter from Kit to Solange, Eden headed straight to the Ellis County jail.

"Have you heard anything?" she demanded of Plum Streeter as she handed over his wife's dress.

"I've made some inquiries around—the saloons, cat houses, barbershops—anywhere folks might gather and talk. Nobody's seen him since I fired him. He was renting a room in a boarding house on Fort Street, but he cleared out that next morning without a word to his landlord, and left a week's rent owing as well."

Eden could not hide her disappointment, but that was nothing compared to the sheriff's announcement that followed.

"Mrs. Murdoch, I took Mr. Randall to court this morning. He pleaded guilty and was sentenced to hang next Saturday."

"Four days from now?"

She ran back to Brad's cell. "How could you do this? Have you lost your mind?"

He looked miserable and in no mood to argue. "Eden, I didn't have a choice. Streeter made sure of that. I talked it over with Mr. Wallace—"

"Mr. Wallace! What does he know?"

"Streeter said if I didn't plead guilty, he'd arrest *you* again and make us both stand trial. I couldn't let that happen."

She returned to Streeter's office, ready to spit nails. "How could you do this behind my back? How could you take him to court before I came back here?"

"I never said I wouldn't. I promised you I'd look for Harry

Knapp, and that I did. I'm not going to neglect my duties to follow you on some squirrel chase. Even if we do run down Knapp again—which I doubt—that still doesn't mean he knows anything important."

"You can't honestly tell me you would knowingly hang an innocent man, just to get re-elected."

Streeter snorted angrily. "I have a duty to serve the people of Ellis County."

"You have a duty to serve justice!"

The telegraph delivery boy interrupted their quarrel.

"I brought this straight away, Sheriff."

Streeter forced a friendly smile and handed the boy a dime.

Eden impatiently paced around the office while the sheriff read his telegram.

He looked up with a strange expression. "Providence has decided to smile upon you today, Mrs. Murdoch. This is from Sheriff Masterson in Ford County. He arrested Harry Knapp last night for public drunkenness and Knapp claimed to still be my deputy. Masterson wants to know if it's true. Impersonating a peace officer is something we all take pretty seriously. He's going to hold him until he hears from me."

"How soon can you leave for Dodge City?" she asked.

"Hold on, now. I need to get organized. If I can catch the noon train to Dodge, I can get him back here by nine tonight."

"Please. You must."

He sighed. "I'll need to find someone to cover for me. This time of year, the county hates to pay for extra help."

Eden stayed with Brad all afternoon and evening while they waited for Plum Streeter to haul Harry Knapp back from Dodge City. They sat together in the greatest intimacy the bars between them would allow—on the brick floor of the jail, holding hands and occasionally exchanging a stolen kiss or two.

"Brad, I don't know if anyone's told you this yet, but the secretary of the Interior—"

"Fired me. I know. I picked up a newspaper when I passed through a town on my way back here. Strange to get the news that way. It was almost like I was reading about a stranger."

"I'm so sorry."

"If I had written the headline, it would read, 'Ten Years of Work Ends Ignobly.' "

"Heroically," she corrected.

"Thanks. That means more to me than you know. I think my entire career was based on a secret desire to win your respect." He sighed. "Now I don't believe my life's work has made the slightest difference. In the last ten years the situation has worsened, not improved. I'm a failure. I've just got to face it "

"You're not a failure just because you tried to solve a problem that was bigger than any one man."

Brad shook his head sadly. "I entered the Bureau with such high hopes."

"You tried to rectify a problem whole armies couldn't solve. Even an entire tribe willing to commit mass suicide didn't end it. The important thing is: you tried. So many others didn't."

"God, Eden, I love you so much."

"The world starts over with each new day."

———

"What are you writing, Kit? Another letter to your sweetheart?" Hadley sat down next to the young man she now looked on as an older brother. She had just donned her nightgown and was brushing out her hair. She wished he would join her in bed. The tiny house was icy cold and the bed would feel even colder when she had to slide under the sheets by herself. She could not understand why he now always refused. He had not shared a bed with her since the unpleasant incident with the Baptist minister.

"She's not my sweetheart. And no, this isn't a letter to Solange. I'm making notes. You and me are going to do some detective work."

The girl clapped her hands together in delight. "Me, too? What will we do? Will this help Mr. Randall?"

"We're gonna get some religion."

"We're going to church? I've never been. What's it like?"

Kit set down his pen. "You've never been in a church, ever?"

She shook her blond head.

"I guess you grew up with some kind of Indian religion, huh? Well, I made some inquiries around town today and found out that this Clyde Summerfield is the choir director for the Methodist Church. You and me are going to say we're interested in becoming Methodists and get kinda friendly with those folks."

"And then what?"

"We're going to listen and learn. Got that? Listen and learn. That's what all good detectives do."

"Why can't Mama be with us?"

"She's got other fish to catch. She thinks some fellow who used to be a deputy in Hays knows more than he's saying and she's going to make the sheriff follow that one up. Ever caught fish with a net, Peppermill?"

"Yes, I have. Well, I've watched."

"We're casting out that net and we're going to yank in the bad guy. Then your daddy can come home to you."

Hadley's face puckered with a frown. "Is he really my daddy?"

"Yep. I'm certain of it."

"But why doesn't my mama just come right out and say it then?"

Kit sighed. "I think she's protecting his reputation. He's still married, you see. Even though he and my Aunt Amanda are getting a divorce, this would make him look bad when they go to court."

The girl looked more puzzled than ever and Kit realized she had not understood anything he had just said.

"Look, Peppermill, just accept the fact that life is complicated."

"Well, look who's outta jail," said Harry Knapp the minute he saw Eden in Plum Streeter's office.

Eden's eyes narrowed, but she said nothing. She clenched her hands to keep from flying at the odious little man and scratching his face off.

"Shut up, Harry," said the sheriff. "Sit down on that bench."

Knapp wore manacles around his wrists and ankles. He moved with a shuffling gait and clanked his way over to the bench.

"Who hired you to follow me?" Eden blurted out.

"How bad do you want to know?" said Knapp with an arrogant smirk.

"Hush up, both of you. Harry, you're spending the night in the shed out back."

"I'll freeze to death."

"Maybe you'd rather share a cell with our Mr. Randall. We've both witnessed how he deals with men who mistreat his woman."

This threat visibly frightened the little former deputy. He sat quietly and avoided eye contact with them after that.

"Are you going to question him, Sheriff?"

The sheriff sighed wearily. "Mrs. Murdoch, it is ten o'clock. I have just spent half a day on a train and have not yet eaten my supper. For all I know, my wife has probably pitched it out. As soon as I lock him up and finish my paperwork to get reimbursed for all these train fares, I'm going to bed. I suggest you do likewise."

"Can I stay here tonight? I haven't made any other arrangements."

"I would think you'd be sick of this hole, but I'm too tired to care where you sleep."

The sheriff returned from placing his prisoner in the makeshift cell in the alley behind the jail. He sat at his desk eating a cold plate of food and filling out forms while Eden and Brad chatted at his cell door.

They all jumped at the blast of a firearm being discharged close by.

"Stay here!" Streeter yelled at Eden. He grabbed his revolver belt from the peg where he hung it and dashed outside.

She and Brad exchanged worried looks. He caught hold of her elbow and held fast, just to make sure she was not tempted to investigate on her own. He knew she had lived with all manner of danger during her years with the Cheyennes and that the sound of a gun firing in the night was more likely to excite her curiosity than frighten her.

Streeter returned quickly, half-carrying, half-dragging a bloody Harry Knapp.

Twenty-Six

Eden rushed to the sheriff's side and saw that Harry Knapp gushed blood from a large neck wound. A bullet, obviously fired at close range, had torn a gaping hole in his throat. He lay on the floor of the sheriff's office fully conscious, but choking on his own blood.

"Did you see who did this, Harry?" Streeter said.

Knapp could only cough blood in reply.

"Who hired you to follow me?" Eden shouted at the wounded man.

A gurgling sound and bubbles of blood were all that issued from his lips.

"What's going on out there?" Brad said, frantic at being barred from the action.

"Tell me who hired you!" Eden yelled. She grabbed the little man's shoulders in desperation, but the sheriff pushed her away.

Harry Knapp's eyes rolled back in his head and the familiar sound of a death rattle rose from his lungs as the air haltingly escaped for the last time.

"Well, that's it," said Streeter.

"No, no," Eden cried. Tears of frustration ran down her cheeks.

The sheriff stood up. "I'm going out to have a look around. You stay here."

Eden returned to Brad's cell. "Harry Knapp is dead. Someone killed him to keep him silent."

They held hands and stared at each other helplessly. "Don't leave here. Bar the door."

"I want to get a message to Kit. To tell him to be careful. I want him to keep Hadley home from school until the killer is caught."

Randall watched Eden return to the front office and stand over the body of Harry Knapp. What she did next both shocked and baffled him: She raised her skirts slightly as though she were about to traverse a mud puddle, then she delivered a vicious kick to the corpse's shoulder.

She halted her strange endeavor when Mrs. Streeter emerged from the door to the back stairway in her dressing gown and nightcap with a lamp in her hand.

"Plum?" she called, as she glanced about apprehensively.

"He's not here," said Eden.

"What's all the commotion?" asked Rosemary Streeter. She walked to the front office and saw the body of Harry Knapp.

Mrs. Streeter gazed down upon the corpse for several seconds. "Miserable scum. Good riddance, I say. Look how he's making a bloody mess of the floor. Like I didn't have anything better to do than clean up this place."

Eden returned to Brad and whispered, "That's the coldest-hearted woman I've ever met. It's a wonder the sheriff doesn't freeze to death living with her."

The sheriff returned just before midnight with several men anxious to join a posse. The undertaker was roused from his bed as well and he and an assistant bore away the body of the slain man.

Eden spent the remainder of the night sitting outside Brad's cell, dozing on and off.

The sheriff returned the following morning, exhausted and disappointed that a night of searching had yielded nothing.

"Now do you believe me that someone else is involved?" Eden asked before the sheriff could retire upstairs to catch a few hours of sleep.

"I have to admit I'm curious now. Before, I was pretty much just indulging you, Mrs. Murdoch. Now, well, I don't know what to think. Harry must have known the man who shot him, that much I'm certain of."

"Why do you say that?"

"The shed out back is built similar to the jail. I put in a barred window when I started using it for my overflow prisoners. There's a shutter on the inside and it was closed when I locked Harry up last night. Somebody had to have convinced him to unlatch that shutter from the inside, then they shot him."

"Someone wanted to make sure he didn't talk to you."

"Possibly."

"Sheriff?" Brad called from his cell. "A young boy came to the jail yesterday while you were in Dodge. He was looking for this Harry Knapp."

"Was it Marcus?" asked Eden with an unpleasant fear.

"No," said Streeter. "My deputy thought somebody paid the kid to come in and ask."

"Brad, did you see him?" Eden said.

"No, I just heard them talking. Whoever paid that boy to come in here obviously learned that the sheriff was bringing Knapp back to Hays for questioning."

"That's what I'm thinking, too. Now if you'll excuse me, I'm going to catch some sleep. It's been a powerfully long night."

The sheriff retreated to his quarters and his part-time deputy, Parker, took over minding the jail. Eden went straight to the telegraph office to inform Kit about the murder of Harry Knapp and to ask if he knew the whereabouts of Clyde Summerfield the previous night.

She next walked over to the Prairie Sunrise Cafe to order Brad some breakfast—the sheriff had not remembered to feed his prisoner that morning. She sat waiting for her order to be prepared when the telegram delivery boy caught sight of her and rapped on the cafe window. Kit had sent an immediate reply:

NEW INFORMATION STOP COME TO BLUESTEM AT ONCE STOP
BRING SHERIFF STOP—CHRISTOPHER RANDALL

Eden knocked, then pounded on the sheriff's door. Finally she heard the sound of steps on the stairway.

Rosemary Streeter opened the door with an even fiercer scowl than usual.

"I need to see the sheriff," said Eden.

"He just got to sleep a few minutes ago. Waking him is out of the question."

Eden shouted up the stairs, "Sheriff Streeter?"

"Hush!"

"I'll fetch him myself if I have to. Or would you rather I speak with the local newspaper?"

Mrs. Streeter gritted her teeth and hissed, "You never give up, do you?"

"I'm the victim, remember? The innocent victim."

"*Maybe.*"

Eden heard the heavy step of Sheriff Streeter on the landing above. He appeared disheveled with long shirttails hanging, far from his usual dapper self. In his stylish, well-cut business clothing he could not be distinguished from a banker or lawyer, but for his badge of office and the holstered six-gun he wore.

"What is it, Mrs. Murdoch?"

"Important new evidence. Brad's nephew, Kit Randall—remember him?"

"Yes, of course."

"He wired me this morning. We need to come to Bluestem immediately. He specifically requested you, sir."

"Can't he contact the local law there?"

"Marshal Bunch is, well—"

"I know Bunch," Streeter sighed. "He's a bit long in the tooth."

"Yes, he's a nice man and square and honest, but . . . his primary job in Bluestem is shooting stray dogs."

Streeter nodded in agreement with this assessment.

"Now, Plum, you need your rest," said his wife.

"My fiancé will hang on Saturday for a crime he did not commit if you do not come and see this through."

"I've gotta go, Rose," said Streeter. He turned and headed back to his bedroom, presumably to finish dressing. His wife ran up the steps after him while Eden returned to Brad.

"I'm worried about you, Eden. And Hadley. And Kit."

"I'll be cautious. I promise. Kiss me for luck."

He pressed his face to the bars and she stood on tiptoe, but before he delivered the requested kiss he said, "I heard you call me your fiancé. Surely you don't think my offer of marriage is still open?"

Eden smiled and frowned in confusion.

"Under the traditional law of contract, an offer, once rejected, is deemed to be withdrawn. Ask your lawyer, Mr. Wallace. He'll support me on this."

He kept a straight face as long as he could bear it.

"You should be ashamed of yourself," she said. "Joking at a time like this."

He pulled her close and finally kissed her forehead.

"The next time you see me, you'll be a free man."

"I hope so." He smiled sadly and she could tell he did not think this a real possibility. "Eden, before you go, could you locate some paper and a pen and ink? I need to write a letter to B.J. Just in case."

Eden and the sheriff rode as swiftly as their mounts would allow, finally pausing to water the horses before crossing the Saline River. A chill prairie wind blew in from the southwest. Eden drew her woolen collar close to her face to brace against it. Yet a south wind was a fair wind, signaling a moderation in the weather to come.

Before they crossed over the Saline, she wistfully looked east. The Vandegaarde Ranch lay just a few miles beyond the horizon. She turned her thoughts back to the most pressing issue.

"Sheriff, isn't there any way to postpone the date of the hanging? Saturday is so close. What if we can't find the real killer before . . . ?"

He looked uneasy. "I've no solid evidence to present to the judge. Not yet, at least."

"But why would someone murder Harry Knapp if not to keep him quiet?"

"Knapp could've had lots of enemies. I sure saw a different side to him the night he attacked you. For all I know he may have outraged other women, too. Maybe some father or brother was coming after him that night to settle the score."

"But you've got to admit you're suspicious."

"I've admitted to being curious. That's all. I'll promise you this: The minute we have any strong evidence that throws doubt away from Randall, I'll ask for a stay of execution. Mr. Randall's lawyer would need to file a writ of habeas corpus."

Eden did not know what all that meant. She knew that corpus was something Latin to do with a body. She remembered that much from her days as a Civil War nurse. They rode on for another two hours without a word between them.

As they approached Eden's homestead, the pace of her heart quickened. Terrible pictures flashed through her mind that Kit and Hadley might both be dead. She kicked her horse into a lope and Streeter followed without remark. Perhaps he, too, felt the danger.

Hadley came running out to meet them the moment they were close enough to recognize. Eden saw that Kit followed carrying her shotgun. He was taking his job as Hadley's protector seriously.

"Kit, what's your news?" Eden called out as they neared.

They all met on the barren, unturned earth. No winter wheat had been laid in for the next summer.

"I don't think Clyde Summerfield is your man," said Kit.

Eden and Streeter dismounted and they all walked toward the house together.

"He was singing his heart out at the Methodist Church choir practice until nine o'clock last night."

"You're sure about this, son?" asked the sheriff.

"I saw him myself."

"We both did," said Hadley as she hung on her mother's arm.

"Well, if the man was in Bluestem at nine o'clock," said Streeter, "he certainly didn't shoot Harry Knapp at eleven."

"But I know somebody who *wasn't* in Bluestem last night. Phin Claypool. And he was out of town the same week as the murder of Lawrence Murdoch. That's my big news."

Eden and Streeter exchanged glances at this. Kit took charge of watering their horses while Eden and the sheriff entered her house for a brief refreshment.

Hadley poured them each a glass of lemonade. Her mother wondered where she had gotten the money to buy such an expensive commodity as fresh lemons this time of year but decided not to ask. She feared Kit's gambling habit had funded such extravagance.

"Well, let's go talk with this Claypool," said Streeter. "Does he even know you, Mrs. Murdoch?"

"Yes, he knows me and hates me, actually. But I can't imagine he knew Lawrence."

"So we have no motive where this Claypool is concerned? Well, Mrs. Murdoch, I'm afraid you made me take a long trip for nothing."

Streeter ate some bread and cheese and then made his horse ready to return to Hays City.

"At least come with me to talk to Claypool," she begged as he mounted his horse.

A wind too warm for January whipped about them and tossed Eden's long auburn braid and heavy riding skirt.

Streeter sighed. "All right. I'm here. I might as well do something."

"Thank you."

Eden ran to prepare her own horse. Kit was at her side in an instant. "Kit, you must stay here. Someone has to stay with Hadley."

"You stay here. I want to go with the sheriff."

"I have to go. I know this man. I'm the one who must ask him questions."

After several more minutes of debate, Kit grudgingly agreed to remain at home. Eden and the sheriff rode to the bottling works at the base of the Solomon Spring.

They entered the small frame building. The interior was dark and dusty. Enormous wooden crates filled with green bottles bearing the label *Solomon Spring Miracle Elixir* lined every wall, floor-to-ceiling.

Clyde Summerfield, the building's only occupant, sat at a small desk, writing in a ledger book.

"Why, Mrs. Murdoch, how splendid to see you," he announced with a broad smile.

"Hello, Mr. Summerfield. I'm afraid this is not a social call."

The smile fell off the round face of Summerfield as he regarded Plum Streeter, who promptly introduced himself.

"Mr. Summerfield," said Eden, "I've learned from Kit Randall that you were at a church choir practice last night. Is that correct?"

"Why, yes, ma'am. Young Mr. Randall is most charming. He brought with him your little girl. He told me they were thinking of joining our church. We would be most glad to see that event and if you were to join also, well, I cannot tell you—"

"Do you know where your boss was last night?" Streeter interrupted. His tiredness was showing itself in a more abrupt tone than usual.

"Phin?" Summerfield adjusted his spectacles. "I can't say for sure. He left yesterday morning without much notice to anyone. Haven't seen him yet today."

"Left town?" Eden asked.

Summerfield shrugged. "You might want to talk to his wife. She would know more than me."

"When he returns to Bluestem, will he show up here?" Eden asked.

"Well, no. I doubt it. He hasn't come out here in nearly two months. I don't know why."

"Where was Mr. Claypool the last week of November?" said Streeter.

Summerfield frowned. "Young Mr. Randall was asking such questions here just the other day. Why do you wish to know?"

"Just answer the question," Eden snapped. She instantly regretted her sharp tone when she saw the hurt look it produced on the soft features of her listener's face. She now felt silly ever thinking Summerfield was a murderer. Seeing him here, an overgrown baby of a man, made this notion seem particularly absurd.

"I believe he was in Kansas City."

"Aren't you certain?" asked Streeter.

Eden liked the quickness with which the sheriff picked up on questionable or unusual details. He took his sleuthing seriously, unlike other frontier lawmen she had met or heard of, who were basically hired because they were talented in the use of a gun or were related to a town council member, usually both.

Summerfield tried to smile but looked ill-at-ease. "He told me Kansas City, but when I spoke awhile ago with Mrs. Claypool, she thought he was in Denver that week. I decided it best not to ask too many questions on that one, if you know what I mean."

"No, I don't know what you mean," said Eden.

Summerfield grinned at Sheriff Streeter in a knowing way. "I thought there might be another lady involved somehow. Someone in Kansas City he didn't want the Missus finding out about. Phin's got an eye for the ladies, if you haven't noticed. More than's appropriate for a married man, I'd say. All those local ladies who audition for his plays—well, he's told me some things that would make a pious man blush."

"Plays," said Eden, breathing faster. "He loves to act in plays. He must have lots of costumes."

"I suppose," said Summerfield.

"And wigs and false beards?"

"Lots of them."

"Oh, Sheriff!" Eden clutched Streeter's elbow in her excitement. She explained to a bewildered Clyde Summerfield, "We think the man who shot my husband was wearing a false gray beard as a disguise."

"How did he get to Kansas City or Denver, or wherever it was he actually went to?" asked the sheriff.

"Same as always, I would reckon. He rode out of here to Hays City to catch the Kansas Pacific. Everybody around here takes the K.P. I suppose you could go north to Nebraska for the Union Pacific, but that's a lot farther. Oh, if only they would build us a trunk line. They promise every year."

"Hays!" said Eden triumphantly. "He was in Hays. I knew it." She squeezed the lawman's elbow more tightly.

"We still have nothing, Mrs. Murdoch," was his reply. He disengaged himself from her grasp. "Tell me this, Summerfield, did Mr. Claypool have an injury of any kind to his hand in recent weeks—say early December?"

The plump man's lips parted in amazement at this question. "How did you know that?"

Eden was tempted to leap for joy and wanted to kiss the sheriff for thinking to ask this crucial question. "That's it! He fired Brad's gun."

"What sort of injury?" asked Streeter.

Clyde shrugged. "He came back from his trip with his hand bandaged and he kept it in a sling for nearly a week. He said he cut it peeling an apple. I never saw it without the bandage."

"Sheriff, this is the break we've needed all along. What more do you need?"

"Let's talk outside."

The tall sheriff guided her out of the dark little bottling works and sat her down on a rough bench in front of the building.

"Mrs. Murdoch, we still have no motive. You say Claypool didn't even have a reason to know your husband."

Eden could not answer this. Claypool hated her, she knew this well enough. But what would he have against Lawrence? Or Brad, for that matter? As the confusion of thoughts collided in her weary brain, she began to speak them out loud.

"Phineas Claypool said I was ruining his business by scaring off his investors. He claimed he might end up in bankruptcy."

"How did you manage to run off his investors? What did you do?"

"I protested his proposed health spa. He's planning to build it here on this sacred site."

"Sacred?"

"It's sacred to the Indians. All of the tribes. He was going to ban them from making pilgrimages here. It was terribly wrong. I made a big fuss and the town marshal arrested me and the news papers wrote articles about me. They started calling me Joan of Arc." Eden glanced up at the sheriff with an abashed smile. "The whole matter got so much bad publicity for Mr. Claypool, his financial backers refused to go through with the project. He told me he was going to be ruined because he had already signed a lot of contracts thinking he could get the money."

"So if he wanted you out of the way—and he didn't mind

killing—why wouldn't he just kill you and solve his problem?"

"If I died, I'd be a *martyred* Joan of Arc. And everyone would immediately suspect him, after so public a quarrel. Just like you suspected Brad of killing my husband. Why wouldn't you after what you had witnessed the day before? *But* . . . if Claypool killed someone innocent and unrelated and made it appear that I did it . . . my credibility would be destroyed and the *state* would hang me."

The unnaturally warm January wind grew warmer still and whipped against them from the south, stirring the dry ground and causing them to shield their eyes from the dust. Mountainous gray clouds churned overhead.

"No more Joan of Arc?"

"No more Joan of Arc," said Eden. "After my arrest, Phin Claypool's investors reconsidered. He told them I was some kind of demented husband-killer, I guess, and that they should ignore me. You can ask Mr. Summerfield. He'll tell you."

Plum Streeter sighed and sat down next her on the bench. "It's a clever theory, I'll give you that. But, it's just a theory. I can't waltz into Judge Blackmore's court and convince him to ignore a signed confession because you thought up an interesting alternative story. We still have no facts, just a string of coincidences."

"Well, I'll just have to find a way to make Mr. Claypool confess."

The sheriff rose to his feet again. "Good luck."

She and the sheriff departed in opposite directions and did not see Clyde Summerfield open the drawer to his accounting desk and find a gray beard stuffed in the back. He stared at it for many minutes.

Twenty-Seven

The afternoon light was fading quickly as Eden and the sheriff parted company at the Solomon Spring. He did not want to start for home so late and rode into Bluestem to find a room for the night. Eden sadly headed to her farm, sick with worry, but determined to find a way to trap Phineas Claypool.

After a glum dinner with Kit and Hadley, she turned in early, but found sleep elusive. She rose just after dawn and went for a walk. The unnatural, warm wind continued. She could not remember a January day as warm as this one. Only a light jacket was needed as the prairie grasses whipped and whispered around her.

Dark clouds rumbled in the distance and threatened a storm for later in the day. Without consciously deciding to, her feet seemed to lead her back to the spring. She mounted the large limestone dome of the sacred place and frowned to see the wrought-iron fence had now been completed. It ringed the upper crest of the spring, though the final section, no doubt the future gate, remained in pieces on the ground.

She stood on the edge of the clear pool and watched the reflection of clouds rolling by overhead. Her long auburn hair had pulled loose from its braid and caught the wild wind, dancing on her shoulders.

She stared deeply into the waters and prayed for a solution to her problems. A crack of thunder in the distance caused her to jump. Then she heard the words of Clyde Summerfield again: *Phin hasn't come out here in nearly two months. I don't know why.*

She smiled at her own reflection in the sacred waters. She knew why Phineas Claypool did not come out here anymore.

She ran all the way back to her house to get her horse, pausing only long enough to argue once more with Kit to convince him to stay behind and protect Hadley.

She rode straight into town to locate Sheriff Streeter. She called at the two hotels and the second one told her he had already checked out. She frantically began to search for him, but soon spotted his horse at the Bluestem City Jail. He had mentioned he would need to pay a courtesy call on old Marshal Bunch.

She practically dragged Streeter to Clyde Summerfield's house and found him just leaving to go to work.

"Mr. Summerfield, have you seen Mr. Claypool?" she asked, trying to control the desperate edge to her voice.

"I believe he's back in town, but I haven't spoken with him yet." He pulled out his handkerchief to clean the lens of his spectacles. He squinted at her and the tall sheriff of Ellis County.

"Mr. Summerfield, we must get him to come out to the spring."

"Why? Like I said yesterday, he hasn't been out there in weeks."

"Has he been acting strangely?"

Summerfield chuckled. "With Phin, that would be hard to say."

"I don't understand," said Streeter.

"I've known Phin for nearly eight years and I still can't predict what he'll do or say on any given day. He can be happy one moment and furious the next without so much as a long breath in between. He's an actor at heart and sometimes I'd swear he's just playacting through a day."

"Isn't he superstitious, Mr. Summerfield?"

"I don't know. He's powerful afraid of thunder and lightning. That's the only thing I know for sure. We have a lot of fun teasing him about it. Him trying to convince us it was his wife made him put up all those lightning rods."

"I think the reason he won't visit the Solomon Spring is because he believes the legend."

"What legend?" asked the sheriff.

"The Indians believe that if an evil man approaches the spring, a great geyser will rise up and drown him."

Streeter and Summerfield exchanged wry smiles over this, but Eden would not be deterred. She had heard the drama in Phineas Claypool's voice the day he told his investors the story of the spring and though he might never admit to anyone—even himself—that he took the legend seriously, a guilty heart can work strange magic on a usually rational mind.

"Mr. Summerfield, you must find a way to get Mr. Claypool to venture out to the spring. It's vitally important. An innocent man will hang tomorrow for his crimes if you don't."

Summerfield took Eden's hands in his. "Mrs. Murdoch, there are many who could love and care for you. Many who could give you the life you so richly deserve." It was obvious from the sincerity in his eyes and his voice he spoke only of himself.

"I appreciate your concern and I am humbled by you sentiment, but . . . I am trying to save the life of my daughter's *father.*"

Summerfield glanced down and let go of her hands. "Oh, I see."

A quick glance back at Plum Streeter told her he felt his time was once again being wasted.

"Please, Mr. Summerfield, will you help me?"

Summerfield looked off into the wide, flat distance for several seconds, pondering that false beard in the back of his drawer.

"You be at the spring by noon. I'll do whatever it takes to deliver Phin to you."

Eden threw her arms around the man and planted a firm kiss on his cheek.

"Oh, my." Clyde grinned and his plump face grew rosy.

Eden and the sheriff returned to her farm and spent a miserable few hours waiting for the noon appointment to arrive. Streeter was clearly displeased to be forced into wasting another day away from Ellis County.

Between begging the sheriff to come with her and begging Kit to stay home, calming Hadley's tormented fears for her mother's safety, and listening to the ticking clock inside her mind that counted down the time between now and Brad's appointment with the gallows, Eden thought she might explode.

Eden and Streeter reached the Solomon Spring well before noon. The strange warmth was such that neither wore a coat or wrap. Tumultuous winds danced over the wide prairie earth and the sky grew dark, cloaking them with a threatening and ominous curtain.

"What exactly are you going to say to him if he shows?" Streeter asked.

"I don't know yet. Just promise you'll agree with anything I come up with. All right?"

"We'll see."

Amidst the shacks and half-dismantled buildings that remained of the abandoned town of Waconda, they saw a two-horse buggy approaching at a strong speed.

Eden strained to see, but felt certain the buggy carried Clyde Summerfield and Phineas Claypool. She drew several deep breaths to try to keep her nerves at bay.

The buggy drew up next to the base of the limestone dome in front of the bottling works.

The thin and agile form of Phineas Claypool was out of the buggy before Summerfield could even draw the rig to a complete stop.

"Clyde, what the devil is going on here? You told me the place was on fire!"

He looked even more annoyed when Eden and Plum Streeter stepped out into plain view. Claypool turned a furious face on his assistant, but got no explanation.

"Good day, Mr. Claypool," Eden said.

"What do you want?" He then looked to the sheriff. "And who the devil are you?"

"The name's Streeter. I'm the sheriff of Ellis County." He did not offer his hand.

"Well, it sounds like you are pretty far from your jurisdiction, Sheriff."

"We need to talk to you, Mr. Claypool," said Eden.

"What can I do for you?" Phin Claypool forced a smile as though he had taken it upon himself to play the gregarious host.

"Did you know Lawrence Murdoch?" asked Streeter.

"Never heard the name before."

"Why, yes, you have, Phin," said Summerfield. "We talked about it a lot. You cut out all those newspaper articles about Mrs. Murdoch being arrested for his murder and you sent each and every one of your investors a copy. Remember?"

"I . . . forgot." He turned a wrathful, warning frown on his subordinate.

Eden took a deep breath and plunged onward. "We have reason to believe that you were the man who killed my husband, Mr. Claypool."

"Horse shit!" Claypool said with a snort.

"There's no call to use such language in front of a lady, Phin."

"Your friend is right," said Streeter. "And I'll thank you to keep a civil tongue in my presence as well. Now we have some pretty startling evidence that you know more than you are saying about the murder of Lawrence Murdoch . . . and Harry Knapp as well."

A distance crack of thunder caused them all to start and Claypool looked more worried by the threatening sky than by the sheriff's accusations. With his black brows drawn down into a troubled wedge, he continued to stare at the dark clouds churning in the southwestern sky even as their conversation continued.

"Where were you on Wednesday night?" asked the sheriff.

"And the last week of November?" said Eden.

"Nowhere of interest to you. I had business dealings out of town."

"Where?" barked Streeter.

Claypool paused before answering and still watched the sky. "Kansas City."

"Why did you tell your wife Denver?" asked Summerfield.

"Shut up, Clyde!"

"We'd like to know, too," said the sheriff.

"It's none of your business."

"I think it is, Claypool. You're under investigation for murder."

"You already caught the murderer. He's sitting in your jail right now waiting to hang. He confessed. It was in all the papers. If you had any sense, you'd jail her, too. She was obviously his accomplice. The gun was found in her hotel room."

"I didn't find the gun in her hotel room, Claypool. Where did you get that idea?" Streeter glared at the man.

Claypool's already pale skin whitened still more. "I just assumed. Now if you'll excuse me . . ."

"You had Harry Knapp put that gun in my room!" Eden shouted triumphantly.

Clyde Summerfield spoke up and asked a question that had tormented him all night. "I want to know why you put that false beard in my desk drawer, Phin. Were you trying to implicate me in all this?"

A great gust of wind tossed dust in the faces of Claypool and Summerfield. As both men drew out their handkerchiefs to wipe their eyes another split of lightning hit the ground a few miles distant. The thunder that followed could be felt as well as heard.

"Claypool, we have strong reason to believe that you injured your hand firing Brad Randall's gun," said Streeter.

"You burned your hand when you pushed my husband into the alley next to the bank and shot him in the back of the head!"

"That's a damned lie! You get off my property right now."

"Or what?" said Eden. "You'll call the authorities? The sheriff is already here."

"I didn't kill your husband! Now go away and leave me be!"

"I'll ask only one thing of you, sir. Repeat that up there next to the Solomon Spring and I will go away and never bother you again."

All the men looked at her as though she had lost her mind.

"I'll do no such thing."

"Why not?" Eden challenged. "Are you afraid?"

"Hell, no. What would I be afraid of?"

"The legend. If an evil man approaches the spring, a great geyser will rise up and drown him. You're afraid that will happen to you. At least afraid enough not to test the promise."

"That's the most absurd—you're a madwoman."

Eden ran up to Claypool and said in a tempting voice, "Then prove me wrong."

"I'll do no such thing."

"This has got me curious now," said Plum Streeter. "Why don't you just do it? Then we'll all be happy."

Claypool tried to laugh. A silly, nervous whinny was all that came out. "If we went up there now, we'd most likely get struck by lightning and that's a fact."

"He's got a point," said Clyde Summerfield, somewhat apologetically.

An eerie smile graced Eden's face. "My Cheyenne husband was

killed by lightning. Clear sky lightning. Not a cloud in the sky. Have you heard the phrase 'bolt from the blue'? It can happen any time, any place. You're never safe."

"You're a damned crazy woman. A witch! An Indian-loving whore!"

"How dare you talk like that," cried his outraged subordinate. "Shame on you."

"I'm asking such a simple thing, Mr. Claypool," Eden continued with her same unnatural composure, her voice carrying an almost dreamy quality. "Just march up that hill and tell me you're innocent and I swear I'll believe you."

"Come on, Phin. What's the hurt?"

"All right, fine!" Claypool glared at Clyde, then headed nearer the path that led to the spring.

No one seemed anxious to be the first to ascend so Eden took the lead with Claypool behind her and the sheriff and Clyde Summerfield bringing up the rear.

Another crackle of lightning jolted them when they reached the top. Claypool was visibly sweating. The day was unnaturally warm, but not enough to produce perspiration. He stopped walking several yards from the edge of the placid pool of water. It sat like a perfectly round mirror of the heavens.

"We're here," said Claypool. "Now what?"

"Stand at the edge of the sacred water and swear your innocence." Eden's voice shook with emotion, but her eyes flashed with solid determination.

"I already told you I'm innocent. What more do you want?" Claypool glanced nervously at the sky. "We're going to get struck by lightning if we stay up here. You all can play the fool for her, but I won't."

"I asked you to stand by the edge of the water. Are you afraid?" She took several steps closer to the trembling man. His fear made her bolder. For every step she took toward him he took a corresponding step back.

He looked over his shoulder and realized he now stood on the edge, but he could not move away because his accuser stood directly in his path.

"Afraid, Mr. Claypool?" She smiled arrogantly, her thin nostrils flaring. "I would be if I were you. If an evil man approaches the Solomon Spring a geyser will rise up and swallow him. Isn't that how the legend goes?"

"Shut up! This is stupid."

"We know you did it. We have proof."

"You do not."

"Oh, but we do. Your fingerprints were found on the murder weapon."

Claypool's narrow face twisted in confusion. "Fingerprints? What are you talking about?"

"The tips of your fingers have little ridges in them. Each person's pattern is unique to themselves. We found yours on the trigger of Brad Randall's gun. How do you suppose they got there?"

Claypool's angry expression melted into a look of alarm. He glanced over Eden's head to the sheriff. "What in hell is she talking about?"

Eden tossed a pleading look over her shoulder, silently praying Streeter would play along with her game.

"Fingerprints are . . . a very promising tool for identification," said the sheriff.

A sudden, enormous gust of wind slammed down the prairie and caused the water of the Solomon Spring to slosh from its banks and soak Claypool's shoes and trouser cuffs. The man jumped in terror and stared for several seconds at the spring.

"Damn you all!" Claypool cried in a quavering voice as he turned back to face his accusers. He lunged forward and grabbed Eden by the waist. He crushed her body against his in a terrifying embrace as he pulled a small derringer from his coat pocket and held it to her temple.

"Don't move," he whispered.

"Put the gun away, Claypool," the sheriff barked.

"Phin," Clyde Summerfield pleaded. "You don't want to do this."

"Sheriff, you lay that six-gun you're wearing down on the ground real slow or I'll blow her brains out."

"Easy now, Claypool."

Eden's face was crushed against Claypool's shoulder and she could only see behind him. It sounded like the sheriff was complying with the order.

"Phin, she's a mother. She's got a little girl. You don't want to hurt her."

"Stay out of this, Clyde! Now both of you start backing down that—"

Before Claypool could finish his sentence, Eden viewed the astounding sight of Kit Randall sneaking up the side of the dome. He then sprung from his crouching stance and seemed to fly through the air as he tackled Claypool sideways.

All three of them tumbled into the sacred waters of the Solomon Spring, with Claypool's derringer firing a wild shot in the air before they hit. Eden heard Plum Streeter cry out in pain before the waters swallowed her.

Eden felt Claypool release her as she sank deeper into the seemingly bottomless spring. Water invaded her nostrils and choked her before she could hold her breath. She felt weightless and disoriented. She did not know which way was up. All was blackness, though she sensed the thrashing presence of her two companions nearby.

Her lungs ached with a strange swelling sensation. A piercing pressure threatened to split her eardrums. Just when she thought she would lose consciousness, she felt herself start to rise as though invisible arms were bearing her upwards.

Her face broke the surface of the water at last and she greedily gulped air.

"Over here!" shouted a voice from somewhere. She flailed about madly, kicking her legs and flapping her arms in all directions. She had never learned to swim. The heaviness of her soaked skirts felt like an anchor.

"Over here!" came the voice again, and she now saw Clyde Summerfield lying on his belly, extending a long shaft of metal—a piece of the wrought-iron fence they were building—the fence that had so enraged her.

After several tries, she was able to grab the end of the pole. She held on with both hands as Summerfield and the wounded sheriff pulled her to the side of the spring.

Once out of the water, she sat on the edge coughing as she frantically strained to see what had become of Kit and Claypool. Clyde dashed about the rim of the spring, trying to see or do something. The sheriff attempted to staunch the flow of blood from his gunshot wound. He had caught a bullet from Claypool's derringer in the flesh just above his knee.

The dark waters of the Solomon Spring—made darker by the heavy sky overhead—churned and roiled, but no men were immediately evident.

"Where are they?" Eden cried.

Just when she felt a nauseating wave of panic set in, the surface of the waters began to churn again and the two men's heads broke through.

"Kit? Kit?" she called.

They were fighting, not with the waters but with each other. Grunts and coughs could be heard as Kit seemed to drag Claypool's struggling body under the water again and they disappeared once more.

Eden, Streeter, and Summerfield watched helplessly from the edge.

They were gone, just vanished. Precious seconds passed. Eden began to whimper. If young Kit died trying to save her she would never forgive herself.

The two men at her side gave up hope and rose to their feet. The sheriff used the metal pole as a crutch since his injured leg would not take his weight.

"Oh, please, dear God, great *Maheo*, save him!" Eden called out to the heavens. The words had not left her lips when Kit's handsome young face popped out of the water. He coughed twice, drew several deep breaths, then tossed his wet curls from his eyes with a jerk of his head. He gracefully swam to the edge of the spring with skilled and measured strokes, then pulled himself out and laid down flat on the limestone. His chest heaved up and down as he sucked in restorative air.

They sat for several minutes more, waiting. Phineas Claypool never reappeared.

Eden turned her attention to Streeter's injured leg. She assured him she knew what she was doing. In her years as a Civil War nurse, she had helped treat every kind of gunshot wound the fighting men knew how to render. Her years as the wife of a Cheyenne medicine man had expanded her knowledge to include the natural world of herbal remedies.

The bullet had passed clear through his lower thigh and had neatly exited on the other side, missing the bone and the large artery. She told him that he should expect a full recovery if the wound did not turn septic—and she would see to it that it did not.

"Can you carry him to my house in your rig, Mr. Summerfield?"

"Most assuredly."

"Kit, do you feel able to ride a horse?"

"Sure, let's go."

"What really happened in that spring?" Eden asked Kit as they followed Clyde Summerfield's buggy to her homestead.

"Mr. Claypool and I engaged in a sport called water polo. I

used to play it in college and was pretty good at it. Obviously better than him."

She shook her head with a doubtful frown, "Whatever the true story is, thank you."

"With all due respect, I didn't do it for your sake so much as Uncle Brad's. He has this crazy idea that dying for you is going to cover him with some kind of martyred glory. But that's just not right. Better to *live* gloriously."

"I agree."

"He's going to get over this and be all right again. All he needs is time. Time and quiet and maybe the love of a good woman, as the saying goes."

"Brad has that, Kit. I hope he knows he has that."

"I'm not talking about his wife."

"Neither am I."

The Randall dimples creased deeply into Kit's cheeks.

Twenty-Eight

The freakish winter thunderstorm hit full force as Eden spent the afternoon bathing and dressing Plum Streeter's leg wound. Lightning split the wide prairie sky over and over, and the thunder it produced rattled the new windows Kit had installed. The sky had darkened to such a degree they were forced to light all of Eden's lamps.

The good Methodist Clyde Summerfield shocked everyone by producing a bottle of whiskey for the wounded man to drink to ease his pain.

"I thought you Methodists preached temperance," Kit teased.

Summerfield blushed. "I'd appreciate you not telling anyone." He then spoke in a more contemplative mode. "This has all been most upsetting. Learning the truth about Phin. There were always aspects to his character I did not admire, but still . . . I would not think him capable of murder." He shook his head fretfully. "I should have spoken up when I found out what he did to the little girl's dog."

Hadley rushed up in outrage. "He was the one who shot Pink?"

The old dog in question raised its furry head at the mention of its name.

"Yes, little one. I'm sorry," said the plump man.

Eden reached out for her daughter and folded her into her

arms. She noticed her patient had an odd look on his weathered features. "Are you in pain, Sheriff?"

He smiled faintly. "Burns like hell, but I'm feeling more relaxed by the minute thanks to this." He took another swig from the small whiskey bottle, then raised it in a salute to Clyde Summerfield.

Kit, now in dry clothes, entered the room from behind the blanket that hung in the far corner as a privacy curtain. He rubbed his hands together to warm them. The sheriff offered him a sip of whiskey and the boy took it without hesitation.

"So, Sheriff, what happens next?" said Kit.

"I've been laying here thinking about just that. We don't have much time between now and noon tomorrow. I'll dictate a message to be wired to Judge Blackmore, telling him I have new evidence in this case and that he'll need to stay the execution until we can hold a hearing."

"I want you to wire my lawyer, Mr. Nicholas Wallace," said Eden. "I want him to file the writ of—what was it called?"

"Habeas corpus," said the sheriff.

"I'll leave for town directly," said Kit.

"I'll drive you in my rig," Clyde offered. "That storm is still fierce."

"I'd rather ride my horse," said Kit. "Faster that way."

Eden took Kit's hand and squeezed it. "Be careful."

———

Kit returned three hours later, dripping wet for the second time that day and without his horse. He burst in Eden's door and nearly shouted: "The storm has knocked down the telegraph lines. I couldn't send the wires."

"Oh, dear God," said Eden.

"Damn," the sheriff muttered. "We're going to have to go to Hays straight away."

"It's nearly dark and the storm's beating like hell out there,"

Kit said. "It took me two hours just to get home. And my horse slipped in the mud and broke his leg. I had to walk the poor, suffering devil all the way home and now I guess I'll have to go out and shoot him."

Eden clapped her hand over her mouth to hold her emotions in.

"We'll have to wait for sunup," said Streeter. "I can travel. I don't plan on dying anytime soon."

"You can't ride, Sheriff," said Eden. "Your wound will open up and start bleeding again."

"All right, this is what we're going to do," Kit announced. "I'm going to leave as soon as it's light. I'll take the best horse we have among us and ride out of here like the devil was chasing me. You all will follow toting the sheriff in the back of your wagon. As soon as I get there, I'll find this judge and tell him he's got to wait and hold a hearing or something."

"Go straight to the jail and tell my deputy—Parker's his name—that I've been wounded but I'm on my way."

"And contact Mr. Wallace, my attorney," said Eden. "Tell him he must help you with the judge and that he must file that writ."

"Habeas corpus," Streeter repeated.

Everyone made ready for the early morning journey as the storm continued to rage outside. The sheriff finished off Clyde Summerfield's little whiskey bottle and dozed into a fretful sleep. Hadley curled up on the floor using furry old Pink as her pillow and bedfellow. Eden covered her with a blanket.

Kit laid out his bedroll in his newly built, but unfurnished addition. As he organized his belongings, he discovered he still had a half-full bottle of morphine in his possession. He thought to give it to the sheriff. When the whiskey wore off, he would be needing some pain relief.

Before he reentered the main portion of the sod house, he heard the sound of weeping. In the darkened room, lit only by the orange glow of the woodstove, he found Eden sitting at her kitchen table with her face buried in her arms, quietly sobbing. He sat down next to her and took her hand in his.

"It's going to be all right," he said.

"But noon tomorrow is so close and Hays City is so far. Even if you rode a racehorse, you couldn't reach there is less than three hours."

"I'll leave as soon as the storm lets up, whether it's light or not."

"No, you might get lost."

"Hey, you're just full of scary thoughts, aren't you?"

"Aren't you worried, too?"

"I suppose I should be." The boy let out a long sigh. "I killed a man this afternoon. I can't seem to think about anything else just now."

"You were so brave. I'll never be able to thank you for all you've done."

"We're not done yet." He reached out and pulled her close, patting her head like she was a child and he, the protective parent. "I'm not going to them hang my favorite uncle."

With every hour of the night, the temperature dropped outside. The mercury fell to zero by midnight and the rain froze as it fell, glazing every surface the prairie offered.

When the first light of morning glowed on the eastern horizon, Eden peered out the frosted glass of her front window to behold a dazzling fairyland of ice. Every tree, every twig, every single blade of grass sparkled diamondlike with the new day.

As she hurried to make the wagon ready to transport her patient, she realized Kit had already left. When she first saw his empty bedroll, she thought he had merely gone to the privy or to the corral to groom a horse, but now she noticed the sheriff's horse and saddle were gone as well.

She and Hadley together helped the hobbling sheriff into the bed of the wagon. Hadley announced she would sit in the back and serve as Streeter's nurse, so Eden wrapped them both with every blanket she owned.

The frigid air stung her nostrils as she guided her sluggish horses out of her yard and onto the main wagon road south. The moisture from her breath froze in the woolen scarf she had swaddled around her face. She relentlessly asked the sheriff for the time. He was the only member of the party owning a watch. Unfortunately, Kit's morphine put him to sleep an hour into the journey so she was left to wonder and worry for the next three hours until he woke up again.

Two more bumpy, icy hours and the city of Hays at last grew on the southern horizon.

Hadley climbed next to her mother in the driver's seat. "It's going to be all right, Mama. I can just feel it."

"What time is it?"

"Quarter after noon," said Plum Streeter from his bed of blankets.

A small painful gasp escaped Eden's lips and she laid her whip on the backs of the horses, though they were near to the point of exhaustion.

They drove straight to the jailhouse at the sheriff's direction. The streets were no busier than a normal winter Saturday, no crowds had gathered nor were milling about. The entire town seemed a brilliant, ice-shrouded still life.

Eden's throat tightened when they passed the town square where the sheriff said they would erect the gallows. She saw a scaffold, but there were no crowds beneath it nor a corpse hanging from it. The only objects hanging from its armature were icicles, as long and threatening as shark's teeth. What did this mean?

She halted the horses at the jailhouse and jumped down from

the wagon, ignoring her injured passenger as she ran for the door. Hadley scrambled after her.

"It's about time!" Kit Randall shouted the moment she opened the door.

Eden frantically scanned the room looking for Kit. To her amazement, he was calling to her from the cell where he stood imprisoned with a very much alive Brad Randall.

The deputy, a young man no older than Kit, jumped up from the sheriff's desk.

"Brad!" Eden ran to his cell door.

Randall's smile broadened with every step she took.

"Kit, what are you doing in jail?" she asked.

"Tell that damned fool of a deputy that I didn't steal the sheriff's horse."

The mention of the sheriff brought Eden to her senses. She turned to the confused deputy and said, "The sheriff has been wounded. He's out in my wagon. Go get him, will you?"

Young Deputy Parker did as he was told and in a moment the limping sheriff was helped into the office of the jail. Eden called upstairs to the sheriff's wife, who rushed down. She dashed to the side of her wounded husband and threw her arms around him.

"Oh, my poor, poor darling Plummie," Rosemary Streeter cried.

"Now calm down, Rose. There's folks around."

Eden covered her mouth to keep from smiling at this tender little scene between Rosemary Streeter and her "Plummie."

The young deputy spoke up. "We had to postpone the hanging. Nick Wallace got a writ and the judge is going to hold a hearing on Monday, I guess."

"Well, we're going to have to cancel the hanging altogether," said the sheriff.

"Thank God," Randall murmured. He sat down on his cot with a gasp of relief. "You're sure?"

"You can breathe easy, Randall," said Streeter. He directed the deputy to unlock the cell.

Lawyer Wallace rushed into the jailhouse, having seen the commotion from his office window.

"Sheriff, you're back. Thank God," said the young attorney. "You do have some sort of compelling evidence to present to Judge Blackmore? He said he would personally horsewhip me if I were—how did he put it?—leading him down the garden path."

"You won't have anything to fear from the judge, Mr. Wallace," Streeter said. "I think I can make things right with him and the prosecutor, come Monday."

Eden grabbed Wallace's arm and planted an impulsive kiss on his cheek. "I knew you would come through for us."

The sheriff looked up at Brad from the smothering embrace of his wife. "Now, Mr. Randall, if I release you on your own recognizance, do I have your solemn word that you'll stay for the hearing on Monday?"

Randall nodded, then whispered to Eden as he gratefully reattached his much-missed suspenders, "Be an angel and fetch me a glass of water, would you?"

She grabbed a nearby pitcher and hurried to the pump just outside the back door of the jailhouse. She had to break the glistening ice that coated the pump handle, but the water ran smoothly. She returned to the office and handed the full pitcher to Brad. He startled her by gulping the water straight from the vessel, draining it in seconds, then wiping his dripping chin on his sleeve. He grinned self-consciously at her wondering expression.

"I was really thirsty. I haven't drank a drop since yesterday."

"Why ever not?"

"Uh . . . no reason." He gave her another awkward smile and changed the subject. "Kit told me what happened at the spring yesterday. I could hardly imagine it all."

"Neither could we and we lived through it," she said.

Brad leaned close and whispered, "How can I ever make this up to you?"

Eden smiled at him. "I think you'll have to marry me. Nothing less will do. Of course, our real hero is your nephew."

"I have something in mind for him. He'll be very surprised . . . and pleased."

Hadley tugged at Brad's coattail. "Mr. Randall?"

Brad knelt to face the girl at her own height.

"I'm glad you're not hanged."

Brad grinned. "Me, too." He leaned close to whisper in her ear. "What would you say if I married your mother?"

"I'd say it's about time."

Brad laughed out loud. He glanced up to Eden and announced, "She's definitely her mother's daughter. No shortage of firm opinions."

"Mr. Randall, will I call you 'Father,' then?" Hadley asked.

"I hope so."

"Will your boy, B.J., mind that?"

"You've as much right as he does, darling girl."

They ate a celebration dinner at the Prairie Sunrise Cafe. Randall could not wait for them to finish their first course before making his announcement. He raised a toast to Kit.

"To the bravest man I know!"

They were all drinking coffee instead of a more festive beverage, but they toasted nonetheless.

"Nephew, I was waiting for your twenty-first birthday to make this announcement, but you've more than earned the right to hear it early. You're due a sum of money. An inheritance, actually."

Kit's dark eyes widened. "Who died, Uncle?"

"Your grandmother."

"But that was—what—five years ago?"

"My mother left the Randall Dairy to all her children. You're entitled to your father's one-third share. Jennetta and I thought it best not to mention it at the time because . . . well, you were underage and your mother had just remarried. . . ."

"Oh," Kit nodded with a bitter smile. "You wanted to keep the money out of the hands of The Son of a Bitch. Pardon me, ladies, but that's my special term of endearment for my *beloved* stepfather."

"That's what he always calls him," said Hadley offhandedly.

"So how much are we talking about?" asked Kit.

"Well, we spent a lot of it on your college education, but there should be at least three or four thousand left in the trust account. Plus the rentals throw off about a hundred and twenty-five a month for each of us."

Kit was speechless. He sat for a moment, then continued his meal, obviously lost in thought. After a few minutes more, he excused himself and left the table.

"I was afraid of this," said Brad.

"Solange?" Eden guessed.

They watched as Kit made his way to the back of the restaurant and waited for Solange to complete an order at one of the tables.

"He's making a terrible mistake," said Brad.

"Maybe it will be all right," Eden said, though she shared Brad's concerns.

Brad shook a disapproving head. "A Georgetown graduate marrying a prairie waitress. A *pregnant* prairie waitress, no less."

Eden took issue with Brad's unexpected snobbery. "And just whom should a Georgetown graduate marry? His boss's daughter, perhaps?"

Brad blushed at this biting reference to Amanda. "Your point is well taken. How about . . . a twice widowed woman with a beautiful daughter?"

She ignored his teasing remarks and forced herself to ask an indelicate question. "Brad, do you really have an income of a hundred and twenty-five a month?"

He laughed. "You make it sound like a fortune."

"To me, it *is* a fortune."

"Well, just sitting here with the two of you makes me feel like the wealthiest man on earth. If B.J. were here, the picture would be perfect."

Eden could not help but think that if Marcus Vandegaarde, born Samuel Murdoch, were sitting here, her picture would be perfect, too.

Hadley pointed to the corner of the restaurant. Kit now had Solange in his arms and was whispering something in her ear. She immediately gave a little jump of joy and covered his face with kisses. They finally broke their embrace when Solange's customers began to demand her attention again. Kit returned to the table, but remained silent.

He resumed eating his dinner as though nothing were new.

"Well, Nephew?" Brad finally said. "Are congratulations in order?"

Kit looked up blankly.

"Did you ask Solange to marry you?" said Eden.

Kit seemed stunned. "No. I just told her I was going to give her the money she wanted to go to school. She needed two hundred and fifty dollars. She says it's a loan, but I don't expect her to pay me back. We men of means can afford to be generous."

Eden silently rejoiced that Solange would be able to attend the school for unwed mothers she had told her about. Perhaps her future would not be so bleak after all.

"School?" Brad asked.

"There's this school she wants to go to for girls who—" He glanced uncertainly at Hadley. "I'll tell you later."

"Kit, you are the most generous boy—man—I've ever met," said Eden.

Kit acknowledged the compliment. He looked pointedly at his uncle with a somewhat challenging smile. "We can all be heroes if we try."

Brad Randall smiled back. "Indeed."

Kit put his arm around Hadley. "I almost forgot my surprise for you, Peppermill. September twenty-eighth."

Hadley looked to her cousin for an explanation as did her parents.

"Your birthday. I had a letter waiting for me here from my friend Dan. I asked him to go to the library and do some research. He says your birthday has to be September twenty-eighth."

Hadley shrieked with delight and everyone at the table clapped their hands, causing the entire restaurant to turn and stare. Kit kissed Hadley's forehead.

Brad took Eden's hand under the table and squeezed it. He turned to smile at her, but noticed her face wore a perplexed frown. She was looking past Kit and Hadley to the nearby cafe windows that ran along the sidewalk.

He followed her gaze and saw the figure of young Marcus Vandegaarde peering in at them. His hands bracketed his eyes against the plate glass. He had been observing them at the table as they laughed and ate and celebrated. There was no doubt of it.

Randall wondered what thoughts were passing through his fourteen-year-old mind as he spied upon them. Envy? Contempt? Longing? He could not imagine.

Eden slowly rose from the table, but the moment she did, the boy vanished, dashing off like a startled rabbit. In an instant he was gone from sight. She wavered for a moment, debating whether to follow him.

She sat down again, saying nothing, just twisting her linen napkin in her lap. She pressed her lips together and her chin trembled with the effort of holding back tears.

Randall watched this all and wished he could mend the breach between mother and son, but knew he could not. His thoughts inevitably turned to another mother and son, separated, but longing to be reunited.

Epilogue

My Dear Amanda,

In denying you access to our son, I have done both you and
him a great wrong. I hope it is not an irreparable wrong. A
mother should not be denied her child, no matter what the
circumstances nor the condition of her marriage. I have recently watched a family situation unfold in which a mother
was wrongfully separated from her child and the result has
saddened me in ways I won't soon forget.

I am posting a letter to my sister immediately to inform her
of my change of heart. I do not forgive you for your infidelity,
nor do I wish to continue the hollow shell of a marriage we
were left with. My only concern now is the welfare of our
son, that dear and innocent boy, so precious to us both.

A certain dreadful anniversary will soon be upon us. Not a
day has passed in the last year that I have not thought of our darling Sarah and missed her. I am sure it is the same with you.

For a long time I have struggled to understand all that has
happened to us. Sometimes I think that what we have suffered
is more than any human beings should have to endure. To
find reasons for the terrible fate we watched take shape has
taxed my mind and heart at times beyond their capacity.

Now I think I may hold a glimmer of understanding that has given me some peace. A man of my acquaintance, an ardent Methodist, placed before me an oft-quoted passage from the Bible. He had been informed of our tragedy and he sought to help me, I suppose. I took it to be polite, but when I sat down and read it, it touched me in a way I never expected.

I know you will laugh to hear me say this—me, the self-professed atheist who never sets foot inside a church but to attend weddings and funerals—finding solace in a Bible verse, but it is true. The passage in question is from Ecclesiastes.

I returned, and saw under the sun, that the race is not to the swift, nor the battle to the strong, neither yet bread to the wise, nor riches to men of understanding, nor yet favor to men of skill; but time and chance happeneth to them all.

Time and chance happened to us, Amanda. I do not know why our beautiful daughter was taken from us. I don't know why the innocent must suffer nor why casual wrongs go unrighted. Maybe I will never know and maybe I will not know because there is no reason. No reason at all. The cruel randomness of life is not to be fathomed by our poor brains.

Know that I once loved you and that the love we shared lives on in our son. I do not hate you, Amanda. I will never speak ill of you to B.J. I ask the same consideration of you in this.

I have instructed my lawyer not to file a petition against you for divorce. To minimize the damage to your reputation, I would prefer that you instead sue me. Men can weather blows to their good name more readily than women. Tell your lawyer to choose any grounds he wishes. I will not contest